Ace Books by Jeanne C. Stein

THE BECOMING
BLOOD DRIVE
THE WATCHER

THE
WATCHER

JEANNE C. STEIN

ACE BOOKS, NEW YORK

THE BERKLEY PUBLISHING GROUP
Published by the Penguin Group
Penguin Group (USA) Inc.
375 Hudson Street, New York, New York 10014, USA
Penguin Group (Canada), 90 Eglinton Avenue East, Suite 700, Toronto, Ontario M4P 2Y3, Canada
(a division of Pearson Penguin Canada Inc.)
Penguin Books Ltd., 80 Strand, London WC2R 0RL, England
Penguin Group Ireland, 25 St. Stephen's Green, Dublin 2, Ireland (a division of Penguin Books Ltd.)
Penguin Group (Australia), 250 Camberwell Road, Camberwell, Victoria 3124, Australia
(a division of Pearson Australia Group Pty. Ltd.)
Penguin Books India Pvt. Ltd., 11 Community Centre, Panchsheel Park, New Delhi—110 017, India
Penguin Group (NZ), 67 Apollo Drive, Rosedale, North Shore 0632, New Zealand
(a division of Pearson New Zealand Ltd.)
Penguin Books (South Africa) (Pty.) Ltd., 24 Sturdee Avenue, Rosebank, Johannesburg 2196,
South Africa

Penguin Books Ltd., Registered Offices: 80 Strand, London WC2R 0RL, England

This is a work of fiction. Names, characters, places, and incidents either are the product of the author's imagination or are used fictitiously, and any resemblance to actual persons, living or dead, business establishments, events, or locales is entirely coincidental. The publisher does not have any control over and does not assume any responsibility for author or third-party websites or their content.

THE WATCHER

An Ace Book / published by arrangement with the author

PRINTING HISTORY
Ace mass-market edition / December 2007

Copyright © 2007 by Jeanne Stein.
Cover art by Cliff Nielsen.
Cover design by Judith Lagerman.
Interior text design by Kristin del Rosario.

ISBN: 978-0-441-01546-7

ACE
Ace Books are published by The Berkley Publishing Group,
a division of Penguin Group (USA) Inc.,
375 Hudson Street, New York, New York 10014.
ACE and the "A" design are trademarks belonging to Penguin Group (USA) Inc.

PRINTED IN THE UNITED STATES OF AMERICA

10 9 8 7 6 5 4 3 2 1

To my sister, Connie. You are a rock.

Heartfelt thanks to the usual suspects:

Jessica Wade of Ace Books and Scott Miller of Trident Media Group;

Writing partners Mario Acevedo, Sandy Maren, Jeff Shelby, Margie and Tom Lawson;

Phil and Jeanette.

To Denver buddies and San Diego friends:

Patty and Jay Salam, Joanne Hoefer, Sam Reeves, Suzy and Dennis Perkins, Susan Mackay Smith, Miyoko Hensley, Ron Jessee—cheerleaders when I need it.

You are all much appreciated.

CHAPTER 1

IT'S LATE OCTOBER IN SAN FRANCISCO AND IF I WERE still human, I'd be freezing my ass off. A frigid wind funnels straight up from the bay making the fifty-degree temperature feel more like thirty. Even my partner, big, tough, ex-football player David Ryan, looks uncomfortable.

But it's not the cold that has him frowning. It's realizing that our whole game plan for this particular snag and drag has gone up in smoke. And *why*.

We're standing in the middle of the block on Hollister, watching the entrance of a bar on the corner a few doors away. For a Wednesday, the place is jumping. Good news and bad news for what we intend. Good news because a crowd offers cover. Bad news because there's always the danger that some pain-in-the-ass innocent bystander might misunderstand and try to intervene. It's happened before. But since we know our skip, Tony Tuturo, is inside—we followed him here—it's a chance we're prepared to take.

And did I mention we had a plan? I'm dressed in a short black skirt, silk halter top, leather jacket, come-fuck-me pumps. The idea was I'd go inside, entice him with my womanly charms, and make him an offer he'd be too dazzled to refuse. Once outside, David and I would hustle his ass into a car. In less than an hour, we'd be off to the airport and home with our bounty in San Diego. Should have worked. Should have been a piece of cake.

David looks at me. "It's a gay bar. Did you know Tuturo was gay?"

I do now. Laughter erupts before I can stifle it. "Would I be dressed like this if I did?"

He frowns. "So what do we do?"

I can't believe he has to ask. "What do you think we do? *You* go inside and I wait here. God, one look at you and . . ."

"Okay." He stretches the word out. He's watching the door and a steady stream of well-dressed twenty- and thirty-something men making their way inside. Melancholy strains of soft jazz float out each time the door opens. He runs a hand through thick, close-cropped hair. "I don't think I'm dressed properly for this."

He's wearing jeans, a black T-shirt and a black leather duster. Underdressed, perhaps, compared to the suits we've seen pass into the bar. But David was a tight end for the Broncos when they were Super Bowl champs and he's in as good physical condition now as then. His muscular 250 pounds is well distributed on a six-foot-six frame. He's model handsome—high cheekbones, smooth tan, generous mouth.

I lift an eyebrow. "Believe me, nobody is going to notice how you're dressed."

He looks down at me, still frowning. "Okay, then." He hands me the car keys. "See you in a few."

David goes inside and I'm left on the sidewalk to twiddle my thumbs. I move off to stand beside our rental car. I like it so much more when I'm the bait. Inactivity grates. It makes me think about how different my life has become since a night very much like this one last summer. Except that skip turned out to be—not what we expected. And when he attacked, the commingling of our blood turned me into a vampire.

I lean my butt against the door and press fingers against my eyeballs.

Vampire.

I've come to terms with it. Mostly. I accept that drinking human blood is my sustenance and immortality my future. But I haven't accepted it all. The balance between the supernatural and the human side of my personality is shifting. I feel it more every day. The animal within me is becoming stronger, harder to keep in check. I have a mentor who is helping me and a support group, of sorts, to make the transition easier. But I also have a human family and a business partner who don't know what I've become and I'm fighting to hold on to them as long as I can.

The door to the bar swings open and David is back, his arm across the shoulders of Tony Tuturo. They're both laughing and Tony puts an arm around David's waist and pulls him close.

That didn't take long, not that I thought it would. I slip into the driver's seat and crank the engine.

David steers Tony toward the car. Tony is a few inches shorter than David, and about seventy pounds lighter. He has brown hair and smooth olive skin that shimmers in the dim light and screams tanning bed. He's meticulously dressed in a gray Armani suit and pin-striped shirt. No tie. No gun, either, unless his tailor had made adjustments for one in the jacket. He's wanted in New York, accused of extortion and grand theft. I bet there's a gun.

They're approaching the car. David lets his hand drop from Tony's shoulders and skim his jacket as he laces his arm through Tony's.

Very smooth. The subtlest frisk I've ever seen.

For the first time Tony notices that David is guiding him toward a car with the engine running. He takes a step closer, sees me, and stops.

The smile dissolves into a puzzled frown. "Who's in the car?" he asks.

David's grip tightens, one hand is still around Tony's waist, the other closes on his arm. "A friend, Tony. My driver."

I flash a smile.

Tony starts to fidget. "We don't need a driver. We'll take my car."

But David has him close enough to the car to drop the subterfuge. He gives Tony a push that sends him sprawling against the side of the car. While he's still off balance, David snaps on the cuffs and with one hand holding him against the car, pats him down.

The gun, a nice little Smith & Wesson .38 LadySmith, is tucked into a nice little ankle holster.

David opens the back door and shoves Tony in. He climbs in beside him, handing the gun to me over the back-seat and clucking his tongue. "Rosewood grip," he says. "A little too fancy for my taste."

I turn it this way and that, admiring the sculptured wood. "Real nice gun, Tony."

Movement from the direction of the bar catches my attention. A man bursts from the door, looking first to the right and then to the left.

"A friend of yours, Tony?" I ask.

Tony doesn't respond.

The guy is moving toward our car. He's handsome in an Italian silk suit and slicked-back hair kind of way. He's trying to see into the backseat of our car but in the dark, the tinted windows are opaque.

"I think this is our cue," I say to David, gunning away from the curb.

The guy watches us pull away. He has an uncertain frown on his face, but he makes no move to rush to follow us. I let myself relax and head for the freeway.

"Wave good-bye, Tony," I murmur.

But once again, there's no response from the backseat. In fact, Tony doesn't say a word all the way to the airport. He doesn't ask who we are or where we're going. His lack of concern makes me all the more attentive. Nobody ever gives up this easily.

There's a commuter flight from San Francisco to San Diego almost every hour until the midnight curfew closes our airport. It's ten o'clock. We'll just have time to catch the last flight out. I stand with Tony near the shuttle bus at the car rental agency, his jacket draped over his shoulders, concealing the cuffs. When the doors open, I climb the steps first. David prods Tony. He takes the first step, stumbles back, knocks David off balance. Quicker than I would have thought possible, he head butts David, pushes him aside and is off across the parking lot.

But as fast as he is, I'm faster. I hear David behind me, but the adrenaline has kicked in. Predator and prey. It's instinctive. I've got Tony facedown on the asphalt before either of them realizes what has happened. I've let the vampire take over, and while David is still far enough away to keep from hearing, I growl in Tony's ear and turn his face to look into mine.

I don't know what my vampire face looks like. I no longer cast a reflection. I can only feel the change—the heat, the quickening of blood. It's been weeks since I've fed. My human job has occupied a lot of my time and the rest has been taken up with—something else. I didn't realize how intensely the hunger has been building until without conscious effort, my lips curl back from my teeth and a hiss erupts from deep inside.

Tony cringes and tries to get away.

Fingers like steel close around his arms. My mouth is at his ear. "Try that again," I whisper. "And I'll tear you to pieces."

His body is rigid beneath mine. I am aware of the frantic beating of his heart. I smell his fear, see his blood pulsing as it rushes through his carotid, just a kiss away at his jawline.

A kiss away.

David puts a hand on my shoulder and I jump.

"Anna, are you all right?"

It takes a couple of heartbeats before I can relax, let go of the bloodlust. I compose myself and sit back. "I'm fine." My voice is harsh, unsteady. Still, I climb to my feet, hauling Tony up beside me. "I was just explaining to our friend here how it works." As I speak, I straighten Tony's jacket and pat his shoulder. "I think we understand each other now. He's not going to give us any more trouble. Are you, Tony?"

Tony stares at me, his eyes wide. His mouth opens and closes a couple of times but his brain is still trying to process what he saw in my face. Obviously, it can't process fast enough to form a coherent thought.

I pat his shoulder again. "That's okay, Tony, you don't have to say anything."

David gives him a shove toward the bus. "Jesus, Anna," he says. "When did you get so fast?"

"I've always been fast. You just never noticed."

Tony draws a deep, unsteady breath and moves to David's side. He looks up at David and says with pathetic urgency, "Keep her away from me, man. She's like a mad dog."

I smile. Yeah. Kind of like.

CHAPTER 2

WHEN WE GET BACK TO SAN DIEGO, DAVID drops me off at the office before delivering Tony to the cops. Tony seems relieved to see the last of me. Imagine that. Maybe he'll think twice before jumping bail again.

I pick up my car, intending to head for home. But the dance I did with Tony set something loose. Hunger is gnawing at me, refusing to be ignored. If I go home now, I'll face a long, sleepless night of restless anxiety. I need blood.

I know where to go. Mexico.

Culebra doesn't seem surprised to see me when I appear at the door of his bar at two thirty in the morning. He's seated at a table with two other male vamps and a couple of human women. There's no one else in the place and disappointment slumps my shoulders. Obviously, the women are the companions of the two vamps. And the feast is over. They wear the sated, content look of females who have been well serviced. And even if they weren't, vampires are not big on sharing blood supplies.

Culebra reads my mood, senses my hunger, in the instant it takes me to cross to the bar and plunk myself on a bar stool. He joins me, handing me a bottle of beer from the cooler at the end of the bar.

Here. This should help.

Only if it's type O. But I take it, pop the top, and drink.

Culebra is a shape-shifter, a gruff old bandit with a rutted face and the ability to crawl inside my head at will. He's my source of sustenance. Movies and TV depict vampires existing on animal blood. It's not like that in real life. We need human blood to survive. Culebra provides a place for vampires to connect with humans willing and eager to be fed upon. Humans find the process highly pleasurable. Combine it with sex, and the experience is as addictive as cocaine and just as dangerous. Most victims of vampires die because they don't want it to stop and an unscrupulous or undisciplined vampire loses control. Culebra keeps a close eye on those who come here to feed and protects both vampires and their human hosts.

Culebra is watching me, eyes hard and bright in the dim light. *Where's your friend Frey? He would not refuse you.*

I shake my head. *Probably not. But he's a schoolteacher, you know, and it's late. I'm sure he's home asleep.*

Daniel Frey is also a shape-shifter. We've had sex and he's let me feed from him, but I'm not about to awaken him in the middle of the night because I've waited too long to feed. Besides, the last time I called him, a woman answered the phone. There was something in her voice when she asked if I wanted to leave a message that made it clear she hoped I didn't.

What you need is a steady human boyfriend, Culebra tells me, shaking a mental finger. *It's much safer than these indiscriminate pairings. You should know that after what happened.*

Culebra is referring to something that happened a few weeks ago. I came very close to attacking and killing a human who had hurt a member of my family. As a result, I risked exposing myself as a vampire to a mortal world not prepared to accept that such things exist.

Yet I'm not ready for the other alternative, either. I had a human boyfriend. Max. I couldn't bring myself to tell him what I had become, which meant I could not and would not bring myself to feed from him. At the same time, I couldn't seem to stop myself from feeding or having sex with non-humans that came my way. No, that's not exactly true. I didn't stop myself because I didn't want to.

And there's another reason. Max seemed suddenly intent on taking our relationship to the next level. There was a time when that might have made me happy. But even though Max is a good man—strong, loyal, beautiful—because of what I am, that cannot happen. Not only for the obvious reasons, but because I've been unfaithful to him twice with other-worldly men, and I know I will be again.

It's the nature of the beast in me.

Max deserves a woman who can love him as a woman—a real human woman. Not a pretender. I've been practicing the speech since the last time we were together. I just haven't seen him to test whether or not I'll have the guts to deliver it.

I drain the last of the beer, place the bottle on the bar and stand up. With a last glance around, I prepare to leave. When I had Tony on the ground, it took every ounce of strength not to open his neck. I know what would have happened if David hadn't been there. I've got to stop waiting so long between feedings.

I don't need to say any of this to Culebra, either verbally or telepathically. He picks my thoughts out of the air like leaves drifting in the wind.

You need blood. What are you going to do?

I shrug. *Go home. Go to bed. Try to sleep. Tomorrow I go see Williams.*

At last I've said something that eases some of the concern from Culebra's face. *I'm glad you have come to your senses about that. He has much to teach you.*

He walks me to the door. *If you come back tomorrow, I'll have someone for you.* He gestures to the table and the four seated around it. *It's been a slow night.*

I nod and start for the door. Before I can push it open, it swings inward. A man is silhouetted against the moonless night, black on black. He takes a step into the light and I step back, startled. It's the last person I expect, or in truth want, to see.

"Max. What are you doing here?"

CHAPTER 3

I'M NOT SURE WHO IS THE MORE SURPRISED. MAX knows of my acquaintance with Culebra. He was around when I brought David here because of what Avery, a vampire who pretended to love me, had done to him. Max thought David's wounds had been caused by a human, of course, a skip we traced to Beso de la Muerte. For his part, Max works for the DEA, and since Culebra helped him with a drug case a while back, it's not inconceivable that he should be here—just unexpected. What is alarming, though, is the way he looks.

Not good. Max is a big man, hard muscled, big boned. He usually carries about 225 pounds on a six foot three frame. Today, he looks haggard. Worn. His clothes, jeans, T-shirt, a leather jacket, hang on his frame like rags on a scarecrow. He looks like he's lost thirty pounds. He's covered with dust and the lines on his face have deepened, his blue eyes are dull.

But not his reflexes. Before he registers who is standing in front of him, his hand is on the gun under his jacket.

When recognition hits, he backs down, though his eyes narrow. "Anna. What are you doing here?"

Culebra answers before I can, "She's working on a case. A kidnapper believed to be living in Tijuana. I had some information for her."

He looks around. "You came here alone? Where's David?"

"He's joining me in TJ," I respond quickly. "But what's happened to you? You look terrible."

A spark of the old Max flares back. "As opposed to the way you look." He raises an eyebrow. "Nice skirt, where's the rest of it?"

"Glad to see you haven't lost your sense of humor along with your shampoo and soap."

He sways suddenly, unsteady on his feet. I gesture toward a table and he follows me. Once he's seated with me beside him, Culebra lays a hand on Max's shoulder.

"I'll get you some food."

Culebra shoots me a look. *Here is what you need.* And then he moves away.

As if Max was in any shape to donate blood. I ignore him, putting my hands over Max's on the tabletop. "Is it Martinez?"

Max doesn't answer. He doesn't really have to. Max is here because Culebra offers protection to his friends, human and otherwise, in this unlikely place in the Mexican desert. Until recently, Max had been in deep cover as the driver of one of Latin America's biggest drug lords, Rodrigo Martinez. The case was made, with Culebra's help I suspect, and the operation closed down. But Martinez got away. He's after Max and Max is after him.

Max rouses himself to squeeze my hands. "How are you? How is your niece?"

I smile. "Trish is wonderful. She's with my folks in Europe. Mom took a leave of absence from school for a couple of months. She thought Trish could use a little time away."

My voice breaks off. Thirteen-year-old Trish suffered

abuse at the hands of her mother and her mother's scum-bag friends. They're either dead now, or in prison. My folks have taken her in, believing her to be the daughter of my deceased brother.

A belief I've fostered for all their sakes.

Max smiles, too. "It's good that she's with them. Why didn't you go along?"

A dozen reasons flash through my head, every one centered on the problems faced by a vampire trying to conceal her true identity from her mortal family and friends.

Friends like Max.

I shrug. "Timing was off. Business is booming. When the economy declines, crime seems to take an uptick."

"The kidnapper in TJ? You know you need to be careful. Mexico does not look kindly on bounty hunters."

"Hence the work clothes," I reply with a smile. "He'll follow me willingly, don't you think?"

I let a heartbeat go by before asking again, "What about you? Are you in Beso de la Muerte because of Martinez?"

But now Culebra is back at the table with a tray that smells of beef and grilled vegetables. He sets it before Max along with tortillas and a bottle of beer.

Max attacks the food with voracious enthusiasm. He pauses once to gulp down the beer and Culebra fetches another bottle before pulling out a chair to join us.

With his hunger satisfied, Max pushes the plate away and looks up at us. "It's been a while since I've eaten."

"Clearly," Culebra says. "There's more in the kitchen."

Max shakes his head and wipes his mouth with the back of his hand. "What I need now is a shower and a good night's sleep."

Culebra looks at me. *Do you wish to stay here tonight with Max?*

Culebra does not know of my decision to end things with Max. Neither does Max. Somehow tonight does not seem the appropriate time nor Beso de la Muerte the appropriate place to break the news.

Culebra reads the answer in my hesitation and pushes

back from the table. "Come my friend," he says to Max. "I will take you to the tunnels. You will be safe. Stay as long as you need to."

Max looks to me and I see the question in his eyes. I touch a hand to his cheek. "I have to go. David is waiting. Besides, you need to rest."

He doesn't argue, a bad sign. He simply places his own hand over mine and kisses my cheek. "I'll see you soon."

His expression says something different and it's a weight on my heart. I don't let go of his hand. "You haven't told me what you're doing here. What is happening with Martinez?"

Once again, he avoids the question, dropping my hand and taking a step away. "I'll see you soon," he repeats, motioning to Culebra that he's ready to go.

I watch them cross the bar and disappear into the back. Indecision and concern for Max gives me pause. Maybe I should stay. Max is in trouble, that's obvious. What isn't obvious is why. I've never seen Max look so lost. And he's keeping something from me.

Still, I understand that in his line of work, you need to keep secrets.

And look what *I'm* hiding from him.

It doesn't make it easy to leave him, though, or keep my anxiety for him from growing.

I can't help Max if I don't know what kind of trouble he's in. He may not yet be willing to tell me, but I bet I know someone who can find out.

CHAPTER 4

ILEAVE THE BAR AND HEAD BACK TO SAN DIEGO. I told Culebra that I was seeing Williams this morning. Warren Williams is San Diego's chief of police. Only he's so much more than that. Williams is a vampire, a very old vampire, who also happens to be San Diego's chief of police. The real-life, honest-to-god chief of police.

For weeks now, I've hauled my butt out of bed at four thirty to join him at his unofficial office in Balboa Park, a kind of secret headquarters for San Diego's supernatural community. I've started working for him as part of his "Watcher" brigade. We keep an eye on the supernatural community and step in when necessary to protect both creatures like myself and our human counterparts. Sometimes we do just what our name implies, watch, but other times . . .

I park in front of the Museum of Art and start up El Prado. It's a spooky place in the cold dark of early morning. The only thing breaking the shadows is the dim fluorescence of tall streetlamps bordering the parking lot. But fog snakes around the top of the lights and slithers at my feet. Even the towers and ornate cornices cast ghostly images on the walkway. Vamps aren't afraid of the dark. Exactly. But since becoming one, I am acutely aware that there really are things that go bump in the night. I quicken my pace.

Hide in plain sight.

The phrase pops into my head as I approach the mystical waterfall that separates the entrance to the underground hideaway from an unsuspecting public. I step through, not entirely a pleasant sensation unless you like walking through cold, wet spider webs. I don't know much about the magic that makes it work, but I do know that once on the other side, I'm invisible to anyone walking past.

I fish around in the bottom of my bag for the shiny brass key that allows me to open the door I'm now facing. On the other side is a reception area with a desk on which sits a computer. A few keystrokes and the entire "office" turns into an elevator that whisks me downward.

No matter how many times I do this, I'm amazed every time. It's *Mission Impossible* meets *Stargate*.

And the comparisons continue once inside.

The elevator opens onto a large, open space filled with desks and populated, even at this early hour, by the league of human psychics whose work funds the operation. Perched on the corner of one of the desks, head bent in conversation with a woman I don't recognize, is someone I do.

"Good morning, Sorrel," I say.

The woman turns and flashes a smile, her calm blue eyes taking their measure of me. She reminds me of Cinderella, tall, wispy, blond. But this Cinderella is dressed to the nines in a Donna Karan power suit and Jimmy Choos. Her expression reminds me of a cat's, testing the air, reading it, until she gets the answer she's searching for. "Good morning, Anna. Didn't get to bed last night, did we?"

Sorrel is blind, though you wouldn't know it to watch her. She's also an empath. "One of these days you're going to have to teach me that trick."

She laughs. "Trick? No. It's a talent. And like most talents, all it takes is practice and concentration." She flutters manicured fingers. "It's all in the air, Anna. You need only to channel it."

I mimic her fluttering fingers. "So my staying up all night was out there floating in the ether?"

"No, but your weariness is. That's what I feel. I can make it better, you know."

Her gift is to bestow serenity. She tried it on me once. It worked. It also erased the edge I need to do the things I do. For me to survive, that's not an option.

I don't need to explain this to her, she knows and understands.

Sorrel smiles. "It's always nice to see you, Anna."

Even without trying, her gift comes through. Her smile lifts my spirits.

She turns back to the conversation I interrupted and I make my way to the offices that line the rear wall. Williams' door is open and he looks up briefly at my approach and waves me in before returning to his reading.

Williams is seated behind a metal desk, his head bent in concentration. He's tall, lean, looks fiftyish because he has his dark hair professionally streaked with gray. Today he's not wearing cop clothes but jeans, a brown leather bomber jacket, a pair of worn Nikes on his feet and a pink polo shirt.

A pink shirt?

He looks up from the paper he had been studying and touches a hand self-consciously to his chest, frowning. *It was a gift from my wife. What's wrong with it?*

Williams' wife is human. She knows her husband's true nature and accepts it. There are many in the supernatural community "married" to mortals, a concept I can't quite wrap my head around. Still, it strikes me as amusing that this powerful old vamp is concerned that I'm disparaging his wife over the color of a shirt. Amusing and touching, at the same time.

He reads all this because I let my thoughts project to

him. *I happen to like pink.* His tone is just this side of defensive.

I raise an eyebrow and drop into a chair. *It's definitely your color.*

His expression softens. "Love," he says, "makes a vampire do strange things." Then he looks at me, really looks at me for the first time. He lets the paper drop onto the desk and frowns at me. "You need to feed. And you've had no sleep for twenty-four hours. I need you sharp, Anna. Particularly today. Now I'm not sure I can trust you with this assignment."

The hair on my neck bristles. Does he have a direct line to Sorrel? "I can handle any assignment you throw at me. I think I've proven that."

He holds up a conciliatory hand, but the grim expression remains unchanged. "The rogue I'm sending you after is powerful and crafty. He's attributed with many deaths. He's only been a vampire for ten years but he killed as a human and his taste for it has grown with his power. He is operating in San Diego now and attracting the attention of the Revengers. We need to get to him fast."

The Revengers are a secret organization of human avengers whose sole purpose is to seek out and kill vampires. *If this rogue is in their sights, why not let them pull the trigger?*

He frowns. *That should be obvious, Anna. The Revengers don't discriminate between those in our community who are good and those who are not.*

He's right. When I had been a vampire only one day, they almost got me.

And there is a second obvious reason: if we are seen as weak and unable to police our own, it strengthens their resolve that they should.

He's glaring at me again. "But this one won't be easy to kill, especially if you're not up to it."

This time I temper my reply. "All right. I admit I haven't had any sleep and I do need to feed. But I can use both to my advantage." I let him read what happened with our skip in San Francisco. "The blood drive is strong in me today."

Williams closes his thoughts to me, studies me with gray green eyes as fathomless as the ocean. *You are waiting too long between feedings,* he says at last.

I wave a hand. *Perhaps. It couldn't be helped. I went to Beso de la Muerte, but there were no hosts.*

He responds with a growl of disapproval. *Anna, you must stop this. Get a human host of your own, male or female, and stick with the one. It's the only way to protect yourself and stay strong.*

It's been three months since I was turned, and it seems like I've heard this same thing every damned day. It grows tiresome. Maybe after a hundred years, I'll be comfortable with the idea that I should keep a human around to feed from once or twice a month like some pet.

Maybe.

But I don't think so. I let my irritation show.

Can we please get back to the job?

I expect another heated torrent about my feeding habits. To my surprise and relief, however, Williams lets it go. An indication how important stopping this rogue must be.

He hands me a piece of paper with a police artist's sketch of a man in his late forties, light skin, dark eyes, gray hair brushed back from a thin face. "Simon Fisher," he says. "Five foot nine, 175 pounds. Wanted in three states. He brought his last two victims to the hidden caves in La Jolla. You know the place?"

I look up from the sketch and nod. "Can I find him there now?"

Williams glances at his watch. "If my sources are correct, he'll be there within the hour. He was spotted leaving his apartment with a female twenty minutes ago. He likes to kill them at dawn."

I fold the paper and shove it into a pocket in my jeans. *I'd better go.*

Williams rises when I do. *Be careful, Anna. He's shrewd and he's powerful. And, Anna, you must leave his body.*

His eyes are serious. He's telling me I can't stake the bastard. I've only had to do this once before and I remember what it was like.

Can you handle it?

I blow out a breath. I know why leaving a body is important. It allows the police to close the case and the victims' grieving families to get closure. But the cost to the vampire who is performing this public service is high. I feel my stomach start to churn.

Still, I nod. I do this to learn to control the beast and to understand the consequences if I should fail.

I'm at the door to the office when my thoughts turn to Max. I look back at Williams. "Do you have any contacts at the DEA?"

"I'm the police chief of a major metropolitan city. I have contacts everywhere."

I think I've offended him. Vampires, especially old ones, seem to be very thin-skinned. I frown an apology and ask, "Can you check on someone for me?"

He doesn't answer, but waves his hand in a "get on with it" gesture.

Quickly, I fill him in on Max and what he's involved in. "I'd like to know more about Martinez. He seems to be eluding both the Feds and the Mexican Federales. Maybe I can do something to help."

Williams tilts his head, his annoyance gone. "I'd forgotten about Max. He may be just what you need."

"Will you forget about what I need? I asked about Martinez."

Again, the dismissive wave of a hand. "I'll see what I can find out."

His attitude makes it obvious his only concern for Max is how he can be of use to me. I'm not going to argue the point now. There's a damsel to rescue, and this Wonder Woman doesn't have an invisible jet. I have to travel across town in a car.

CHAPTER 5

B UT IT'S A DAMNED NICE CAR. I DRIVE A TWO-YEAR-old, British Racing Green Jaguar XKR convertible. It makes the run between Balboa Park and La Jolla a snap, especially since it's too early for commuter traffic.

I know the spot where Williams is sending me. It's deep in Torrey Pines State Park where there is no convenient access to the secluded beach, only a steep path down a sheer wall of rock. Because of its isolation, it's become a popular "suit optional" beach, favored mostly by those who should never be given that option. But at this time of morning, and for a vampire who can climb like a mountain goat, it offers the privacy one needs for what Fisher has in mind.

I'm neither nervous nor anxious about what awaits me. I've done it before. For the last month, I've worked with Williams doing what the human justice system cannot, taking supernatural rogues to task for their criminal acts. Williams and others as yet unknown to me act as judge and jury. I am one of the enforcers, or executioners, as the verdict dictates.

It's simple. It's quick. It makes sense.

And I've found I'm good at it.

Not that the irony isn't lost on me. My day job is tracking bail jumpers and turning them over to a system that will likely release them back onto the streets to claim more victims. The otherworldly way offers more protection to the innocent and is a hell of a lot more efficient.

I pull as far into the park as I dare and cut the engine. I don't want Fisher to bolt at the unexpected arrival of a strange car. It's almost six, and the late fall sun will soon cast its bright, brittle gaze to the sea. I don't have time to waste.

Before climbing out of the car, I reach into the glove compartment. There's a knife there, in a nice little leather holster. I clip it to my waistband, at my back. If I turn my back on Fisher, he will see it. I don't intend to turn my back on him.

Then I step out, toss my jacket into the front seat, kick off the heels, and I'm off, running through the trees with an ease borne of belonging as much to the animal world as the human. I pass a dark sedan, tucked into a small clearing at the trailhead. I detect no sound from the car as I approach. It is empty. The keys are in the ignition and the doors are unlocked. I pull open the passenger door and release a heady bouquet of blood, lust and fear.

Fisher's scent, commingled with that of his victim. There are a few drops of blood on the headrest. I brush my fingertips over the stain and they come away wet. The taste of her blood is rich on my tongue, sends a thrill of anticipation through me. Tonight I'll head straight back to Beso de la Muerte. I'll have to.

Quietly, I push the door shut. Ahead of me is the path to the caves, still hidden by the deep shadows of predawn.

Head tilted, I listen. Below the ridgeline that hides the path from sight, I hear the rumble of the waves, the skitter of claws on sand as something big frightens smaller creatures back into the sea. That something is treading with heavy, certain steps—one set, not two.

I hope I'm not too late.

The path descends in a rocky, precipitous slope to the entrance of the first cave. I send out a silent, tentative probe, careful to mask my identity and close off my thoughts, seeking only to identify the thing below. Like a bat's radar, the echo bounces back—vampire.

It's all I need to know. I race down the path. I want to surprise this Simon Fisher. Give him something to take his mind off his victim. Something he'll want more than a mortal woman. Something better.

At the bottom yawns the entrance to the first sea cave. It's open, hollow, allowing a straight shot through the sand to the sea. It's the way most beach goers head. Unless you knew what else was down here, you'd miss it. To the left, behind a jagged outcropping of rock that looks solid, is another entrance. Invisible, dark, forbidding. Behind it, I pick up steady footfalls, heavy treads, someone carrying a burden. And soft, uneven breathing.

Vampires don't breathe.

I may not be too late after all.

Another probe tells me that the vampire is only a few yards from the entrance. His thoughts are feverish, the bloodlust is high. He is looking forward to the kill. He will take the woman sexually first, he can barely contain his excitement. Then he will drain her, savoring an even greater sexual pleasure as her life flows into his.

I step around the rocks, into the open. He is too involved in his fantasy to notice. He lays the woman on the ground, strikes her cheeks with the palm of his hand. He knows the drug he used on her should be wearing off. He slaps her again.

She groans, stirs.

I send out the first message. *Simon Fisher?*

His body jerks toward me. His eyes glow with a savage inner fire, then become flat and unreadable. He stares at me. Tries to probe my mind.

I don't let him.

What are you? What are doing here?

As I step forward, he takes a reflexive step back. His

hands are curled in fists at his sides. His face is familiar—
the face of the animal that claims us both. The face of the
vampire. He growls a warning.

I hold up a hand. *My name is Anna Strong. I am a
Watcher. I came to warn you.*

Of what?

The police know you are here.

The woman on the ground takes a deep, gulping breath.
Her eyes are open, but clouded in confusion. When at last
she can focus and she sees Fisher, the vampire, she tries to
scramble away.

He reaches out, grabs her wrist, yanks her back close to
him. He applies pressure to her jugular until she slumps
against him.

I take a cautious step forward. *Let her go. If will be
worse for you if they find her here.*

He grins, presses her limp hand to his lips, licks her
wrist. *I will claim my prize first. The human police cannot
hold me. You know that.*

*But the Revengers can. You have attracted their atten-
tion with your carelessness. They are sending one of their
own with the police. He will be the one who takes you into
custody. You will never be seen again.*

Fisher considers my words. It is well-known in the vampire community that the Revengers have members on the
police force. It's how they identify criminal activity that
can only be attributed to a vampire. It only takes a few
bloodless bodies to raise their suspicion.

The woman's eyes open. She struggles against Fisher's
restraining hand. When his grip loosens, she brings a knee
up into his crotch. But it's not a solid kick and instead of
letting go of her, quick anger darkens his face and he raises
his hand to strike her.

I'm there before he connects, stopping his hand in
midswing with mine.

I pull him toward me. *Let her go. I am offering you
something better.*

There's an instant when I think he's going to fight me.

But I take the chance and drop his hand, let him read what I am offering.

Interest sparks in the depths of his eyes. He keeps his thoughts closed to me but I can guess what's going through his mind. His eyes travel from my breasts to the hem of the miniskirt.

The sexual drive in a male vamp is powerful—more powerful even than in a human male. And sex between vampires is the best sex of all. The combination of blood and sex transcends anything experienced with or by mortals. His eyes still focused on the point where my skirt ends and legs begin, Fisher's mind opens to me in a heated rush of what he wants to do and how he wants to do it.

I nod agreement. *Let the woman go first.*

He glances down at her dismissively. *There are more like her. It is no loss.*

He releases his grip and takes one step back.

The woman is on her feet, confusion and fear casting a shadow on her face.

"There's a car at the top of the trailhead," I tell her. "The keys are in the ignition. Get out of here."

She shakes her head as if to clear it. "What about you? You are coming, too, aren't you?"

"No. I'll be all right. Just go."

Still, she hesitates.

I turn an animal face to her, growl the order. "Go. Now."

She gasps and bolts, stumbling on the wet sand. She doesn't look back.

While my attention is on the woman, Fisher makes his move. He grabs me. With one hand at my neck and one hand at my crotch, he forces me down on the sand. When I'm trapped beneath him, he rips at my blouse with claw-like nails, gathers my skirt up until it's bunched around my waist. His eyes glow yellow and for an instant, I'm transported back to a dark parking lot on a hot July night when another vamp claimed me.

This night will be different.

Fisher pauses, lets go with one hand to fumble with his belt. It's all the hesitation I need.

I jerk my hands free and fling him off, not giving him even a moment to recover before I've reversed our positions. He's beneath me now, his hands pinned behind his back by the weight of our bodies.

He's grinning. *You like to be on top. That's okay with me. But you'll have to open my collar. I can't seem to reach it.*

His words mock me. It's all right. I smile back and do as he asks.

He squirms, positioning his pelvis against the fabric of my panties. I feel his excitement. It sickens me. Just like the thoughts he's projecting and the lust that burns my skin like acid wherever his flesh touches mine.

Come on. Let me in.

His tone is the high-pitched plea of a demanding child.

I want to drink a little first, I tell him. *Get in the mood.*

Irritation sparks along with the beginnings of anger. He raises his head to glare at me. *No. We fuck first.*

I leverage myself against him, forcing his head back on the sand with the heel on my hand. *No. I drink first.*

For the first time, he realizes that I'm stronger than he is, that he is not in control. He reacts predictably, struggling and cursing.

Like a cat with a wounded bird, I play with him. Let him try to wriggle out from under me, to work his hands free. I want him to feel the same helplessness his victims felt, know some of their desperation and fear. He tries to probe my mind, asking if this is a game. I swat away his attempts to read my thoughts. He is baffled with the turn this thing has taken.

What are you doing?

A smile. *Why, I'm playing with you. Isn't this what you like?* I bring my knee up into his groin. Press down until I see his face twist. *Pain. Terror. Helplessness. Isn't this what gets you off?*

He gasps. Tries to burrow his body into the sand to release the pressure. When he realizes he can't, he bucks against me. *You bitch. You tricked me. I'll kill you for this.*

From far away, I hear the faint howl of a siren. It's time to end it.

His skin is salty to my tongue. When he feels my teeth at his neck, his body relaxes, his thoughts flash that this is more like it. He presses his engorged sex against me and starts to move to the rhythm of his heartbeat. I open his throat with a single bite and start to drink.

He thinks he's won. He tells me again to let him in, demands sex. It's not until I refuse, refuse to stop feeding, refuse sex, refuse to give him access to my neck, that he realizes what is happening.

By then it is too late. It doesn't take long. I'm caught up in the hunger. He grows weak, his thoughts diffuse, froth, like foam on the crest of a wave. All the pain and death he's inflicted on his victims flows into me. The horror trips a gag reflex, but I can't stop. Even when he's a shell, a brittle husk, I keep sucking until I feel it. The shudder as his soul is released. Only then can I stop. Only then is the life force gone. Only then do I sit up, climb off his body and collapse on the sand.

There is still one more thing. I roll on my side to look at Fisher's face. When a vampire dies the second death, by staking or burning, he dissolves into dust. There's nothing left. Being drained is different and results in a kind of fast-forward aging. If Williams were to die like this, for instance, his two-hundred-year-old body would shrivel into something that might resemble a mummy's. Fisher, though, had only been vampire for ten years. His face and body look like that of a forty-year-old man.

I have to make it look as if a human killed him. I draw the knife from the sheath at my waist and slice across Fisher's jugular. I work at the bite marks with the serrated edge, opening a wide gash to hide them. A few drops of some clear liquid bubble from the wound. I then grab his ankles and pull his body into the water. I wade out a few feet from shore holding onto him until the current catches his body and carries it away. I want the sea to batter the remains, though it won't be a problem if the police have enough to determine cause of death. I doubt they'll waste serious manpower over the demise of a serial killer wanted in several states.

Now it's over.

I'm wet, bone weary, and sick inside from the infusion of Fisher's blood. If I were human, I'd stick a finger down my throat and vomit until my system was rid of the poison. But vampire physiology doesn't work like that. His blood is already coursing through my system. I'm stuck with it until I can purge it another way.

Brushing sand from my torn clothes, I start up the path.

The sirens are closer. Fisher's victim must have called for help. I need to be gone before anyone arrives. But Williams and I are going to have a talk.

A stake would have been so much easier.

CHAPTER 6

I HEAD FOR HOME PLOTTING HOW QUICKLY I CAN
get to Beso de la Muerte. Fisher's blood burns through
my system. But I know I have to check in with David first
and after our late night in San Francisco, I doubt he'll be
in before ten. Unlike me, David is not a morning person.

My cell phone rings just as I'm walking in the front
door. I flip it open. "Anna Strong."

"Hey, partner."

David's voice is cheery and much too alert for this early
in the morning. "David?"

"When are you coming in?"

"You're at the office already?" I may be able to get away
earlier than I expected.

A chuckle. "Don't sound so shocked. How soon can you
get here?"

I glance down at my wet, bedraggled form and torn
clothes. "I haven't even showered yet."

"Well, get to it, girl. I have a surprise for you."

"A surprise? What kind of surprise?"

"If I told you, it would spoil it. See you in a few."

He rings off and I'm listening to dead air. The enthusiasm I felt over the possibility of getting to Culebra's early vanishes with the suspicion that I'm going to hate his surprise. I always do. They usually involve his girlfriend, Gloria. For a man who is smart and sexy and a great business partner, his taste in women sucks. To make matters worse, he's oblivious to the fact that we hate each other.

I look around my sun-filled cottage. I want to take a shower, a long, hot shower, and fall into bed.

I heave a sigh and toss the phone onto the couch. Oh well, one out of two isn't bad. Before starting upstairs, I flip on the coffeemaker. I don't care what David's *surprise* is, it can wait until I've washed Fisher's foul taste from my mouth and off my body.

The shower revives me though I scrub so hard, my skin tingles when I'm through. I lather on a rich, perfumed body lotion and slip into a clean sweat suit to head downstairs for coffee.

I'm a purist when it comes to coffee, no flavored blends for me. I like the rich, dark taste and aroma of a Jamaican or Kona coffee, mellowed with real cream and a little sugar.

I fill a mug and take it back upstairs. I've only been back in the cottage a month. It burned to the ground not long ago, another of Avery's legacies. When I rebuilt it, I added a deck off the master bedroom. I furnished it with a wicker table and two chairs, though I've yet to have anybody up here to occupy the second. I sink into one now and cast a glance toward the empty one. It seems I've more than one itch that needs scratching. I've fed, in a matter of speaking, but a different kind of hunger remains. My sexual appetite is as strong as my appetite for blood.

I selfishly wish Max were here. Except for the one time when I scared myself by almost drinking from him, sex with Max is great. But what am I thinking? I've got to stop this. I'm breaking up with Max the next chance I get. I have to.

So then what? Maybe David's surprise is a hot friend

who just got into town and David wants to set us up. Maybe I should wear something sexy to the office. Maybe . . .

Maybe Williams is right. If I had a mate, I could be inside right now sweating up the sheets instead of sitting here alone thinking about it.

So stop thinking about it.

My coffee is at perfect drinking temperature—body temp—and I suck at it greedily. It's still too early for the beach to be crowded, but there are a couple of surfers bobbing hopefully on the water. Hopefully is the operative word, the swells are as flat and listless as I feel. Still it's a distraction from a body aching for release.

I focus on the surfers until my cup is empty, then rouse myself to a standing position. I may as well get this over with. I change into jeans, a cotton sweater and running shoes. Hardly sexy. I just can't imagine what David has waiting for me. I have a nagging suspicion it won't be anything good.

IT'S NOT.

I smell her as soon as I walk into the office.

David is sitting alone at the desk, but her perfume, some expensive, flowery signature brand made exclusively for her, emanates from his clothes and skin like deadly fumes from toxic waste.

Gloria.

I was right. I'm going to hate this.

He looks up, sees me standing at the doorway and frowns. "Jesus, Anna. What's wrong? You look like you're going to be sick."

"Where is she?"

The frown dissolves into a grin. "How did you know?"

It takes every bit of effort not to roll my eyes skyward and groan. My sinuses are still revolting from the onslaught. I haven't felt like this since I was exposed to a creep who had binged on garlic. I cross the office and open the slider. Wide. "A lucky guess. Where is she?"

He sits back in his chair, still grinning. "She went across the street to get some rolls from the deli. Should be back in a minute. Are you hungry?"

I grunt a noncommittal reply and drop into my chair. I'm sure it'll take Gloria longer than a minute to get back. Someone will recognize the goddess and beg an audience. It happens all the time. If I'm lucky, she'll be detained a long time.

Gloria Estrella is a model. Tall. Beautiful. Rich. She and David became an item when he was playing football. Why they are still together is one of those great mysteries of life. She hates what he does for a living, hates that he lives in San Diego alone instead of L.A. with her and most of all hates that he has a female partner. Or more precisely, she hates me. She met Max not too long ago and got it into her brain that if David insists on doing what he's doing, Max would be a more suitable partner for him. David won't admit it, but I know in my gut she tries to impress that upon him at every turn.

I must have a glazed look on my face, because David leans across the desk and asks, "Seriously, Anna. What's wrong? You look a little green."

I shake off his question with a curt shrug. It would do no good to tell him what's wrong. I've tried before. Now my indigestion is coupled with disgust. So, I ask, "What's she doing in town?"

He gives me a raised eyebrow. "You can't have forgotten. The restaurant grand opening. It's this weekend, remember?" He flourishes a fancy envelope with gold engraving. "Your invitation. We expect you to be there, you know."

I can't keep the aggravation out of my voice. "*That's* your surprise?"

The corners of his mouth turn down. "I know you and Gloria don't get along but this is a big deal. She wants you to be there. It's a peace offering."

Gloria is at the door trying to sneak up on us. A tightness in my shoulders puts me on alert. That, and the insipid smile that appears suddenly on David's face.

"And Max, too, if he's in town."

Even expecting it, her voice from the doorway makes me jump, which is a pretty good indication of how she affects me. She dulls all my senses except an overwhelming feeling of revulsion.

I don't bother to swivel around in the chair to face her. David, however, jumps to his feet like an eager puppy and motions for her to take his seat.

She does.

We're face-to-face. Unless I pretend I'm blind, I have no choice but to raise my eyes to hers. I have to look up. Even sitting down, she's tall. My shoulders start to bunch together again.

The last time I saw Gloria, her hair and eyes were dark. Today, hazel contact lenses complement auburn hair touched with silver. The face is the same, though, heart shaped and delicate with flawless skin made even more radiant by artfully applied makeup, subtle makeup. Only a critical woman would notice the paint. I peer at her, searching for an imperfection.

Not even a solitary laugh line.

She knows what I'm doing. She sits without moving and lets me take inventory. She's wearing black slacks and a sweater the color of jade. It's tight. It would be. Got to get your money's worth out of the implants.

I make a vampire note to look her up in thirty years when she's sixty and I'm—the same as I am now.

I'd smile if I didn't hate this woman so much.

She is smiling, though, idiotically, as if the expression on my face was not poisonous. "Hello, Anna. You look much better than the last time I saw you. Your hair is combed. Well, sort of."

Every muscle in my body clenches in preparation for attack. The last time Gloria saw me I was in the hospital, recovering from being beaten, raped, and turned into a vampire. How nice of her to remember how awful I looked.

My jaw locks. Probably a good thing. Forces me to swallow the "fuck you" response that springs to my lips.

David jumps in. "Gloria. Anna had just been assaulted. Did you forget?"

His tone is scolding, but his face betrays how he feels about her. He's so fucking in love, it rolls off him in waves like her obnoxious perfume.

It's disgusting.

She tilts her head as if listening, but her eyes never leave mine. "Oh, that's right. Then she got involved with the doctor that treated her at the hospital. I hear he resigned not long after and disappeared. And what about Max? Seen much of him lately?"

Her implication is obvious. I get a mental picture of throwing Gloria on the carpet and gnawing at her throat like a dog with a bone. The fantasy makes me smile.

"Saw Max just last night," I reply.

"Really?" One perfectly plucked eyebrow jumps skyward. "How is he?"

"Fine." Didn't ask about you, though.

She reaches out a hand and David grabs it. "Then we can expect you both at the opening. It should be so much fun. Lots of celebrities. Lots of good food." She smiles with deadly sweetness. "Oh, and I have a designer friend in town. I told him you might need a dress. You're about a size eight, right?"

Jesus. Used to be an eight before the liquid protein diet. She damn well can tell the difference. Everybody can tell the difference. "Four, actually."

"Really?" Her tone tips beyond disbelief to incredulity.

My jaw is locking up again. "And I can find my own dress, thank you."

I realize my mistake as soon as the words escape my lips.

So does Gloria. "Wonderful. Then you'll come." She bats mascaraed eyelashes up at David. "See, I told you. Now you don't have to be worried you won't know anyone at the party. Anna will be there." Flashing eyes back in my direction. "And Max, too, I hope."

My cell phone chirps, saving me from having to answer. I dive for it in my bag and flip it open.

"Anna Strong."

"Anna, it's Williams."

I rise from the desk and turn my back on the lovebirds. "Are you calling about this morning?"

"No. I figured if I hadn't heard from you, either Fisher was dead or you were."

His tone, however, is light.

"Thanks. I appreciate the vote of confidence."

"Actually, I'm calling about Max." He's serious now, the undertone of humor gone. "I had a talk with Max's boss over at the DEA. He's sending someone over to police headquarters in half an hour. He thinks you should talk to him."

My heart starts pounding an alarm. "Why?"

"Max hasn't checked in for over a month. Not since he quit. They think he's gone rogue."

I don't know what's more shocking—Max quitting the DEA or the idea that he's a rogue agent.

Both concepts are ridiculous. I almost blurt the same out loud. But I stop myself. Gloria and David are watching me. I feel it and when I turn around, sure enough, David's face reflects curiosity, Gloria's reflects the profound hopefulness that this is a permanent summons to somewhere far away.

"I'll be right there." I flip the phone closed. "Sorry. I have to leave. David, I'll check in later, okay?"

He opens his mouth but I'm out the door before he gets a word out. I do catch Gloria muttering "same old, same old," under her breath.

I really hate that bitch.

CHAPTER 7

MAX GONE ROGUE? IT'S BEYOND RIDICULOUS. Yet, I knew something was wrong when I saw him last night. I thought it was fatigue and weariness. Maybe it was guilt that he'd kept something as big as quitting the agency from me. Especially if he was now after Martinez on his own.

Why would he not tell me that?

The drive from the office to SDPD headquarters isn't a long one. Morning commuter traffic, though, is heavy and it's slow going. I have more than enough time to run through every scenario I can think of to explain Max's actions. None of them makes sense.

The lobby of SDPD headquarters is quiet when I arrive. And there's a familiar face behind the counter—Patrolman Ortiz, a fellow vamp who works for Williams. I don't know how old he is in vamp years, we've never had the opportunity to discuss it, but in human terms he looks to be in his early twenties, five foot ten, 160 lean pounds. He's cute with an aquiline nose, dark hair and eyes, and olive skin stretched over high cheekbones. The only creases in his uniform are straight and sharp, and exactly where they're supposed to be.

"You stand up there behind that counter all night?"

He greets me in his usual chivalrous Latin way, with a little bow and a smile. "Good morning, Anna. Williams is waiting for you." Even though we're all alone he leans forward like a conspirator and adds, "Good work this morning. I take it you are unhurt."

I pat my stomach. "Only a raging case of indigestion."

He nods. "I understand. Cleanse yourself as soon as possible."

Fisher's blood roils in my system. I want nothing more than to rid myself of it. Drinking of Ortiz would at least get the bad taste out of my mouth. I get a flash of ravishing him behind the counter, putting some wrinkles in those perfectly ironed slacks. I lean toward him. "Is that an offer? Because I might just take you up on it."

He caught the image, too. He grins and holds up a hand. "I'm afraid my girlfriend would not approve. Not even if I explained it was a favor for a friend." He hands me the code and points deliberately to the elevator. "I will tell Chief Williams you are on the way up."

Girlfriend, huh? Curiosity prompts the next question. *Vamp or human?*

Human. He mimics my gesture of a moment before, patting his stomach. *Keeps me strong and off the streets. You should settle down, too, Anna.*

I fear Ortiz has been inducted into the "let's get Anna a human of her own" club. I can't face another lecture. I ward it off by heaving an exaggerated sigh. *Okay, okay, I'm on my way.*

I sense his amusement and it follows me into the elevator. When the doors slide open on the top floor, Williams is waiting to greet me. He's not laughing, though. He's frowning.

"When did you see Max last?" he asks without preamble.

I catch myself before blurting out the answer. "Why?"

He motions me to follow him to his office. He's changed

into formal chief of police mode, tailored gray suit, white shirt and gray-striped silk tie. I can feel him probing my mind, but I learned early on in the vamp game how to close off my thoughts if I need to.

Which is a kind of giveaway in itself to an old soul as powerful as Williams. He waits until we're both seated to comment. "It must have been recently or you wouldn't have asked me to check on him for you. Well, maybe it's just as well that you don't tell me. The Feds have you in their 'bad news' file after what happened with your niece."

Old news. I wonder why he's bringing it up?

That he picks up. "I'm not going to get involved in whatever is going on with Max, Anna. I'll let you handle it on your own."

It's not surprising that the Feds don't like me. I sent an FBI agent away for what I hope amounts to life. But the last part of Williams' statement is. He's always been reluctant to unleash me without being somewhere in the background to mitigate the damage. "Any particular reason why?"

Do you need my help?

I have to consider that a minute. Having an ally in the police department, especially such a powerful one, is something I've come to take for granted. At the same time, this is not the Watcher organization. I follow my own counsel on most things and that can put Williams in a precarious position. So far, he hasn't had to choose between his job and me, though what happened with Trish came close. I don't want that to happen again. Ever.

I don't know what's going on with Max. That's the truth. I have no problem meeting with the Feds on my own. Do you know anything about the agent they are sending? Is he likely to tell me anything?

Williams shakes his head. *The only thing I know is that his name is Foley.* He glances at his watch. *And he should be here any minute.*

We spend the time waiting for Foley by talking about Fisher and what happened on the beach. Williams is satisfied with the way I handled it, a great compliment in itself. He starts to shift the conversation toward a different subject, Avery again, but his phone rings.

Good. I caught the gist of what he was about to say and I don't want to discuss Avery. What happened with the vampire who first seduced and then betrayed me hangs like an ever-present specter between Williams and me. I just want to forget it.

Williams replaces the receiver. *Foley is here. He's on his way up.*

Williams comes around the desk to stand by me and we wait for the knock that announces Foley's arrival. I don't know what to expect since the last time I had dealings with the Feds it ended badly. So I'm surprised when the guy Williams invites in actually has a smile on his face, a smile that doesn't fade even when Williams introduces us.

The guy holds out a hand. "Name's Matt," he says.

I take his hand and shake it. Briefly. My hands are always cold. "Anna Strong."

If he notices the icy hand, he doesn't remark on it. Williams makes his excuses and leaves us. Foley motions to a chair. He's dressed in traditional Fed garb, dark suit, cream-colored shirt, discreet tie. He's short, shorter than me, probably just made the height requirement, and carries a little extra weight around his middle. He has a good face. Not handsome in the traditional sense, but even featured and square jawed. He looks *friendly*. Unusual for a Fed.

He watches me as he settles into the chair. "I know about the trouble with your niece. I'm sorry one of our own was involved in it. If you haven't gotten an apology from the Bureau, I'm here now to offer it."

The Bureau? Surprised, I ask, "You're not DEA?"

He shakes his head. "FBI." Before I can comment, he follows with, "You are exactly as I pictured you. Or rather, as Max described you."

Another unexpected revelation. "Max told you about me?"

Foley nods. "Of course. Max and I are friends. I know a lot about you. I know how you and Max came to be acquainted. How it was your contact that supplied the information needed to get Max that job with Martinez."

Okay. I suppose if Foley was Max's friend and a fellow federal agent, he might know about that, know that a skip I caught was a drug runner for Martinez. He used me to leverage a deal with the Feds. Information in return for immunity. It's how Max got his job as Martinez' driver.

But then Foley continues, ticking off the items as if reading from a mental checklist.

"I know that you were a schoolteacher who left education to pursue a rather unusual career path as a bail enforcement agent. I know you have been at odds with your family about that decision, but that they have come to terms with it, probably because of what happened with your niece. I know you have a relationship of some kind with Police Chief Williams, though not the details of that relationship . . ."

He seems prepared to go on but I hold up a hand to stop him. There would be no reason for Max to share any of this with Foley. "Max told you all that?"

Again, the slow smile. "Not exactly."

Suspicion turns to anger. "Have you been investigating me?"

"It's routine."

"Routine?"

He nods. "You're involved with Max. It's policy to run a background check on anyone close to an agent—especially an undercover agent. Don't look so disapproving. It's for your protection as well."

"Does Max know what you're doing?"

"He set it in motion."

"How?"

"I told you. Anyone involved with an undercover agent comes under scrutiny. Max knows this."

"Scrutiny? Or invasion of privacy?" But the rankling goes deeper. "Max didn't tell *me* about this."

Foley sits back in his chair. "You think he should have?"

I don't know what I think. I only know what I feel—anger. What else has Foley found out about me? When I meet his eyes, he seems to read the question reflected in mine.

"Max doesn't know everything," he says quietly. "I didn't see the point in telling him about your lovers—Dr. Avery, that teacher at your mother's school. I will tell him, if I think it necessary."

Foley's kindly demeanor suddenly rings false. The smile is the same, the straightforward manner relaxed and open. But there is an undercurrent. He's playing a game with me. The only consolation is that I get no vibe that he thinks I'm anything other than a female who likes to sleep around.

"What do you want from me?"

"Your help. We need to find Max."

"Is he in trouble? Because I don't believe he quit the agency."

Foley shrugs. "I can only tell you that he hasn't checked in in a month." His eyes narrow a little. "In fact, the last contact we had with Max was the day after he spent the night with you. Do you remember?"

I do. I was chasing the scumbags who exploited my niece at the time—including the one who turned out to be an FBI agent. I knew then something was going on with Max, but I was too involved in my own troubles to follow up on it. Maybe I should have.

I shake off the thought. Max is a successful and resourceful undercover agent for the DEA. He wouldn't have accepted help from me even if I'd offered it.

I look up at Foley. "Why are you here? What is the FBI's involvement?"

"Interdepartmental cooperation."

"Bullshit. I know enough about government bureaucracy to know there is no such thing as 'interdepartmental cooperation.' What's the real reason?"

Foley lets a sigh escape his lips. It comes off as dramatic and practiced, something meant to divert suspicion.

It doesn't. I don't move a muscle and I don't lower my eyes, forcing him to be the one to shift in his seat and look away. He does, finally, pushing himself to his feet. He crosses to the window and says over his shoulder, "Max is a friend. We've known each other a long time. If he's in trouble, I want to help. Before he gets in any deeper."

A friend? Somehow I don't think so. "Gets deeper in what? Isn't he doing his job?"

Foley isn't looking at me. If I wasn't aware that he would surely notice that I cast no reflection in the window he's so determinedly staring out of, I'd jump up and force him to meet my eyes. I don't buy this friendship thing and I don't trust his motives. "You think he's in danger because of Martinez?"

At that, Foley turns. "No, Ms. Strong." He isn't avoiding my eyes this time. "I'd say he's in danger because of you."

CHAPTER 8

WHAT FOLEY SAYS IS SO RIDICULOUS, IT'S ALL I can do to keep from snickering. But I stay quiet and stare right back at him.

The silence stretches while Foley eyes me. What is he expecting? That I'll crumble under his thousand-mile stare? He's a manipulator and, I suspect, a liar. I'm beginning to *really* dislike him.

"Wow, Foley, you're pretty good." I let sarcasm drip off each word. "Just the right amount of threat and concern. You've convinced me that *I'm* the danger to Max, not the vicious, murdering drug lord he's worked to bring down these last two years."

Foley's mask slips. The open, frank expression morphs into anger.

"Max has been in deep cover for years," I say. "He's put his life on the line every day getting close to one of Mexico's most dangerous men. And you tell me he's in trouble now because of me? Why on earth would I believe that?"

Foley comes back to the chair and sinks into it, holding

up both hands as if offering up an apology. "You're right, of course. I shouldn't have said that."

"Then why did you? What do you think I know?"

Foley lifts one shoulder. "Where Max is, maybe. What he's doing. Why he's gone off on his own."

For once, it's nice not to have to lie. "I can't answer any of those questions."

His eyes narrow. "You're telling me you haven't had any contact with him?"

Define contact. We spent only a few moments together last night. Hardly qualifies as "contact." And I'm sure Max is long gone from Beso de la Muerte. I shake my head. "I can't help you, Foley. And I don't believe Max has gone off on his own. He's too much of a company man. If he hasn't been in contact for a while, there's a good reason."

I've risen from my chair. Foley stands up, too. He fishes in a jacket pocket and comes up with a card. He holds it out. "Call me if you hear from him."

I push the card away. "When Max shows up, he'll contact his superiors in the DEA. But if he does get in touch, I'll be sure to tell him a *friend* in the FBI was asking about him."

Again, there's a spark of dark anger that's smothered before it does more than tighten the corners of Foley's mouth. It's instantaneous and almost undetectable. If I weren't such a suspicious bitch, I would have missed it.

Foley realizes I caught his little display of temper, too.

He pushes the card back into his pocket, smiling now with smooth concern. "Have it your way, Ms. Strong. But remember what I said. Max is in trouble. You can believe it or not. I hope you won't have cause to regret refusing my help."

Help? What help?

He tries the stare again, but when I don't stutter my thanks or recant and beg him to stay, he takes his leave.

Williams is back almost before the door closes. His eyebrows lift. "What does the FBI want with Max?"

Good question. I wish I knew.

Williams' phone rings and he crosses the office to answer it, giving me the opportunity to slip away. I feel Williams' thoughts reach out to me, telling me to hang on a minute. I pretend not to get it. All I want to do is be alone to figure out what this "friend" of Max's was really after.

It doesn't make sense.

Not this minute. And not a few minutes later, when I'm sitting behind the wheel of my car, trying to decide what to do. I'm restless and antsy. As far as I know, David and I don't have any jobs today. If I go back to the office, Gloria and her love-struck minion will no doubt try to drag me into their plans for the big party. I need that like a stake through the heart.

My stomach rumbles in distress. Fisher's poison. What I do need is an infusion of good, clean, human blood to rid myself of it. I could head for Beso de la Muerte now, not wait for tonight. Also, Max was just there. I don't expect him to be there still, but maybe he told Culebra something that might point me in the right direction to find him.

Because the one thing I'm sure of is that Max needs to be warned that the FBI is on his tail.

CHAPTER 9

I THINK I COULD DRIVE TO BESO DE LA MUERTE IN my sleep, I've done it so many times. And even though it's almost November, a warm Santa Ana wind has turned up the heat and chased all traces of clouds and smog out of a sapphire sky. Even the Bay sparkles with diamond-tipped swells. I put the top down on the Jag and let the wind tickle my skin and play in my hair. It's the kind of day that I imagine the chamber of commerce pays photographers to capture. Postcard perfect.

The kind of day even a vampire enjoys. Makes me glad for adaptation. A few centuries ago, I could have only dreamed of days like this. I'd have been confined to some dark hole to await the safety of the night.

We've come a long way.

I've come a long way.

But not far enough, evidently. I pick up the tail in my rearview mirror just as I get on 5 South, heading for the border. I noticed the car first on Pacific Coast Highway, a blue late-model sedan. It stuck with me as I cruised along the Bay, turned up Grape, and now it's two car lengths behind on the freeway. Coincidence? Could be. But more likely, it's Foley. I've had experience with the Feds. They don't take no lightly. And they don't believe anything you tell them that doesn't fit into their preconceived notions. Foley believes I know more than I told him and he's damn well going to prove it by letting me lead him straight to Max.

Sorry to disappoint you, Foley. I slow down and swerve onto the right shoulder. May as well let the jerk know that I've made him.

The blue Ford cruises past, the driver, not Foley, neither slows nor looks over at me. And he doesn't get off at the next exit, either.

Okay, I overreacted. I wait for a break in traffic and pull out. Still, I keep a lookout for anyone appearing to take undue interest in where I'm headed. Not an easy trick, since Mexico is a popular tourist destination from San Diego. But when I've crossed the border and set out on the road less traveled, away from Tijuana, and there's no one behind me, I start to relax. I guess I've let my imagination get the better of me.

Culebra is standing outside the saloon when I pull up, talking to a woman I don't recognize. She's human, I sense that right away. She stands with her back to me, weight evenly distributed on both feet, almost defensively. She's tall, taller than Culebra, with brunette hair drawn back in a scruffy ponytail. There's more hair out of the rubber band than in it. She's dressed in jeans and a tank top. Through the veil of hair that has escaped the rubber band, I see a tattoo at the nape of her neck, a snake coiled around a rod of some sort. There's another tattoo at the back of her shoulder. That one is a skull with a crimson rose where the mouth should be. She's in good shape, well-muscled arms and shoulders, small waist, narrow hips.

She turns at the sound of the car, glances my way, turns back to Culebra. Dismisses me with that one glance.

I immediately don't like her.

Still, I need to feed. And this is a human.

A host? I ask Culebra, climbing out of the car. My salivary glands have sprung into action.

He gives a rough shake of his head. His eyes never leave the woman's face and he's listening intently.

I can't tell if the shake is meant for me, or his companion. I step closer.

Go inside.

Culebra issues the order in a tone I've never heard him use before on anyone, let alone me. Cold. Belligerent. It makes the hair on the back of my neck stand up.

The woman turns again in my direction. Her face is thin, her mouth generous, despite the tight frown. She fixes me with a look designed to scare me or send me fleeing into the safety of the bar. It's a practiced scowl, full of venom.

Biting this one's neck will be a pleasure.

I look at Culebra. *Is she kidding?*

I don't get the reaction I expect. Culebra actually grabs my arm and propels me through the saloon's swinging doors.

I'm so startled, I let him.

His eyes are on fire. *Please, trust me on this. Stay here.*

I nod. It's all I can do, I'm still dumbstruck by being manhandled by Culebra. He drops my arm and whirls away from me, back through the doors.

I look around. The place is empty. Unusual. There are always desperados of some sort hanging around. Was it the woman outside that scared them away? Are they cowering in the caves waiting for her to leave?

I take a step toward the door. Culebra didn't tell me I couldn't *listen.*

Culebra is speaking in rapid-fire Spanish.

Damn. If he was having a telepathic communication with her, I could understand. For some reason, language is no barrier to thought transference. But he's speaking out loud and quickly. Because of me? Does he suspect I'm listening? Dumb question. Of course, he suspects. More than suspects.

I wish I had a better command of the Spanish language. David is fluent. He takes over when the need arises. I can only pick out a few words here and there. Culebra and the woman are arguing, that's obvious, but about what? So far, the words I snatch out of the conversation are disjointed. Someone or something wants to come here. Culebra doesn't want it. The woman is insisting.

And she's threatening him in some way. I don't need to know the words to grasp the implication. She's dangerous. Otherwise, Culebra would have gotten rid of her. Or not allowed her to come to Beso de la Muerte in the first place. His powerful magic would have prevented it.

She's a human and exerting enough pressure on Culebra to force this kind of confrontation. Who is she?

Their conversation teeters back and forth between threat and counterthreat and finally some sort of compromise must be reached because the tone softens into conciliation. I venture a peek outside. Culebra is embracing the woman. His face is to me and his expression is hard. She pulls back and lays a hand against his cheek. Then she walks away, down the steps, toward—what? The only car outside is mine. By the time I've registered that and look around for her, she's gone.

How did she do that?

I start outside, to question Culebra. But he pushes right past me into the saloon. He can't have forgotten I'm here, yet he doesn't so much as glance my way as he makes his way behind the bar. His mind is as black and impenetrable as ever I've experienced. He stoops to take a beer from the cooler, pops the top, and drains the bottle in one long, gurgling swig.

When he reaches for a second, I hold out a hand. "Mind if I join you?"

The sound of my voice startles him. The bottle slips from his hand and crashes to the floor. I jump, too. He stares at me, eyes dull until recognition sparks them back to life.

"Anna. What are you doing here?"

"You're kidding, right? You forget our conversation last night?"

He doesn't respond. And he doesn't look like he's kidding. I jab a thumb toward the door. "Who was that?"

"A friend."

"Friend? I don't think so. I may not be able to understand Spanish, but I understand friendship. That was not a friendly conversation. And why are we talking like this? Why don't you let me into your head?"

Culebra presses the palms of his hands against his eyes, as if reinforcing the barrier that's keeping me out. "It's better you don't know about this."

In two steps I'm across the room and beside him at the bar. "You can't be serious. She was threatening you in some way. Do you think I'll let that go?"

Culebra looks up at me and laughs softly. "No. You are too stubborn to do that."

He adds, *And not bright enough to know when you should.*

He watches for a reaction.

I don't give him the one he expects. *You are probably right. So stop fighting it. Tell me what she is.*

What she is? Not who?

She felt human. But she disappeared.

Culebra reaches again under the bar. This time when he straightens up he has two bottles of beer in his hand. He pops both tops, comes around, slides onto a bar stool and holds one out to me. When we've both taken a drink, he places his bottle on the bar and swivels to face me.

"You are right that she is not entirely human. She calls herself a Wiccan."

The phrase throws me at first, but then I remember what it is. "You mean she is a witch."

"She prefers Wiccan."

Semantics. I recall that Wiccans prefer the other title because "witch" conjures up evil associations. It also conjures up black cats and broomsticks. "So, is that how she did it? She had a broom stashed outside that she hopped on? Off to a Quidditch match maybe?"

But if Culebra catches the reference, he doesn't acknowledge it. Neither does he smile.

"Okay," I say. "Not a Harry Potter fan. But witchcraft is mostly dancing naked in the moonlight and love potions, isn't it? She was threatening you."

Culebra lowers his eyes. "It's not important."

The words are spoken softly, the tone almost indifferent. But the air around us shimmers with negative energy. He's sending me a message in a way he's never done before. He's telling me to back away. It's a threat—but not quite. Ice forms along my spine.

I stare at him, not understanding, not accepting. When he raises his eyes to meet mine, the feeling is gone.

"You must not come back here for a while," he says.

"What?"

"Go home, Anna. I have seen to your needs."

"My needs? What are you talking about? I'm not going anywhere."

He isn't listening. "I will let you know when it is safe to return."

"Safe? Who the hell was that woman?"

There's no answer. I'm looking right at him.

Then suddenly I'm not.

Because in the blink of an eye, Culebra is gone.

CHAPTER 10

JUST LIKE THE WOMAN MINUTES BEFORE, CULEBRA is *gone*. Not shape-shifted. I'd see a snake. He's disappeared. I'm so shaken, it takes me a few minutes to get up off the bar stool and search the place. He's not in any of the back rooms.

Could he be in the caves?

I wasn't aware that teleportation was one of his talents.

But then, I just saw a human do the same thing, didn't I?

The path from the saloon to the caves stretches like a dusty ribbon in front of me. I've taken it a hundred times. It's the middle of the day. Why does it seem menacing now?

I swallow down the feeling of trepidation and force myself to set off for the caves. It's eerily quiet. No buzzing of insects, no rodents scurrying for cover at my approach. Even the hum of the generator on Culebra's lighting system is silent. When I reach the entrance, I call out.

There's no answer. Not from Culebra. Not from anyone. Because there is no one at all in the caves. Not one shred of evidence to indicate there was *ever* anyone in the caves.

I find myself tiptoeing from one chamber to the other in inky darkness, panic so close it sits like a specter on my shoulder. Even the medical supplies are gone, the makeshift hospital nothing but a rock-strewn cavern. This place is a refuge for those under Culebra's protection. David was saved here. There are always twenty or so fugitives hiding from human or otherworldly threats. How did Culebra manage to clear everyone out? Where did he send them? Was Max with them when it happened?

The air is suddenly suffocating, pressing against my chest like a weight. Dank and foul, it seeps into my head like an insidious fog until I can't think.

I have to get out of here. The smell of mesquite and sage and the dry dust of the desert are like a powerful magnet pulling at me. I start to run toward the cave entrance. Even when I'm outside and the sun kisses my skin, I keep running. Back toward the saloon. It looks more forlorn and abandoned than ever. Some instinct tells me I don't want to go back in there until Culebra is back, too. So I skirt around it, head for my car. When I'm inside, when I manage to still the shaking of my hands long enough to fit the key into the ignition and crank it over, I glance into the rearview mirror.

A shadow moves across the road behind me.

I swivel around to take a closer look.

A dark shape, floating, ethereal. How could something as inconsequential as smoke exude such a feeling of menace?

Then, the shadow, too, is gone and all that's left is my fear.

CHAPTER 11

MY FOOT JAMS THE ACCELERATOR AND THE JAG lurches forward as if it, too, can't wait to get away.

I don't scare easily. Didn't when I was human, and as a vampire, I can count on one hand the number of times my skin has crawled the way it is now.

But what just happened is freaking me out.

A human woman disappears into thin air. Culebra gone, his hideout emptied. A shadow not cast by anything I could see, moving of its own volition across the road and into the desert. A feeling that I'm being driven out of Beso de la Muerte by a malevolent spirit that hovers just out of reach, ready to manifest itself if I should make the mistake of turning back.

I don't. I'm not sure I could.

The panic recedes as I drive farther away from Beso de la Muerte. My grip on the steering wheel relaxes, my head clears, my heart rate slows. The relief is enormous. Brain function returns, rational thinking creeps back, though each thought unfolds slowly like a paper ball released from a tight fist.

Culebra disappeared.

I had no idea shape-shifters could do that.

I chew on the possibility all the way back to San Diego. I know one other shape-shifter, Daniel Frey, but it's a weekday and he'll be teaching now. I'm not going to interrupt his class with my questions. I have too damned many.

I can drop in on him at his condo later.

Which leads me back to why I went to Beso de la Muerte in the first place.

The need to rid myself of Fisher's blood. I can't wait much longer. If I play my cards right, Frey will let me feed from him. We've done it before. It also occurs to me that the panic I felt in Beso de la Muerte might have something to do with the bad blood circulating in my system. I learned the hard way that it's not good to wait too long after feeding from a rogue to cleanse myself. It's vampire dialysis. A dose of untainted blood purges the toxins. And like dialysis, the longer you go without it, the harder it is to separate out the bad stuff and flush it away.

But I've always counted on Culebra. What am I going to do now? He's the link to my blood supply.

The thought sends another chill up my back.

I have no idea when I'll see him again.

My cell phone rings just as I pull into my garage.

I flip it open. "Anna Strong."

There's a moment of dead air before an unfamiliar voice whispers, "Tell your boyfriend. I'm coming."

Then the connection is cut.

It takes me a moment to process what I just heard. When I realize I should check the caller ID, I find the number is restricted. Of course. You can never use star 69 when you need to. I snap the phone closed and toss it into my bag.

Then I get mad.

More than mad. Furious. Because I have a strong feeling I know who made that call. Foley. Counting on spooking me into calling Max or even better, going to see him. Instinct tells me he's sneaky enough to try something like this.

I head into my cottage, looking around for a car I don't recognize. My home is on one of those small streets in Mission Beach where there is no motor vehicle access in front so all the garages open onto an alley. I know everyone on my block. There's not an unfamiliar car in sight.

So, he's probably somewhere on Mission Boulevard. No use looking there. It's one of the most popular beach thoroughfares in San Diego, fronted with restaurants, boutiques, bike and surf shops.

The tumblers on the lock to my back door fall into place with the turn of the key. I push inside, pausing to savor the one good thing in this bitch of a day—my home. The kitchen is filled with sunlight, the air smells of coffee and cinnamon. I toss my purse on the counter and head for the stairs.

Into darkness.

I stop at the foot of the staircase. Someone has pulled the curtains closed, down here and upstairs, too.

I tilt my head, listening. Nothing. I sniff the air. Under the aroma of coffee and the tang of salt air, is something else. Something I hadn't noticed at first. Musk. Testosterone. Senses springing to life, I breathe it in. It's human, I smell the blood. And male.

Is this what Culebra meant when he said he'd taken care of my needs?

But he doesn't have access to my house.

Does he?

I don't care.

Noiseless as a cat, I run up the stairs. Every molecule in my body vibrates in anticipation. I know whoever is here, was sent for one purpose. I know it without understanding, just as I know I'll take what I need and be whole again.

Thank you, Culebra.

He's in my bedroom, asleep. I hear deep, regular breathing. When I approach the bed, I can only make out a form under the covers. He's on his side, his face turned away from me. I'm shaking with need and sudden lust.

I want more than blood.

I strip off my clothes and slide under the covers. He

doesn't stir. Should I say something? No. Culebra sent him. He is here for one purpose.

I abandon thought, close my eyes, lose myself in pure tactile sensation. I fit my naked body against his, slide a hand around his waist, breasts pressed against a broad back, thighs cupped around buttocks. I move my hand down a flat abdomen, skim rock-hard thighs, come to rest between his legs.

He's awake now, I sense it, but he doesn't move. He lets my hands arouse him, moans softly in pleasure. I'm on fire. I position myself so that my mouth is at his neck. I want to take him inside me when I feed, but the thirst is too great. I can't help myself, can't stop the hunger from taking over. I open his neck.

Blood flows into my mouth, into my being, flooding me with warmth and consolation. Relief and release. Peace. I feel all Fisher's negative energy fade until he is no longer a part of me. My host feels it, too, the euphoria, the joy. His body burrows against mine, seeking greater closeness, wanting more. This is why humans offer themselves to vampires. We are not yet united physically, but currents of desire shake him as I feed.

The first primal hunger satisfied, I begin to stroke him.

Thank you, Culebra.

Caught in the vortex of pleasure, the man cries out.

"Anna."

My eyes open, my heart races.

He starts to roll toward me. "Anna."

I hold him still, not wanting to face him. I know the voice. I start to shake. I want to pull away, creep back down the stairs, hide until the shaking stops. Because I know the voice. The man beside me, the man whose blood is now commingled with mine, the man I didn't recognize in my lust to feed is Max.

I've just done what I swore I would never do. I've fed from Max.

Without thinking, without consideration. I took what I needed.

Worse, I didn't *know* it was Max. I didn't recognize his body. Didn't recognize his smell or touch. I didn't try. I didn't care.

Max is still on his side, his eyes closed. He's moaning that he wants more. He takes my hand and pulls me closer. He's violently aroused, not realizing that the pleasure he feels comes not from any human stimulus, but from the act of an animal. The vampire. Me.

I've got to stop it. I've got to close the wound and make it disappear. I've got to make Max forget what he's just experienced.

In a panic, I move closer, lap spilled blood from his neck and chin. Suck gently on his torn skin until I feel the cells repair themselves and nothing physical remains to indicate what I've done. But he'll remember.

Max rolls over, pins me beneath him, forces my legs open with his own. He takes his pleasure the same way I just took mine—aggressively, fiercely. I'm drawn into the current of *his* need and when it's over, and he collapses against me with a muffled gasp, I know, I *know* things will never be the same between us.

Because Max has experienced it now, and he will know the difference. Not the reason, he can never know that, but the sensation, the thrill.

Damn you, Culebra.

CHAPTER 12

MAX IS SITTING UP, PROPPED AGAINST THE HEAD-
board. His skin, where it touches mine, is hot,
flushed with what passed between us.

The weariness and tension that were so evident last
night are gone. His eyes are clear blue again until he looks
at me and a frown clouds them and tightens the corners of
his mouth.

"What just happened?"

I try to laugh. It sounds more like a strangled yelp. I
clear my throat, try again, going for more of a tease this
time. "If you have to ask, it *has* been too long since we've
had sex."

He shifts, turning so that he is looking straight into my
eyes. "This was different. More than sex. You must have
felt it."

Oh, yes. I did. But how to explain it? Especially since I
know it will never happen again.

He's waiting, body tense.

I take the coward's way out, counter with a question of
my own. "How did you get here?"

He stares at me a second before answering, "Culebra said he got a message from you. That I was to come here and wait." He relaxes a little, smiling. "When you weren't here, the temptation to take a nap in a real bed was just too strong. I hope you don't mind."

"Why would I mind?"

Max shrugs. "I can't always tell how you'll react to things. The last time we were together like this"—he motions to the bed—"you seemed different."

I start to argue that of course I was different, I'd just found out I had a niece in big trouble. But he stops me with a curt wave of his hand.

"I know what you're going to say. You were worried about Trish. I understand. But there was—is something else going on, too. Something you won't share with me. I feel it. It started the night you were attacked. You act differently around me. You hold back." A small smile lifts the corners of his mouth. "At least you did until today."

I don't know how to respond. He's right. I hold back for a damned-good reason. Vampires aren't known for their self-control as I've just so dramatically proven. Yet, I don't dare tell Max the truth. I know he goes to Beso de la Muerte and he's admitted to me that some of the strange characters he's met there are a little different. But while "different" to Max means delusional, maybe even criminally psychotic, all the same, he believes they're human. How would he react if he found out some of those characters are not only inhuman, but immortal? And I just happen to be one of them?

Max isn't making this easy. He won't look away, won't let me off the hook. He wants an answer.

"I don't know what to say, Max. If you feel I've been holding back, I'm sorry." I decide to turn the tables. A dirty trick, but he's backed me into a corner. "And if you want to talk about holding back, how about what you've been doing? I heard that you haven't checked in with your boss in over a month. I had a chat with an FBI agent this morning who says you're in trouble. You didn't mention any of that last night, did you?"

Max turns away from me. "Is that the reason you wanted to see me?"

"Is it true?"

His voice cuts like a whip. "Who contacted you from the FBI?"

"His name is Matt Foley. He says he's a friend."

There's no expression on Max's face. None. I'm looking at a mask. I wanted to take his mind off me. It seems I succeeded. His skin is suddenly cold. "Max, he isn't a friend, is he?"

Max throws off the covers and climbs out of bed. He goes straight into the bathroom without looking back. In a minute, I hear the shower running.

I sink back onto the bed. Christ. I don't know whether I should follow Max into the shower, press for answers, or get dressed and out of here before he gets back.

I know I can't do that, though. He needs to know what I suspect about Foley following me and I need to know what's going on between them.

So, I lie there for the ten minutes it takes Max to return to the bedroom. He's dressed and heads straight for a chair where he picks up his gun and clips it to his belt. Then he reaches for his jacket. He doesn't look my way or say a word.

I barely have time to shrug into a robe before he gets to the bedroom door. I stop him with a hand on his arm. "You can't leave. Not yet. I think he's watching me."

Max turns around. "Why?"

I tell him about the call I received. "I thought it was a trick to get me to contact you. Now I'm afraid he knows you're here."

Max lets me lead him back to the bed. He sinks down on the edge. "I'm sorry he dragged you into this," he says.

"Who is he?" I ask, sitting beside him. "Why is the FBI investigating you?"

Max tosses the jacket aside. "The *FBI* is not investigating me. Foley is. I thought I'd covered my tracks. Especially where you're concerned. I'm sorry, Anna."

I take his hand, squeeze it gently. "He knows a lot about us. About me. He said you told him."

Max shakes his head. "Foley works for Martinez."

I'm not sure I heard that right. "What?"

He pulls his hand out of mine. "He's a mole for Martinez."

"In the FBI?"

Max nods.

"And how many people know this?"

Max looks away. "The better question is how many people believe it?"

I've known Max for two years. He's the most stable, reliable man I know. His instincts are better than good. And my own impressions of Foley were less than favorable. Still, why wouldn't Max's own people believe him?

Doubt must be reflected on my face because Max's expression darkens. He reaches again for his jacket and starts to stand up.

I don't let him, stopping him with a hand on his arm. "Wait a minute."

"You don't believe me, either. I can see it on your face."

"Hey, don't jump to conclusions. I met Foley today. He's clever and manipulative. What I wonder is what makes you suspect he's working for Martinez?"

"I saw them. Together."

"Did you report it?"

Fury makes the muscles at his jawline tighten. "Of course I did. My boss in the DEA checked it out. Trouble is, Foley had an alibi for the time I 'claimed' he was in Mexico with Martinez. He and his partner were working a kidnapping case in Arizona. The investigation was dropped." He pauses, his eyes become cold. "And my boss looked at me the same way you are now."

He takes my hand with his own and removes it from his arm. "I'd better go."

"Not yet. What do you think Foley wants?"

"That's easy, Anna," he says. "He wants me. Foley is the one who told Martinez that I worked for the DEA. Martinez put a million dollar bounty on my head. Foley plans to collect."

"He's not being very subtle about it. He met me in the police chief's office."

"He brought Williams into this? Great. I suppose your friend issued an APB on me already."

Max knows of my connection to Williams because of Trish's case. He thinks my family has stayed in touch because we're still awaiting word on whether or not Trish will have to testify at trial. And then, of course, I deal with police all the time in my capacity as a bounty hunter. Max doesn't know about the other . . . services I perform for Williams. I shake my head. "Williams is hardly my friend. Anyway, he only got Foley and I together as a courtesy. Foley asked for the meeting. I'm more concerned because Foley doesn't seem to care who knows he's after you."

"That's because he's been telling people that we're friends. And we have known each other a long time. We went to high school together. But we lost contact after that. A fact no one seems much interested in. Now he's got everyone convinced I've gone rogue."

"But your boss in the DEA, he can't believe that. Why don't you tell him what you just told me?"

Max's eyes narrow. "I tried. He wants me to come in. If I do that, I'm dead. I have only one choice. Get Martinez and Foley before they get me."

"How? Do you have a plan?"

Max passes a hand over his face. "I had one chance. I knew where Martinez stashed his family."

The expression on his face, the way his voice drops off sends alarm racing up my spine. "What happened?"

He doesn't look at me. "The Federales found his safe house first. There was a shoot-out. His wife and three kids were killed in the cross fire. Martinez got away. He blames me. Thinks I gave up the location."

"You didn't?"

He shakes his head. "Martinez is a stone-cold killer but he loved his family. I would have gone there to bargain with him, never to send a hit squad against him. I didn't give up the location but someone did."

"Foley?"

"Foley just wants the money. And I doubt he knew where Martinez had gone. Even Martinez' men didn't know where the house was."

"But you knew."

He nods.

"So Martinez blames you for the death of his family?"

Max doesn't answer. He doesn't have to.

"Last night. Did you know I'd be in Beso de la Muerte?"

Max grunts. "No. I was being tailed by Foley, Martinez and, I suspect, some of my fellow agents. I needed a few hours rest. Culebra offers sanctuary."

"And you weren't afraid they'd catch up to you while you rested?"

"It was a chance I had to take. Martinez knows about Beso de la Muerte, of course, but he hasn't shown up there since his business with Culebra concluded. It's almost as if once it was done, he forgot the place existed."

Probably not far from the truth. I think Beso de la Muerte is protected by some powerful glamour. What happened today may be part of that but this isn't the time to venture down that path. "What can I do to help?"

"Nothing." Max's eyes flash. "There isn't a damned thing you can do. If you try, you'll only make things worse and maybe get us both killed."

"But what about Foley?"

He stops me with a determined shake of his head. "I mean it, Anna. You can't fix this. I know what I have to do. Find Martinez and bring him in. If you want to do something, let me stay here until dark. I've got a car parked on Mission. If Foley is watching, create a diversion so I can get to it."

"That's it? What if I go to Williams? He has contacts in the FBI."

"And tell him what? You think he's going to believe me when my own people don't?"

Max looks tired. Arguing is not going to accomplish anything except add me to his list of things to worry about.

"I won't interfere if you don't want me to," I say.

"Do you mean that?"

I blow out a breath. "Do I have a choice?"

The cloud lifts from his eyes. He smiles and pulls me to my feet. "So, it looks like I have a few hours to kill." He puts his hands on my shoulders and works the robe down my arms. "What about you? You and David have anything going today?"

David and I? Not a thing, especially with Gloria hanging around. I start unbuttoning his shirt. "What shall we do?"

"Whatever you did before? Do it again."

My head is screaming, never. But my heart is thudding against my ribs and my traitorous body is already warming to the idea. Max leans down to kiss me and I feel his excitement. I can control myself. I can.

The ugly voice of reason starts screaming in my head. *You are supposed to be breaking up with this man. What are you doing?*

But it's too late. I'm already kissing him back.

Then the damned phone rings.

CHAPTER 13

M AX GROANS.
"I don't have to answer it," I whisper. "The machine can pick up."

We stand, wrapped in each other's arms until the answering machine clicks on.

"Hey, Anna. It's David."

Max steps back and gives me a little push toward the phone.

Reluctantly, I cross to the other side and punch the speakerphone mode. "What's up?"

"You're there. Good. We have a job. Can you meet me at the office?"

My eyes slide to Max. "This isn't such a good time."

There's the briefest of hesitations before David says, "Sorry. But it's now or never for this. If you want, I'll call Jerry. See if he has someone else I can use for backup."

There's an undertone in his voice that gives me pause. He sounds both annoyed and angry. I glance over at Max. This time, Max gets up and starts toward me, gesturing that I should go. "I'm on my way."

Max takes the phone out of my hand and replaces the receiver on the cradle. "Go."

"Will you be here when I get back?"

Instead of answering, Max starts rebuttoning his shirt. I fish my clothes out from under the bed where I kicked them in my haste to jump into bed.

Awkwardly, I wriggle into my jeans, pull my sweater over my head. Max waits until I'm dressed to reach down and pick up my bra. It was lying half-hidden among the bedclothes. He twirls it around a finger. "Forget something?"

I take it from him, stick it in a drawer. "I'll be back as soon as I can," I say. "Stay here. I'll let you know if I pick up a tail."

Max doesn't reply.

I reach up and touch his cheek. "I'm sorry I have to go. Wait for me, okay? Promise you won't leave until you hear from me."

Max smiles and wraps me in a hug. "Be careful," he says.

He doesn't say he'll wait for my call or me. He is smiling though, and that's a better image to carry away than the one last night at Beso de la Muerte.

I back out of the garage and head up the alley toward Mission. I idle longer than I need to at the intersection, hoping if Foley is watching, he'll give himself away by starting his own car. But when I finally negotiate the turn, the only car behind me is a battered woody with a surfboard on top and three mop heads inside. No one else pulls away from the curb. No one else seems to take any interest in my progress downtown.

When I call home, to let Max know that if Foley is watching the place, he's probably still there, he doesn't pick up. I speak the message to the recorder, not knowing if Max is listening or not. Maybe he decided not to wait for dark to leave after all.

But David *is* waiting. In the parking lot, standing beside his Hummer. He's wearing jeans ripped at the knee and a dirty Windbreaker. He hands me a paper bag and a small gun case and motions for me to climb inside.

I raise an eyebrow at the sight of the case. "You brought my gun? Who are we going after?"

He waits until we're both belted in to answer. "Remember that police officer who was killed in Chula Vista last summer?"

How could I forget? Big story with an unhappy ending. The victim was a young officer just out of the academy, making what he thought was a routine midday traffic stop. Only the car ended up being stolen and the driver was a Mexican national wanted by the FBI on drug trafficking charges. The cop was shot before he got the report back on the car. And Alvaro Guzman made it across the border before his identity was confirmed.

"Guzman is back in San Diego? I can't believe it. If he's caught, he's as good as dead. What would bring him back here?"

David smiles. "Love." He draws out the word. "Jealousy. Getting high on his own supply. He has a lady who took up with his cousin the minute he was gone. The cops know it, too, and have been watching both of them. So has a friend of mine. From the inside. He says Guzman has already made it across the border. He's just waiting for the chance to catch his cousin with his girlfriend."

"And this friend told *you* this why?"

"Best reason of all. The reward. It's over half a mil now. He's in for a third and he doesn't have to be the one who turns Guzman in. He's our silent partner."

"This is the first I've heard of any of this."

David lifts a shoulder in response. "I wasn't sure it would lead to anything. But I got a call today. Guzman is hanging out in the swamps behind Qualcomm Stadium. If we can get to him before the cops do, the reward is ours."

Quite a payday. I open the gun case and withdraw a weapon I haven't used since becoming a vampire. Still, the little .38 Smith & Wesson feels comfortable in my grip. Then I open the paper bag. Inside are a torn Windbreaker not unlike the one David is wearing and a ratty black knit cap. I slip on the Windbreaker and check the cylinder on the .38 before clipping it onto the waistband of my jeans.

The stadium comes into view. David's ripped jeans, the tattered Windbreakers, the caps. All designed to let us blend in with the inhabitants of San Diego's infamous tent city.

San Diego is, for the most part, reclaimed desert. In years of drought, Mission Valley is an arid depression, every inch developed up to the banks of what is known euphemistically as the San Diego River. Occasionally, though, in times like the last couple of years when we've had three times the average rainfall, the San Diego River actually becomes one. The riverbanks come alive with man-tall reeds, scrub oak and chaparral, a family of plants indigenous to Southern California. The seeds of these plants lie dormant for decades and germinate at the first really good rainfall. In a matter of weeks, a desert forest blooms where dust used to reign.

It's that way now. Even a few of the roads connecting Hotel Circle and Friars Road have collapsed or are under water. The embankments on either side of the roadways form a shelter under which the homeless, and often the lawless, pitch their tents, hidden away from prying eyes in a tangle of dense brush.

One of those flooded roads is Fashion Valley Road. As we near it, David pulls the Hummer to the curb in front of a large condominium complex. He motions to our right. We can just make out the pitched tops of a makeshift tent city under the bridge.

"Guzman is supposed to be in there," he says. He pulls a flyer from the pocket of his Windbreaker and unfolds it. Then he hands it to me. "Here's Guzman's wanted poster. My contact says his hair is longer now, but he's still clean shaven. He has a two-inch scar on his left cheek."

I look at the photo, committing it to memory. The stats say he's five foot ten, 175 pounds. "Any idea what he's wearing?"

David shakes his head. "No. But we can be sure he's armed, so don't take any chances. Dead or alive, we collect the reward."

Something in his tone makes me shift my gaze from the paper in my hand to David. He's looking at me with uncharacteristic intensity. "What's up?"

He waits a beat too long to shrug off my concern.

"David?"

He expels a breath. "Guzman has nothing to lose. He's facing the needle."

He has shifted in his seat, turning his face away from me. It doesn't take much to read the meaning behind the words. He's thinking back to an evening last summer. "Hey. David." Anger sparks like a flare. "You didn't have this problem a few days ago. What's changed?"

Color creeps into his face, his jaw tenses.

"I thought you'd gotten over what happened last summer. You called me a half hour ago and now suddenly, you're . . ."

When the truth hits, it's like a fist to the gut. "Oh, god." I jam the cap over my hair to keep from reaching over and punching him. "You were with Gloria when you got the call from your friend, right? Gloria told you I couldn't handle this. She said you should bring someone else in. That's why you said you could call Jerry for backup."

It's clear now, David's sudden change in attitude. Jerry Reese is the bondsman we often work for. It doesn't surprise me that Gloria would suggest David contact him instead of me. What does surprise me is that David actually had the guts to go against her. At least until now.

"That's it, isn't it?" I'm so angry I'm shaking.

I shove open the car door and jump down. "When are you going to see what's going on? Gloria is an asshole. She wants to break up our partnership."

David climbs out and comes around to meet me at the front of the Hummer.

"I've really had it with that bitch. How long are you going to let her pull this crap?"

But David isn't listening. His attention has been drawn to something else. I can tell because his eyes are not focused on me, but over my shoulder. Irritated, I turn to follow his gaze.

There are three men walking on the other side of the road, heading toward the embankment under the bridge. All are dressed in jeans and Western shirts. The one in the middle glances over at us and looks quickly away.

Guzman.

I grab David by the shirt and swing him toward me, raising my voice. "Are you listening? I won't go through this again. You have to make a choice. Gloria or me. You can't have us both."

The men on either side of Guzman are watching us.

David picks up the cue. "I'm sick of your ultimatums. You're crazy if you think I'd choose a junkie like you over that sweet piece of ass."

One of the men laughs and says something to the others in Spanish. Guzman still does not look our way.

Without thinking about it, I reach up and smack David across the face.

He isn't expecting it and he recoils in shock. "What the fuck?"

We have the attention of all three now. Even Guzman is smiling. But they've reached the edge of the bridge and without pausing, they disappear into the brush.

We wait a minute to be sure they're really gone, then David rubs at his cheek with the palm of his hand. "Ouch. That hurt."

I strip off the Windbreaker and the cap. They've seen us. No way will we blend in with the residents of tent city now. No use in trying.

David glares down at me. "I *said* that hurt."

"I had to make it look good, didn't I?"

He slips out of his Windbreaker, too. His Glock is nestled

under his armpit. He draws it from the holster and checks the safety. "Next time," he grumbles, "come up with something that doesn't involve slapping me, okay?"

I have to struggle to keep the smile from my face. I won't tell him how really *good* it felt to give in to a purely human impulse and whack him. The only thing better would have been if it had been Gloria's face. I force the corners of my mouth into a frown. "So how do we do this? It looks like Guzman has picked up a couple of friends."

David is quiet for a couple of seconds.

A smile tickles my mouth. "Let's continue the farce. They heard you call me a junkie. I'll go down there and try to score."

"Wait a minute," he says. "You can't go down there alone. It's too dangerous."

"I won't be alone for long," I counter. "Will I?"

"No. But—"

I knot the Windbreaker around my waist to cover my gun. "I'll go in the same way they just did. You cross to the other side. I'll give you five minutes to get set."

David looks across the street and then back at me. "Okay. But don't do anything stupid like approach Guzman on your own. Wander around looking sad." He narrows his eyes at me. "After all, you just lost your boyfriend. Let him approach you."

"I know how to handle this," I snap. "You just be ready."

I turn and walk across the street.

David calls out, "You junkie, skank whore. I'm gone, you hear me? I hope your low-life friends take care of you because I'm out of here."

He climbs into the Hummer and screeches away from the curb.

Good job, David. A little too enthusiastic maybe, but they should have heard that all the way to the stadium.

I raise a middle finger to the departing car and plunge into the undergrowth.

I don't have to hide the smile anymore. I've fed and my body hums. True, I fed from someone I never intended to but Max's good, pure, clean blood restored my equilibrium in spite of whatever misgivings I have about us. The adrenaline has kicked in, triggering a purely human sense of excitement. This is why I became a bounty hunter. This is going to be fun.

CHAPTER 14

I HEAR VOICES COMING FROM THE ENCAMPMENT.
Spanish, English, male, female. Even the squeals of a
couple of kids at play. But it takes a few minutes to push
through an overgrown tangle that rips at my jeans and
catches at the hem of my Windbreaker. When I finally do
break free, I feel as though I've stumbled onto a gypsy
camp located like a bad joke in the middle of the city.

There's no one in sight as I walk through a narrow aisle
formed by ragged tents and cardboard lean-tos. Whoever
belonged to the voices I heard a moment ago vanished at
the sight of a stranger wandering into their camp. The only
interest I attract is from some kind of huge winged insect
that buzzes relentlessly around my head.

I hate bugs.

The second time I swat at the thing, my ineffectual gesture brings forth a gale of childish giggles. I look around to
find I've been followed by two tots, neither older than five
or six, both little towheads, wearing dirty jeans and faded
Chargers T-shirts. They hide their faces behind their hands

when I turn to face them, their narrow shoulders shaking with laughter.

I squat down to their level. "You think that's funny, huh?"

The taller of the two spreads his fingers to peek out at me. "Don't do no good to swat. You're too slow and the bugs are too fast."

I consider that for a minute, looking around to see if we've an audience. It appears we don't. When the swamp creature with the wingspan of a small helicopter comes back at me, I snatch it out of the air and hold it captive in the palm of my hand.

Both kids look at me with wide eyes and open mouths. I hold the bug out to them and they look like they're ready to bolt. With a shrug, I open my hand and the creature takes flight.

"Show me how to do that!" The talkative one squeals, jumping up and down.

I stand, wiping bug dust from my hand by rubbing it against my jeans. "Maybe later. Right now, I'm looking for someone."

He squints up at me. "Who?"

"Don't know his name. But I just saw him come down here a few minutes ago. He was with two friends."

The kid tilts his head. "Why are you looking for him?"

So young to be so suspicious. But maybe that's what comes from living in a dump under a bridge.

When I don't answer right away, he pantomimes taking a hit on a joint, and then slaps the crook of his right arm with his left hand. "Weed or smack?"

The gestures and the question coming from this angel-faced kid remind me that this is not a game. My cavalier attitude undergoes immediate adjustment. I have to get the hell away from these kids and find Guzman.

I stand up abruptly. "You going to show me where the guy is or not?"

The chatty kid's face droops into a sullen mask. "He's in the last tent. Down there."

He and his silent companion start to follow me, but I whirl on them. "Get out of here. Playtime's over."

The glare, the heat in my voice roots them to the spot. But I want them gone. I sense the approach. When they still don't make a move to leave, I flail my arms at them. They turn tail and run.

I keep my back turned. I know someone is right behind me.

"Those kids bothering you?"

The words come from over my shoulder, a soft male voice.

I pretend to be startled, flinch and turn on my heels. One of Guzman's companions from a few minutes ago is now standing right in front of me.

I make a quick mental calculation. David should be around here somewhere by now.

The guy is doing some calculating of his own. His eyes sweep the length of my body. He has the look of a predator. "Didn't I just see you up on the street? With a big guy? You got him good. Big slap for such a little lady."

I draw myself up. "He deserved it, the asshole. Thinks he's such a big shit. Thinks he can treat me like dirt and I'm going to take it. I don't need the fucker. I don't need anybody."

I let a hint of desperation seep into the tirade. He picks up on it just the way I knew he would. His kind always look for weakness. It doesn't matter if it's man or vampire, the wiring is the same.

His face takes on a solicitous expression—you have to look closely to read the truth behind the mask. The eyes remain hard and cold but the voice is like a caress. "What can I do for you, pretty lady? You didn't come down here by accident. How can I help you?"

I start to fidget. "I heard I could buy what I need here."

He tilts his head, narrows his eyes. "Why here?"

I let my temper flare. "Why here? Gloria." I spit the name. "The cops know me in my neighborhood. They watch me all the time. I think David's bitch, Gloria, ratted on me. She's trying to get rid of me." I shove a hand into my pocket. "Look, I have money. Can you help me or not?"

He reaches out a hand of his own and stops me from going any further. Glancing around, he says, "Easy, *chica*. I can help you. Come with me to my tent. It's not safe for a girl to flash money. There are others here who would take advantage."

I haven't seen another soul except for those two kids. Still, I let my shoulders slump. "Thank you. I've never had to do this before. Not like this anyway."

He puts a hand on my arm and rubs my wrist, tugging gently until I follow him toward the tent at the end of the row. I pretend to stumble, and he helps me regain my balance with an arm around my shoulders. When he pulls me against him, I feel the gun tucked into his waistband under the oversized Western shirt.

A big gun.

His arm remains across my shoulders until we get to the tent. The second guy we saw walking with Guzman stands like a sentinel in front. My guy sweeps back the canvas covering that serves as a door, leans forward and says something in Spanish.

Great. Is he alerting Guzman that he's bringing someone in or telling him to start shooting?

He steps aside. If I balk now, it's over. I steel myself to take a defensive posture if needed and duck into the tent.

The air in the small tent reeks of dope and unwashed male. To make matters worse, it's muggy as a steam room and just about as hot. My skin prickles in revolt.

Guzman is seated cross-legged on the cardboard covering the floor of the tent. I needn't have worried about being greeted by a hail of bullets. He doesn't show the least bit of interest in me. He has a cell phone in his hand, and he keeps looking at it as if waiting for a call.

My drug-dealing friend has to bend low as he creeps to the back. He reaches into a knapsack, asking over his shoulder, "What's your pleasure?"

I fidget and scratch at my arms and chest. Junkie itch is what I'm going for but the fetid atmosphere inside the tent makes it more a shudder of disgust.

He watches and smiles knowingly. "Ah, *la chiva* then."

Heroin. That word I know.

He turns his back to me again as if not wanting me to see his stash but it's obvious he's shaking something into a baggie. "You got your works?" he says over his shoulder. "I can sell you a needle, too."

He's pinched the baggie closed and shoved the rest back into the knapsack. When he turns around again, I shake my head. "I'm good." I dig my hand into my pocket. "How much?"

The cell phone in Guzman's hand trills loudly. He motions for us to be quiet and snaps it open. He listens for a couple of seconds then, *"Estás seguro."* Another moment of silence. Then he speaks again.

He looks up at me and barks a command, voice harsh. His eyes burn.

The few words I recognize make me wonder if Guzman's cousin isn't in for a surprise. The rest seems to be an order for the dealer to hurry. Pronto translates in many languages. His expression makes ice form along my spine. I wonder if he's about to pull a gun and start blasting. One way to make things go faster.

I take a step back as he climbs to his feet, every cell in my body prepares for attack. But he pushes past me without another word.

"Two hundred."

The words pull me back. The dealer's eyes have gone as stone-cold as his boss's. *Come on David,* I think, *make your move.* My pockets are empty. How long can I stall?

"Two hundred," I whine. "What ever happened to dime bags?"

He smiles. "Supply and demand," he says. "Do you want it or do you want to take your chances with Gloria?"

The dealer's expression hardens, his hands move to the waistband of his jeans. I know I can make quick work of him but not without *noise*. The last thing I want to do is alert Guzman that something is wrong.

Damn it. I shift to another pocket. "No. I just forgot where I put the money."

He is neither amused nor indulgent. He doesn't drop his hand. "*Rapido.*"

The word is a threat. If David doesn't show up soon, I'll have to come up with something besides money to offer him. Since he hasn't already suggested exchanging bodily fluids for the drugs, my options are limited.

Outside, there's an exclamation of surprise, a thump as a body hits the ground, and David's voice. "Anna?"

Finally.

My guy doesn't look to see what's going on before reacting. He goes for his gun.

I'm quicker. Once the constraint of keeping silent is removed, I tackle him. I hit him low on his body, chopping at his gun hand. He yelps and the gun falls free. But I've hit him too hard. There's a support pole in the middle of the tent and he falls against it. The pole cracks, the tent shudders, and we're wrapped in a canvas cocoon. He manages to land one good solid punch to my cheek before I pin his arms down. The punch hurt. My teeth are about to retaliate when the canvas is pulled away.

David peers down at us. He's got a cuffed Guzman lying on his stomach, his face pressed to the ground. David has one foot on the small of his back. Guzman is quiet, not struggling.

"You okay?" David asks.

I haul the dealer to his feet. "Peachy. What took you so long?"

David stares at a spot on my face. He smiles. "He got you, didn't he?"

The smile stops me from rubbing my cheek, which I was just about to do. "You don't have to sound so smug."

He hands me a pair of handcuffs. "Did it hurt?"

I yank the dealer's hands behind his back instead of answering. Mum, I snap on the cuffs and give him a shove.

David is still smiling. "Good," he says.

Since the tent is in shambles around us, we're standing out in the open. Guzman has yet to make a sound, his other buddy is out cold. The dealer I have in cuffs starts to yell in Spanish.

David grabs Guzman by the scruff of his neck and hauls him to his feet. "Let's go," he says to me. "He's telling his friends that we're robbing them."

"What about the other two?"

David motions with his gun to a scrawny tree a few feet away. "Cuff your guy to that. This one is still out. Quick. Time to go."

He says the last because we now have an audience. Heads poke out from tent flaps, men, mostly, with bad teeth and hungry looks. I don't waste any time. I shove the dealer to the tree and cuff him, press his face into the rough bark in retaliation for the punch. The scratches and trickle of blood don't shut him up. He's still yelling.

It's not having the desired effect, though. No one steps forward to help him. I'd bet they're just waiting for us to leave so they can loot his stash. I call to David, "Tell them we're calling the police for the other two so they'd better work quick and get out."

David nods that he understands and relays my message. The hungry looks become keen with anticipation.

I glance back when we get to the top of the road. About a dozen bodies are closing in on the dealer and his pal. He's still yelling, threats now probably. But the pack ignores him and descends on the tent. Even the two kids are dancing around with glee.

Christ. What a world.

David calls the police as soon as he has Guzman secured in the backseat of the Hummer. They tell us to bring Guzman in through the security gate at the back of police department headquarters. Not surprisingly, they want to be the ones to usher Guzman on his perp walk to the arraignment. I don't blame them. It was one of their own that he killed. They can take all the credit for his capture as far as I'm concerned. As long as we get the reward.

They also tell us we'll have a police escort that will pick us up on Friars Road. No lights or sirens, just added insurance that Guzman will get where he's going. We spot two cruisers and an unmarked car almost instantly.

Guzman is mute on the ride. I glance back at him once and he has his eyes closed. I can't tell if he's asleep or just plotting revenge on whoever turned him in. I don't care either way.

I expect Chief Williams to be among those waiting for us when we get to SDPD. He's not. Guzman is taken away quickly, disappearing into a special elevator that will take him to a holding cell in the basement. David and I are escorted upstairs, handed paperwork to complete and shown into an interview room to complete it.

A first.

Usually we're treated with about as much respect as the fugitives we turn in. Handed a clipboard and pen, if we're lucky, and sent to the same bench as the collared and cuffed miscreants to fill out the forms.

"Wow," I say to David when we're seated at a scarred table and brought coffee by a smiling deputy. "Never been treated to this kind of service before."

David thanks the deputy and waits for him to depart before replying. "Never brought in a cop killer before."

He starts in on the form.

"Want me to do that?"

David snorts. "We want them to be able to *read* it, don't we?"

"Good point," I reply without rancor. There's a lot of money at stake. I sip at my coffee, surprisingly not too bad, until the cup is empty and I'm getting antsy. I push away from the table and stand up. "I'm going to find the john."

David nods in an absentminded way, and I leave him with his head bent over the table, pen moving across the form, no doubt detailing the capture. I make my way to the lobby. I have no need of a restroom, one of the advantages of being vampire, but I want to try to contact Max again. Now that the job is over, my thoughts are back on him.

There's no one behind the desk. Everyone must be downstairs hoping for a chance to take a shot at Guzman. I walk outside and call my own number. There's still no answer. I'm saddened by the thought that Max is gone and I don't know when I'll see him again.

I return to the lobby and wander over to a bulletin board. There's a poster on it with mug shots and rap sheets—San Diego's most wanted. Guzman is number one but someone has already marked a big X over his face with thick black marker.

My cell phone rings as I peruse the rest of the list. I flip it open.

"Good job today, Anna."

The whispered voice.

"You didn't get yourself killed. I'm glad. That's a pleasure I reserve for myself. Tell your boyfriend."

But the threat hardly registers. My attention is diverted by the poster. Specifically, by number ten.

A woman with dark hair and hooded eyes.

The woman from Beso de la Muerte.

CHAPTER 15

I DON'T WAIT FOR THE CALLER TO SAY ANYTHING else. The only response he gets to his threat is a curt, "Fuck you, Foley." I guess I should be happy that he's following me and not Max. Just shows how stupid he really is.

I snap shut my phone and look more closely at the picture of the woman I last saw arguing with Culebra.

She looks older in the photo than in person, probably because the lighting in booking isn't all that flattering. But the stats—height, weight, hair and eye color—are the same. She's wanted for attempted murder, aggravated assault and burglary. Considered to be armed. Last seen fleeing the scene of a crime in Lakeside. I grab a pen and jot down the name: Belinda Burke. Unassuming name for a witch.

I wonder if I have time to get to Williams and ask about her but before I can, David is crossing the lobby toward me. He's folding a piece of paper and slipping it into a jacket pocket. He's smiling.

"Time to party," he says. "I just called Gloria and she wants us to come to the new restaurant. She's having the chef prepare a celebratory meal. Kind of a dry run for the opening Saturday night."

For a moment, the witch, the call, *everything* fades with a rush of irritation. David doesn't get it. He thinks I was acting—really acting—on that sidewalk an hour or so ago just for Guzman's benefit. I fumble for a way to express vehemently enough how spending an evening with Gloria is *not* my idea of a celebration.

I don't get the chance. David has already turned away and started for the door.

I cast one last look at Belinda Burke. I'll ask Williams about her tomorrow morning when I see him at the park. He should know what she is.

It's not until I'm sitting in the Hummer nursing my irritation and planning how to make my escape once we're back at the office when the phone call pops again into my thoughts. How did Foley manage to follow us to Mission Valley? Could he have been waiting at the office instead of at my house? I'm damned sure he didn't follow me when I left Max. Or does he have some connection at SDPD who is feeding him information? Another question for Williams tomorrow. This time, the idiot actually threatened me. What would be the purpose of that except to draw Max out to protect me? Another dumb mistake on Foley's part.

David keeps glancing my way. I feel it like the flutter of one of those irritating insects. I turn my head to look at him. "What?"

"You don't look very happy for a woman who just earned herself a shitload of money for a couple of hours work. What are you thinking about?"

I let my head fall back against the headrest. Should I tell David about Max? About the calls? If I'm being threatened, he really has a right to know. He's my partner and while it's unlikely I'll meet my immortal end at the hands of an unsuspecting human, David has no such protection. What if Foley makes good on his threat and David gets caught in the cross fire?

Still, I hesitate. If I tell David, he'll no doubt tell Gloria. It will be just one more weapon in her arsenal against me. No, before I say anything, David and I have to settle this Gloria thing. He's a good man but he has a blind spot where she is concerned.

I suck in a breath and plunge in. "I'm still pissed at you, David. You let Gloria interfere in our business. We've been together almost three years. We're good. Damn good. But every time I think things are going great, Gloria opens her mouth and you start questioning if I can do the job. Why? Have I ever let you down?"

I get it all out in a rush.

I should have taken my time. When after a minute he still hasn't responded, I prod him with an elbow in the ribs. "Did you hear me?"

David keeps his eyes on the road. "Yes."

"Yes? That's all you've got to say?"

He shrugs but the muscles are bunching at the base of his skull. His jaw is so tightly clenched, I actually see it tremble.

Finally, he says, "It's not *your* letting *me* down that bothers me."

He says it so quietly, I think I must have misunderstood. "What are you talking about?"

This time he takes his eyes off the road to look at me. "Maybe Gloria is right. Maybe we should take a break. Evaluate what we want to do before something bad happens again. Last summer I almost got you killed. I couldn't live with myself if it happened again."

My first inclination is to laugh. I *did* get killed, after all, but not in any way he can imagine. Instead I give rein to the second impulse. Anger.

"You son of a bitch. I got over it. Why can't you?"

Again, the aggravating hum of silence.

"Are you trying to piss me off? What do you want me to do? Make it easy for you and quit?"

I don't know why I said that, but once I did, the picture snaps into focus. I swivel toward him. "You want to dissolve our partnership? Because you're afraid I'll get hurt or because of Gloria?"

We're still on Broadway headed back toward the coast and David pulls the Hummer to a stop on the side of the road. His hands remain on the wheel and his eyes stare straight ahead, but he says quietly, "Not because of Gloria, exactly." He pauses, draws a deep breath. "I'm thinking of moving to Los Angeles."

Rage rises in my throat until I think it will choke me. I have to swallow hard a couple of times before I can get words out. "Los Angeles? Where Gloria lives and this has nothing to do with her? When did you decide this?" My voice is shaking.

His shoulders hunch. "It's not definite yet. It's something I've been thinking about for a while. You know it hasn't been the same for us since the attack. It's like we're going through the motions but we're not *friends* the way we used to be. We don't go out to eat anymore, we don't even work out together. You make excuses to avoid spending time with me except on the job. It's obvious you only think of me as a business partner and you can always find another one of those."

He runs out of breath and words at the same time. I'm too stunned to do anything but stare. Everything he said is true. There are reasons for all of it, of course. Hello. Vampire. But David doesn't know that. He doesn't *know*.

And I can't tell him.

He clears his throat as if to dispel the awkward silence, then forges ahead. "Once we collect for Guzman, you'll have plenty of money. You can find another partner if you want or go out on your own. You're so good at the business, you really don't need anyone else. Or you might think about becoming a cop. I'm sure your friend Williams would like that. I suspect that's why he spends so much time with you. And I'm sure Max wouldn't object. I never thought he liked the idea of what you do for a living. Too outside of the box."

I can't stand hearing another word. "David." I bark his

name so loud, we both jump. "Will you please shut the fuck up?"

The afternoon sun has fallen low in the sky. The glare through the driver's side window makes it impossible for me to see David's face clearly. I'm overwhelmed with sadness and regret. Sadness because I don't know how to make this right and regret because I'm suddenly not sure I should try.

I grab my purse and reach for the door handle.

He turns in the seat. "What are you doing?"

But I've already opened the door and climbed out. I close it quietly behind me and walk away. I don't answer because I can't.

What am I doing? At this instant, I don't have a clue.

CHAPTER 16

I F SOMEONE HAD TOLD ME EARLIER WHAT HAVOC
this day would wreak on my life, I would have come
home from Beso de la Muerte this morning and gone
straight to bed. I wouldn't have gone to see Williams,
wouldn't have answered David's telephone call, and certainly wouldn't have gone back to Mexico. If I had
stayed home, I would have known it was Max in my bed.
I would have avoided Gloria at all costs. I might even
have told David to bring someone else in on Guzman's
capture just to avoid that last conversation.

If I had known.

What good is it to be immortal if you can't see the future? A serious design flaw.

"Another drink, miss?"

At first glance, the bartender doesn't look old enough to
be working in a saloon. His skin is blotchy, his hair
bleached, his pants baggy. His eyes, though, are not young.
They reflect what he's been exposed to—cynicism, remorse, regret. Like breathing second-hand cigarette smoke,

exposure to pathetic creatures like me must be a hazard of the job.

Or maybe it's what I'm projecting through a haze of scotch.

I nod. "Yes. Please."

He nods, too, and upends the Glenlivet bottle. Single malt, eighteen year Glenlivet. At the rate I'm drinking, I'll go through Guzman's bounty before sunrise.

I don't much care.

The guy at my right elbow eyes me. He's been watching me for the last hour, biding his time, waiting for the right moment to speak. He thinks if I'm drunk enough, I won't notice the bad skin, thinning hair and shiny spots on the elbows of his jacket. He thinks if I'm drunk enough he may get lucky.

I turn toward him and smile.

He may be right.

"ANNA. HEY, WAKE UP."

I pull the covers over my head.

"Come on. We have to get out of here."

Dragging myself to consciousness is painful. Like cold on a sensitive tooth. My head throbs, my limbs are heavy as lead, even my hair prickles on my scalp. It takes me a minute to realize I don't recognize the voice speaking in my ear. Worse, I don't know where I am. And I'm naked.

When I peek out from the covers, all I see is the lower back of a naked male torso bent over at the waist. He's dressed, at least half of him, in a pair of Levi's. He's perched on the other side of the bed. I shift to sit up, and a bottle rolls out from under the covers and hits the floor with a thud.

The back straightens and turns around. The face is vaguely familiar. It splits into a grin. "So you finally came to. It's about time. Come on. Checkout time is ten. We've got about fifteen minutes."

I don't want to embarrass myself by asking the obvious—who the hell are you?—so I gather a sheet around my chest and sit up.

The guy is bent over again and I see now that he's tying his shoes. I look around the room. A motel room. Nondescript. A table and two chairs in the corner, one of which is piled with my clothes. Bed, chest of drawers, armoire that I assume houses the television. The double doors are closed. Obviously, we did not watch television last night.

So, what did we do?

As soon as I try to move, I know.

Jesus. I'm so sore, a gasp escapes my lips before I can stop it.

The guy turns around again. "Are you still in bed? Come on, we've got a long trip ahead of us. We have to get to El Centro by noon."

"El Centro?"

He frowns. "Don't tell me you forgot. You promised to help me. My daughter, remember?"

No. I start to say it out loud, but his face is so full of hopeful anticipation, I swallow hard and say nothing. Instead I rub at my eyes. "I'm not quite awake yet." I look up at him. "And to be honest, I'm a little confused. Did we meet at the bar last night?"

He laughs and reaches out a hand to smooth my hair. "I guess I should be insulted," he says. "But you did have a lot to drink. No, we didn't meet at the bar. You and my brother met at the bar. He told you about me and you agreed to help. He brought you here, to my room. We were talking and—well, one thing led to another."

I guess so. The ache between my legs begins to throb. We must have had some night. But it's daylight now and I haven't a clue where we are or what I agreed to do for this guy. I missed my appointment with Williams in the park, the first time in weeks. I wanted to ask him about the witch and what happened at Beso de la Muerte. I don't know if Max has tried to get in touch with me, or David.

The guy has crossed to the chair. He picks up a T-shirt

and slips it over his head. His arms and torso are well muscled, his waist and hips slender. He has calloused fingers, strong hands. A carpenter maybe? He's probably in his early forties. He has short, sandy hair, thick, well cut. His face looks familiar, not quite handsome but rugged and appealing. The shadow of his beard adds an unpretentious air of strength. When he turns once more to face me, I realize what it is that's familiar.

The guy last night, sitting next to me at the bar. This is the polished version of that guy. I see the similarities now. Brothers. God, did I screw them both?

I throw back the covers and pad naked into the bathroom. No need for coyness. I can hardly walk.

I lock the door behind me. Can't risk my fuck buddy walking in and noticing no reflection in the mirrors that line three of the walls. There are a couple of wet towels on the rim of the tub. He's evidently already performed his morning ablutions. I turn on the shower and step inside. I splash water on my face, duck my head under the stream and finger comb the knots out of my hair. I wash the smell and residual vestiges of sex off my skin. There seems to be a lot of it. I wonder if I fed from him while we had sex. I don't feel the rush that accompanies feeding, but I've never been dead drunk with a stranger before, either.

Dead. Drunk.

I'd smile if my face didn't hurt so much.

When I come back into the bedroom, wrapped in a towel, he's laid my clothes out neatly on the bed.

Jeans. Sweater.

And my gun.

I look around for my panties. They're probably around here somewhere, but it's too awkward to ask about them. Kind of a flashback to yesterday morning with Max and my bra.

Max.

Jesus.

Can't blame this one on the hunger.

I ignore the sick feeling in the pit of my stomach and go

through the motions of getting dressed—slip the sweater over my head, pull on my jeans, clip the gun to the waistband.

I've stalled as long as I can. I turn around.

"This is really embarrassing, but I don't remember much about last night. Can you kind of refresh my memory?"

The guy has been gathering up his wallet and keys and shoving them into his pockets. He pauses, concern flitting across his face. "What don't you remember?"

"Well. Truthfully, I don't remember *anything*."

The concern settles in. Color rises in his cheeks. "Anything?"

I shake my head. "No. Sorry. You said I agreed to help you. Help you with what?"

If I'd kicked him, I don't think I would have gotten a more startled reaction. He stares at me, a terrible awareness springing into his eyes. "Are you even a bounty hunter?" he asks quietly. "Because that's what you told my brother you are."

I nod, relieved at least that I hadn't made up some fantastic tale about being a model—or a vampire. "Yes. I am a bounty hunter. Is that what you needed help with? Fugitive apprehension? Because I can do that. I just need a few facts."

Relief replaces some of the alarm on his face. "It's my ex-son-in-law. He's harassing my daughter. We've gotten a restraining order, but he's avoided being served. You said you could do it for us. That you could make him agree to stay away. You seemed pretty confident . . ."

His voice trails off as if maybe he's not so sure I can pull it off.

"Hey—" I stop, realizing I don't know his name. Another humiliation to add to the list. "Piece of cake. But I have to make a phone call first." Williams will be wondering about me by now. David, too, maybe, unless he's already packing for the move to L.A.

I look around for my purse. It's half-hidden under the

Windbreaker on the chair. I retrieve my cell phone but realize when I flip it open that the battery is just about dead. There's a phone in the room, but I don't want to leave a call record in case I've been followed here. Williams will just have to wonder.

I snap the phone shut and turn it off to conserve what little juice is left. "No battery. Oh well—this shouldn't take very long. I can be back here by late afternoon, right?"

The guy nods. "No problem. My brother left this morning to tell Sylvie that we are on our way. You can ride back with him."

I take it that "Sylvie" is the daughter. He asks me then if I want breakfast. When I shake my head, he grins.

"It's no wonder. I've never seen a woman throw them back the way you did. But you can hold your liquor, I'll give you that. And it certainly didn't affect your performance, if you get my drift." His right hand drifts to his crotch in a cupping gesture that's both self-conscious and protective. "Ouch. You wore me out, lady."

Too much information. At least he's smiling. And I don't see bite marks on the guy's neck. If we had more than sex, I seemed to have cleaned up after myself.

He slips into a jacket and looks around the room. "I guess that does it. Are you ready?"

I smile and nod. No use telling him I wish to hell I could remember what it is I'm supposed to be ready for.

CHAPTER 17

BEFORE WE GET ON THE HIGHWAY, WE STOP FOR gas at a filling station. It's the first indication of where I ended up last night. We're in Santee, in East County. If you asked me when or how I got here from a bar in San Diego, I couldn't tell you. We're in a late-model Ford pickup. One of the big ones with a bed liner and toolbox. Clean. He uses a credit card to pay at the pump, then leans in to ask me if I want coffee. When I nod, he goes inside giving me a chance to open the glove box and look for a registration or insurance card—anything to help me put a name to the body I evidently spent last night enthusiastically fucking.

Dan Simmons. Local address, El Centro.

I snap the glove box closed just as he reappears in the door, two jumbo cups in hand. He hands them in to me, climbs in, takes his back, and we're off.

Luckily, Dan does not feel the need to keep up a constant stream of chatter as we hit the highway. It's a long, boring ride to El Centro through some very unremarkable country. I lay my head back and close my eyes, pretending to sleep so I can properly berate myself for being so careless. I can't believe I did what I did last night. The last time I had indiscriminate sex I was a kid in college. Even then, I never got so drunk that I lost control. And I always took precautions. After what I saw in the shower, I'm pretty sure there were no precautions. If I weren't a vampire, I'd be beside myself with concern.

I'm still beside myself with concern. What if this guy had turned out to be a Revenger? He could have as easily staked me as fucked me. I could be a pile of dust right now. Dan is human, and that's fraught with its own consequences. Up until now, I've excused my extra-relationship dalliances on the basis that it was of necessity. I needed to feed. I'm pretty sure I didn't feed last night. Last night was all about being pissed off, getting drunk and getting laid.

Shit.

Well, now I know. Vampires can get shit faced and stupid just like humans. What I don't know is how it affects my physiology in the long run. I no longer have a functioning digestive system. Like intravenous feeding, liquids are absorbed directly into my bloodstream. Obviously, liquor is absorbed as quickly as blood. Will I gradually get last night back? Don't think it's a question I should ask Williams. Physical injuries are quick to heal. Even the soreness I experienced earlier is gone. Which makes me wonder what we *did* last night. This guy must be hung like . . .

What am I thinking?

What is wrong with me?

An inkling of understanding blossoms in my brain. This is why Williams and Culebra harp about avoiding or at least limiting human involvement to one dependable host. It's safer. Disillusionment leads to reckless behavior in vamps as well as humans.

It's warm in the car and before I realize it, I actually have drifted off to sleep. I know it because I'm awakened by the grip of a hand on my arm. The sensation brings me to consciousness with a snap and a growl.

Dan pulls his hand back. "Anna? Wow. That must have been some dream." He gestures to the road ahead. "We're almost there. Do you have any questions before I take you to meet Sylvie?"

I rub my eyes and sit up. I have a lot of questions. "Tell me again about Sylvie's ex."

Dan pauses a moment before speaking. He keeps his eyes on the road, but his grip on the steering wheel tightens. "His name is Alan Rothman. He's a construction worker. He and I did some jobs together a few years back. He seemed a nice enough guy. Good at his job, friendly. Sylvie had just graduated from college and gotten a job at a local bank. She didn't have many friends here so I introduced them."

His breath catches. He stops and collects himself. "I introduced them. That's the hell of it. They dated awhile, got married. Everything was fine at first. Then he started getting jealous—of Sylvie's work, of her friends, of me, for Christ's sake. We used to go to lunch once a week. One day, she didn't show up. When I called the bank, they said she hadn't been in for two days. I went to the house."

Another pause, another sharp intake of breath. I remain quiet. When he can continue, he does. "I found her. So badly beaten she could hardly speak. I took her to the hospital. That's when I found out it wasn't her first visit. I knew one of the nurses. She told me Sylvie had been to the ER twice in the last month. A sprained wrist, cracked ribs. She hid it all from me."

His sorrow is so acute it infects me, too. In a different way. A quiet rage begins to build. "When did this happen?"

Dan drags a hand across his eyes. "A month ago. When she was well enough to be released from the hospital, I took her home with me. She filed charges. He got out on bail. She filed for divorce. But he won't give up. He follows her everywhere, leaves threatening messages on her cell phone."

"You contacted the police?"

He nods. "They took the threats seriously, but they

couldn't follow her twenty-four hours a day. We took out a restraining order. He's avoided being served. He moved out of their apartment in the middle of the night. The landlord doesn't have a forwarding address. He quit his job. Emptied their bank accounts. All the time the calls continue. It's getting worse. He says he'll kill her and I believe him."

We're on the outskirts of El Centro now, and Dan turns into a housing development. Middle-class, stucco ranch-style homes with tile roofs, landscaped lots. The desert is held at bay by a wide swatch of grass that surrounds the perimeter. Sprinklers send plumes of water cascading into the air, capturing and reflecting rainbows against the blue of the sky. Palm trees rise here and there like slender sentinels against the encroaching sand.

We pull into a driveway already occupied by a big SUV. At the front curb, a vintage Chevy Impala is parked, the convertible top down. Dan gestures to the car. "That's Burt's."

The brother I assume. I don't want to embarrass myself further by asking. I had the impression as Dan relayed his story that he told me all this before. He's gracious enough not to say it.

"What were you doing in San Diego last night?" I ask.

Dan is leading the way up a brick path to the front door. "My brother needed some finishing work done on his house. Sylvie agreed to stay at a friend's for a couple of days so I could help him. He was waiting for me at that bar when he met you."

He gives me a sideways glance, which I quickly avert. I can't even imagine what kind of conversation we had that led me to that motel room.

Dan has his keys in his hand. He's a step or two in front of me. Suddenly, he stops so abruptly I almost bounce off his back. "The door," he says.

I look up. The path is flanked by tall bushes and at first, I don't see anything. But when I move around Dan, I do. The front door is open, the frame splintered in several places. It looks like someone kicked it open.

Dan starts to yell for Burt, for Sylvie.

I grab his arm and stop him from bursting inside. I pull him behind me and motion for him to stay where he is. I doubt he will, but at least I'll go in first. I let my senses do a quick initial reconnoitering. I don't feel or hear anyone inside.

Dan whispers urgently in my ear. "Your gun. You may need it."

I doubt it, but the panic in his eyes lessens a little when I unclip the gun from my waistband and hold it at the ready.

I slide around to the side of the doorway, flatten myself against the wall, peek in. It's quiet. I crouch low and move inside. My toe comes in contact with something soft and yielding. I know without looking. A body. When I glance down, the body stirs. It's a man. A man I recognize from last night. Dan's brother.

Dan is right at my heels. He gives a little cry and kneels down. "Burt. What happened?"

The man groans and tries to sit up. The effort brings a wave of retching. He has a nasty cut on his scalp. He grabs at his head and moans, blood oozing between his fingers.

I squat down beside him. The scent and the sight of his blood makes it hard for me to keep from touching my own fingers to his wound. Instead, I rock back on my heels and ask softly, "Is he still here?"

He shakes his head, slowly and carefully. When he meets Dan's eyes, there are tears in his own. "Alan got her. He has Sylvie."

He says it apologetically as though it's his fault she's gone. Dan puts his arms around his brother. "Did he say anything? Do you know where he was taking her?" His voice is calm, controlled.

Only I see the fury burning in his eyes.

Burt struggles again to sit up. "He said something about 'getting it back.' Sylvie fought him but he was too strong. He was going to kill me if she didn't agree to go with him. She did, and he hit me anyway. God, Dan, I am so sorry."

I stand and place a hand on Dan's shoulder. "Do you know what he meant by 'getting it back'?"

When he looks up at me, resolve hardens his features. "Their first date. He asked me for suggestions. I said take Sylvie hiking in Palm Canyon. She loves it there. Later, he told me he fell in love with her that day. That's where he's taking her. I know it."

"Can you show me?"

He nods.

Burt is moaning again, his eyes glazing. He may have a concussion.

"Call an ambulance for your brother. Then we'll go."

Dan moves stiffly, pushing himself to his feet, walking with measured steps to a cordless phone on a side table a few feet away.

There's a photograph on the table. Dan and a young woman. I memorize what she looks like while he speaks softly into the receiver. I have a feeling, glancing back at Burt, that serving her ex-husband with a restraining order is not going to solve their problems.

Dan brings the phone to his brother.

"They want you to keep talking to them until the ambulance comes. Can you do that?"

Burt takes the phone. "Go," he says. "Find Sylvie."

Dan turns but instead of starting for the front door, he disappears through an interior doorway. He's back in a second. His studiously vacant expression triggers a spasm of suspicion in my brain.

"Dan, where did you go?"

He ignores my question, and heads outside.

I follow, too, but pause once, to turn at the doorway. "Tell the police where we've gone."

Burt nods. I breathe the scent of his blood one more time before hurrying to catch up with his brother.

CHAPTER 18

PALM CANYON IS A DESERT ANOMALY. AN OASIS tucked between canyon walls fed by an underground stream. When we pull into the parking lot, there are a half dozen cars lined up near the ranger station. Hikers, no doubt. There's no one on duty in the station on a Friday afternoon, though. State budget limitations have made it impossible to have full-time rangers.

Dan hasn't said a word. Wouldn't look at me or answer the question of where he went when he left his brother and me. I know how afraid he is for his daughter. I also know that kind of fear leads you to try stupid and desperate things. I'll have to keep an eye on him.

When we've parked and are out of the car, I stop him before he heads for the trail. He looks at me with the same blank expression.

"Let me take the lead," I tell him. "Alan doesn't know who I am. He does know you. If I go first, we may be able to surprise him."

He shakes his head. "You don't know what he looks like. You don't even know what Sylvie looks like."

"Dark hair, shoulder length, about five feet five inches tall, 120 pounds. She has her father's eyes."

He looks like I've just performed a magic trick.

"There was a picture on the table in the living room."

"You got all that from a picture?"

"It's what I do. Trust me. I'd ask you to stay here, but I know you wouldn't. All I am asking is that you don't try anything foolish and you don't get in my way."

His nod is wooden and not very convincing. But I understand. When my niece was in trouble, no force in the world could have stopped me from helping her.

We start into the canyon. It's after two in the afternoon and shadows are already lengthening. When we come to the first fork in the trail, Dan doesn't hesitate, but points to the right. We pass a group of hikers coming out.

I stop them. "We're looking for friends of ours. A couple. Did you pass anyone in the last half hour or so?"

A blonde wearing biker shorts and a tank top steps forward. She glances over my head. "We did pass someone. Your name isn't Dan, is it?"

Dan gives a startled jerk beside me. He steps in front. "Yes."

She frowns. "He said to tell you that they'd wait for you. That you would know where."

She looks to her companions with an expression that makes me suspect she wants to say more.

"Was there something else?" I prod.

She nods. "I may be reading too much into this, but I don't think the woman wanted to go with him. She was crying. I asked if she needed help, but she said no. The guy kept stroking her hair. He wouldn't let go of her arm. It was creepy. I was going to report it at the ranger station."

Dan doesn't wait to hear more. He starts down the trail at a run.

The blonde and her friends look like they might follow him. I touch her arm to get her attention. "There's no one at the ranger station. Call the police. Tell them which trail we took but warn them that it's a hostage situation."

The girl and her hiking buddies still look more excited than concerned. "Don't follow us," I snap at them. "This is not a game. There's a woman in danger, and you could get her killed. Get out of the canyon and call the police."

I can't wait to see if they'll do as I ask since Dan is out of sight. Once I make sure no one can see me, I race to catch up with him, vampire speed kicking in. I have no idea where we're going, but I do know I want to get there first. In seconds I've caught up with him. I drag him to a stop with a hand on his arm.

He whirls around, his face a mask of rage. "What do you think you're doing?"

But it's not the expression on his face or the anger in his voice that gives me pause. It's the gun. He's holding a gun. A Glock that's now pointed right at my chest.

I have to fight my first impulse, to wrench it out of his hand and hit him over the head with it. I understand now why he disappeared for a minute back at the house. He went to get this—a wicked-looking Glock.

I hold out my left hand, palm up, and increase the pressure on his arm with my right. I use my best calm voice to reason with him. "That gun isn't a good idea. You'd better give it to me."

He ignores my outstretched hand as completely as he ignores my reasonable voice. He tries to pull away, but I'm too strong. If he was thinking clearly, he'd probably wonder about that. Instead, he tries to fight me.

It's no contest. When I've got the gun and his face is contorted with the pain of my grasp, his expression crumbles. "What are you doing? We have to save Sylvie."

"We will. But we'll do it my way."

He stops fighting and I let go of his arm. To his credit, he doesn't grab his forearm and rub even though I know it must hurt like a son of a bitch.

I slip his gun into the waistband of my jeans, unclip my own. "How much farther?"

His eyes start to clear. "About half a mile. There's a

wading pool at the end of this trail. At this time of year, there won't be anyone around. The water is too cold."

I nod. "Are you going to be all right?"

"When we get my daughter back." His voice is thick with worry.

"Then let's go."

We walk quickly and quietly along a dirt path that cushions our footfalls. The path winds through thick vegetation, screening our approach as effectively as it hides the location of our quarry. When I hear the spill of water into the rock basin, I know we're close.

I put a finger to my lips and whisper, "Where?"

Dan points ahead and to the right.

But before I can react, a taunting voice from that direction calls out. "Dan? Is that you? Come out, come out wherever you are. Sylvie needs you."

There's a whimper and a short cry, as if he's yanked Sylvie's hair or pinched her so that she'd do just that.

He called for Dan. No mention of anyone else. I pull Dan's head down so that I can whisper in his ear. "Go out. I'll be right behind you. Keep him talking."

Dan nods. His face has lost the sharpness of his anger. The only emotion stamped there now is concern.

"We'll get Sylvie out safely."

I'm not sure he hears me. He walks away, calling out, "Sylvie, honey, it's Dad. Where are you, baby?"

A small voice answers from about one hundred feet ahead. "Here. By the pool."

Her words are cut short and in their place, the male voice snaps out in contempt, "Yeah, Daddy. By the pool. Come join us. We wouldn't think of starting this party without you."

Dan gets several steps ahead before I veer off the path and let his voice guide me. My plan is to go around the pool, get behind Sylvie and her abductor and spring myself on him before he realizes I'm there. I allow the animal to take control of the human. I make no noise at all as I move toward them.

Dan's voice is plaintive. "Why are you doing this, Alan? You love Sylvie, I know you do. Why would you want to hurt her?"

"I do love her. But you've spoiled it. You've made her think I'm not good enough. Well, it worked. I'm not good enough. But no one would be. I'm going to spare her the pain of finding that out."

"Please. Think about what you're doing." Dan's voice is abruptly silent. Then, "Sylvie. I'm so sorry. What has he done to you?"

He must be with them now. And I gauge that I'm only a few yards from the target. I push closer.

Sylvie is crying. "Dad. I'm sorry. I begged Alan not to bring you here. I agreed to go with him—anywhere—if he'd promise not to hurt you or Uncle Burt." Her voice breaks. "I think he killed him."

"No. Don't worry about Uncle Burt. He's going to be just fine. We got to him in time."

I realize Dan's mistake the same instant Sylvie's captor does. *"We?"* His voice ratchets from contempt to suspicion with that one word. "Who is 'we,' Dan? Did you bring someone with you?"

I can see them now, the three of them. Sylvie and her ex-husband have their backs to me, Dan is in my line of sight. I know Dan doesn't do it on purpose, but his eyes shift to me and away, and in that instant, Alan reacts. He whirls around, his grip on Sylvie's throat forcing her to move with him. He can't see me, I've already ducked out of sight, but he yells in my direction.

"Who's there? Tell me. I've got a knife and I'll cut her throat if you don't show yourself."

I gather myself to spring. Dan moves first. I hear the scuffle as I launch myself up. Alan pushes Sylvie at Dan. He raises the knife to plunge it into her back but I stay his hand with a growl. He spins to face me, but confusion slows his reflexes. He expects to see a human face, not a two-legged animal.

The shock lasts only an instant. He twists his hand and lashes out with the knife. The blade cuts through my jeans, opening a gash high on my left thigh. Blood follows the path of the knife in a crimson arc.

The smell of my own blood triggers an uncontrollable urge to spill his. The change is complete. The vampire takes over. I hear the gasps as Dan and Sylvie see what most mortals never will. I let my gun drop to the ground and prepare to attack the way an animal would, with open jaws and snapping teeth.

Alan starts to scream. I don't care. He's cowering behind upturned fists, trying to back away. I close in on him. He raises the knife and I let him. I'll give him that last flicker of hope before I rip out his throat.

The gunshot is so loud, it makes me jump, clapping my hands to my ears. A spray of blood and tissue settles like a crimson veil on my face and clothes. For a moment, I'm not even sure who's been hit. The painful sound continues to resonate like the toll of a bell long after understanding reaches the brain. Alan crumples slowly to the ground, his face gone.

I drop on all fours. I don't know who shot Alan, but I don't want to take the chance that whoever it is isn't through firing yet. Bullets hurt.

It gets quiet in the clearing. Too quiet. Sylvie moves first, coming close to stare down at Alan's body. Dan grabs her and pulls her back. She reacts as though slapped, jumping away from her father with a small cry. Then she collapses against him and starts to sob.

Neither looks in my direction. I'm back to the human Anna, but I have an image of me growling and gnashing my teeth at Alan's throat a moment before. I imagine they do, too, and that may have something to do with the fact that they aren't rushing over to see if I'm all right.

But there's a bigger puzzle.

Neither Dan nor Sylvie is holding a gun.

I look down at Alan's body. The shot took out the back

of his head, exiting through a gaping hole just below the bridge of his nose. The shot could only have come from behind. From the bushes. And from a high-powered rifle.

My eyes probe the dense brush. Nothing.

Until all hell breaks loose.

The echo of the gunshot has barely faded before uniforms surround us. State police, local police, detectives, even a couple of rangers appear out of the shadows like a swarm of gnats. Evidently they were close on our tail and the sound of the shot was like the discharge from a starter's pistol. It brought them at a run, guns drawn. Between Burt and that group of hikers, no stone was left unturned.

When commanded to place our hands on our heads, we do and the cops approach.

Our guns are secured. We're separated to tell our stories. I have no doubt they'll be remarkably alike. Dan and I came to save Sylvie from an abusive ex-husband. She has fresh bruises on her cheeks and her father and injured uncle to back up her story that she feared for her life. The question of who shot Alan, though, is the big mystery. The fact that none of us were in a position to pull off the shot, or had a rifle, pretty much lets us off the hook, at least for now.

During his interrogation, Dan hardly glances my way. I keep waiting for him to say something about the ferocity of my attack on Alan, but maybe he's too busy feeling grateful that I didn't do the same to him last night. I have a feeling it will be a long time before Dan beds a strange woman.

Darkness has fallen. Lights are set up so that the ME can finish his work. When it's finally my turn to tell the story, I'm handed off to a uniform from El Centro PD. Not considered important enough, I guess, to warrant either of the detectives who questioned Dan and Sylvie. The cop is short and built like a box, square shoulders, square jaw, squat little legs. He's abrupt and listens only perfunctorily to my answers. He's heard the story from Sylvie and Dan and I'm hardly more than a bystander in the drama. The fact that I was fighting Alan at the time he was shot and could very well have been killed, too, is pretty much ignored. In fact, the only detail I'm asked to clarify is my occupation and if I have a license for the gun. I tell the cop yes, that it's in my purse back in the car. He passes that information to the detective who tells the cop to escort me back to the parking lot and verify the license. Noticing the blood on my thigh, the cop does ask if I want a doctor to look at it. It's long since stopped bleeding, I can feel the skin repairing itself. I tell him it's just a scratch and he doesn't push.

Then he says that once he verifies the information on my carry permit, I'll be free to go.

Go where?

But I don't have time to dwell on that detail. About the same time I'm being excused, the press shows up. With lights and cameras and microphones. How they got wind of what happened out here so quickly, I can't even guess. Maybe the hikers. In any case, the detective in charge turns livid with anger. He circles the troops and orders them out. My cop friend and I get rounded up with them and herded back toward the trailhead.

Halfway to the ranger station, someone from the press notices the ragged tear in my jeans, the blood stains. All of a sudden, I'm a target for questions and cameras. The officer with me manages to deflect most of the attention. He directs me to sit in the back of Dan's car while he secures the area. I watch as the media people, still protesting, are loaded into their vans, wondering who I can call now for a ride home.

I power up my cell phone. It chirps that I'm getting a text message. Puzzled, I flip it open. There's just enough battery left for the message to come through.

"Feeling lucky? You should be. I could have killed you, too, but this is much more fun. Say thank you, Anna."

CHAPTER 19

THIS GAME IS GETTING OLD. SAY THANK YOU? MY "unknown" messenger has just announced that he is the one who shot Alan. The message is written out, no text-speak. Could definitely have come from Foley. He doesn't strike me as cool enough to know how to compose a message the way anyone under thirty would. But he's made a serious mistake. How does he think he can get away with the shooting?

Any reservation I may have had about the veracity of Max's claim vanishes. Foley *is* in league with Martinez but he's on my trail now, which means he's not on Max's. But being so blatant about it is puzzling. What does he hope to accomplish with this cat-and-mouse game? And he's just killed a man and not come forward to acknowledge it. How is he going to spin that?

The cop comes back to the car and opens the door, an invitation to step out. He dutifully notes that it's my name, address, phone and license numbers on the gun permit. I'm just about to ask him for a ride into town when another car pulls into the lot.

It's not a police car, but a dark, late-model Chevy with tinted windows. The cop starts toward it, undoubtedly ready to order it out of the park, but the driver's door opens and a familiar figure steps out.

"It's all right," I tell the cop. "I think it's my ride."

A uniformed Ortiz approaches. "SDPD," he says, holding out a hand. "If it's okay, I'll take Ms. Strong home."

The cop looks puzzled but shakes Ortiz' outstretched hand and doesn't object. As we walk toward the car, I open my mouth to ask Ortiz how he knew to come after me.

I never get the chance. He opens the back door and motions me inside.

"Get in, Anna."

The voice comes from the backseat. A familiar voice. I lean down to look in.

It's Williams.

And he's pissed.

CHAPTER 20

WILLIAMS' EYES FLASH RED IN THE DIM INTERIOR of the car. His anger is palpable, radiating outward in a burst that I feel like heat on my skin.

"Get in."

For just an instant, I consider turning around and beating it back into the canyon. But Williams would probably send Ortiz after me and what would that accomplish but to delay the inevitable? I toss my purse inside before folding myself into the backseat.

Williams doesn't wait for me to get settled or for Ortiz to get the car back on the road before he starts in.

"Tell me something, Anna, do you have a death wish? Could you have called any more attention to yourself? How the hell did you get involved in a kidnapping in El Centro?"

He's speaking quietly but with great agitation. The softness of his voice makes his anger more intimidating than if he'd been yelling. He stops abruptly and waits. I swear he's growling, he's so furious.

"Well," he snaps when I don't reply quickly enough. "Are you going to answer me?"

I feel like a kid who's a hairbreadth away from being smacked if she gives the wrong answer. The fact that he's completely shut me out of his head confirms how close I am to unleashing the beast. I let a few seconds go by to give Williams a chance to cool off.

When his shoulders become less rigid and the frown lines around his mouth retreat from exasperation to mere annoyance, I ask, "What would you like to know first?"

"How did this happen?"

The version I offer Williams is sanitized. No mention of a drunken tryst. I compose my words as carefully as my thoughts to give nothing else away.

When I'm done, he says, "You want me to believe you ran into this 'old friend' by chance in a bar last night and he told you his daughter was in trouble and you rushed to her aid."

"That's my story and I'm sticking to it."

He doesn't appreciate my attempt at humor. Watching his face is like watching an approaching storm. There may be blue skies overhead now, but you know trouble is coming.

Since he's not asked another question, I venture a few of my own. "How did you find out about it? How did you get here? Why didn't you let the local cops know who you were?"

He passes a hand over his face. I suspect the gesture is a delaying tactic. I sense his anger boiling again to the surface. I don't push.

Finally, he says, "The report of a suspected kidnapping is broadcast statewide. An alert was issued as soon as that girl's uncle spoke to the police. He said you and her father were going after her. He named you, Anna. It is all over the news. The press will be waiting for you at the cottage, at the office. David has called me a dozen times already."

He says all this in a clipped tone, as if I've done something wrong. It's beginning to tick me off but it does clarify one thing. How Foley knew where I was. "I was trying to save a woman's life. What's wrong with that?"

Williams turns in the seat. "What's wrong?" he snaps. "How were you going to do that, Anna?"

"What do you mean?"

"I mean did you bring your gun? Were you planning to use human self-defense techniques? If you'd gotten shot, what would you have said to avoid being brought to a hospital? How would you have explained a wound that heals almost instantly? The anomalies that would have appeared in your blood had samples been taken? Or would you have simply told the doctors not to worry, that you're a vampire and have no need for human medical assistance?"

His sarcasm is as heavy-handed as his anger. And he doesn't wait for me to answer. He points to the blood on my clothes, his eyes so intense, I feel the pressure of his gaze. "Blood. Yours or his? Did you control the bloodlust and hide your true face?"

Again, he gives me no opportunity to confirm or deny. "You didn't, did you? You took the easy way, unleashing the animal. You exposed your nature yet again to mortals. It's in your head. I see it."

Then there's no point in denying it. And yet, if I hadn't used my powers, I never would have reached Sylvie in time to prevent Alan from plunging a knife in her back. I want to remind Williams of that, but he's not in a receptive mood.

He continues to stare at me in stern disapproval. "You are so ignorant, so impatient. I protected you when your niece was in trouble because I could. But now you have exposed yourself again. This time to strangers over whom I have no control."

I know it's not smart to argue, but *smart* is hardly what I've been lately. "I think you're overreacting." I say it in a very small voice. "I didn't kill this guy."

"Oh? What did you do, Anna?"

The image is sharp in my mind. Lunging at Alan, growling, snapping at his throat.

"It will be clear in the minds of this woman and her father, too." Williams says it softly. "Anna, did you not learn anything from what happened with Trish? The mortal world has its own rules. We have to abide by them if we are to coexist. As much as we may want to, we cannot use our powers impulsively. We cannot call attention to ourselves."

"That's a funny statement coming from a chief of police."

As usual, the mouth engages before the brain is in gear. Williams is holding himself in check, I can tell by the way his hands curl into fists and his lips form one thin line of irritation.

I hold up a hand. "Okay, that was stupid. You have never shown anything but your human face in public. I think I understand why you chose to be a policeman. It puts you in the position to use your powers to protect those who are most vulnerable. But you do it discreetly. I get that. I respect what you do."

The frown softens.

I take that and the fact that he hasn't tried to rip my head off as a signal to press on. "I think you and I have the same instincts. So how could I have ignored a father's plea for his daughter's safety?"

Williams drops his head a little and looks at me with brows drawn in pained tolerance. "You could have called the police—called me—when you first heard the story."

"There wasn't time. I swear I thought I was just going to serve the guy with a restraining order. Things got out of control."

He nods. "And why was that? How did you find yourself in such a situation to begin with?"

His tone is deceptively neutral. He is looking at me with an expression that says more clearly than words that he already knows the answer. I cross my arms over my chest and nod for him to continue.

"You got into a fight with David and crawled away to nurse your wounds in a bar. You got drunk, Anna, and ended up with a stranger in a motel room. Do you have any idea how irresponsible that was?"

"Irresponsible?" It comes out whiney and childish but I don't like being put on the defensive for trying to help, even though I called myself worse this morning. "Funny word to use considering how it turned out."

He's clearly not impressed. "What would you call it then? You did get drunk last night, didn't you? Did you feed from the guy while you were having sex? Did you take care to obliterate the marks? Do you even remember?"

How does he know so much?

Williams shakes his head. "How do you think? You smell like sex and a distillery."

He's looking out the window. I'm glad. He can't see the color that floods my face. I'd been careful to keep my thoughts compartmentalized, hidden away from his scrutiny.

Shit. While I could screen the thoughts, I could do nothing to block that sensitive vampire nose. A hundred showers wouldn't have been enough to erase the scent.

Williams isn't finished. He turns in the seat. "That woman's uncle, the one you met last night in the bar, told the El Centro PD the whole story. The real story, Anna. You never laid eyes on either of those men before last night."

So he knows every damned gruesome detail. I shouldn't be surprised.

I hunch a little lower in the seat. "You said David called you. What did he say?"

Williams is frowning again, not the least bit fooled by my lame attempt to change the subject. But he says, "Not much. Just that you and he had a fight. He's very upset. He cares for you. Too much, probably."

Well, that shouldn't be a problem for very much longer.

Williams picks up on that. *What does that mean?*

There doesn't seem much point in trying to hide the reason David made me angry enough to jump out of his car and head for the nearest bar. I let Williams pick the details out of my head. He actually smiles as he absorbs the implication of what transpired between us. He especially likes the part about David suggesting I become a cop.

Hey. I hold a hand up to stave off his too obvious enthusiasm. *Who said I want to be a cop? I like being my own boss. Working for you would be*—I have to fumble for the right word. He is a powerful vampire, after all. *Difficult. You and I don't see eye to eye. On anything.*

You mean we don't see eye to eye on your personal conduct. And with good reason, I'd say. His tone becomes even colder. *Well, you'll have time to reconsider.*

I don't like the way he says that. The words are uttered in the same tone a judge uses when passing sentence— with finality, offering no recourse. I stare at him, waiting.

His eyes bore into mine. *Here's the deal, Anna. Until we know that you will not be exposed as a vampire, you will not go home. You won't go to your office or your parents or anywhere you might be recognized. You will not try to contact David. You will not come to the park or to my office. I don't want to see you or hear from you.*

He blows on the tips of his fingers and opens his hand as if dispersing the seeds of a dandelion into the wind. *You're going to disappear.*

CHAPTER 21

DISAPPEAR? WHAT THE HELL DOES THAT MEAN?
What do you think?

I don't like his expression or his tone. He's talking to me like a kid being sent to bed without supper. *Where would I go? And for how long?*

Williams shrugs. *Can't say how long. Until we can be sure Sylvie and her father aren't going to cause trouble.*

And how will my disappearing help?

Williams waves a hand. *Out of sight, out of mind. If we're lucky, Sylvie and her father will want to put this behind them as quickly as possible. Maybe they'll attribute the way you attacked Alan to adrenaline or fear. But if they start asking questions, especially to the press, you run the risk of being marked as vampire to those who watch for just this sort of story.*

And my disappearing won't cause a problem? Won't that look a little suspicious?

Williams shakes his head. *Maybe. But it's far less dangerous than if you attract the attention of the media.*

I can't believe what I'm hearing. How much worse can

my life get? Acid churns in my blood. *And just where am I supposed to go?*

I've given that some thought.

What he projects is unacceptable. "Not Avery's. I won't even consider it." Speaking it aloud sounds more forceful than projecting it mentally.

"Why not?" He responds in kind. "It's a beautiful house. Secluded. There's a caretaker living there so the neighbors won't be suspicious of lights on in the house at night—"

"Caretaker?" I screech in protest. "Who hired a caretaker?"

"I did. You can't leave a house like that unprotected." He doesn't sound the least bit apologetic. "He's one of our own. And he's discreet."

"And you didn't think to ask me before you hired this caretaker?"

"What would you have said?"

"No, of course. I want that place closed down. I'd burn it to the ground if I thought I could get away with it."

"Then you are even more foolish than I thought."

This time it's me rubbing my hands over my face. "I won't go there."

He accepts the finality of my answer. "Beso de la Muerte, then? Won't have quite the amenities of the house in La Jolla."

The mention of Beso de la Muerte snaps my attention like a rubber band. It also reminds me of what I'd intended to ask Williams this morning. "Who's Belinda Burke?"

Williams looks at me. "Where did you hear that name?" His tone is mildly curious, but his face reflects more than that. I feel his interest pique.

"Yesterday. I saw the poster when we were bringing Guzman in. Who is she?"

"If you saw the poster, you know who she is."

"Okay then, what is she?"

For the first time since I got into the car, Williams'

expression is more anxious than put out. He doesn't answer right away. When he finally does, it's with cautious undertones. "She's a very dangerous woman," he says.

"And?"

"And what?"

"I know she's more than a dangerous *woman*."

He acts reluctant to answer so I add, "Culebra called her a Wiccan."

Williams abandons caution. "Culebra knows her? How?"

I tell him. When I finish the story, he says, "Burke is much more than a witch. She's the most powerful practitioner of the black arts I've ever known."

"You mean she deals in more than love potions and black cats?"

He looks positively grim. "Much more, I'm afraid. If you've seen her, I need to know. We have to find her before midnight tomorrow night."

"Why? What happens tomorrow night?"

"It's October thirty-first."

"October thirty-first? Halloween?" I'd completely forgotten. "So?"

There's an instant when I think Williams isn't going to answer. He seems to be weighing options, but not for long. "It's Samhain, the Celtic New Year," he says. "Do you know anything about Wiccans?"

I shake my head.

"At midnight on October thirty-first, the worlds of the living and dead—human dead—converge. It produces a crack in time that lasts only an instant. But during that instant, a door to the underworld can be opened. Belinda and her coven are preparing to use their magic to bring forth a demon from the underworld. A demon who will do their bidding."

He falls silent.

I stare at him, waiting for the punch line because this has to be a joke.

He stares back. He's serious.

After all that I've experienced, you'd think I would accept what he's telling me. We're two vampires having a conversation about a witch who is about to summon a demon. Another day at the office. Instead, I do the only rational thing a person can do in a situation like this. I laugh. It erupts from my gut like spew from a volcano.

Williams' expression darkens. "You think this is funny? Well, maybe that will change if she succeeds. Demons have an interesting predilection. They like to eat vampires."

I see the seriousness of his expression, hear the concern in his voice, feel the anxiety rippling off his skin. But it doesn't change the image I have in my head of a leathery skinned, horned *toad* trying to eat me. I can't help it. The more I try to suppress the laughter, the more it takes control until my shoulders are shaking so hard, I almost fall over on the seat.

ENOUGH.

When someone yells in a closed car, it's bad enough. When someone yells in your head, it hurts.

I sit up straighter in the seat, wiping tears off my face. When I can form a coherent thought without hiccoughing, I say, *Come on. A crack in time? Demons who eat vampires? Why wouldn't I have heard of this before? And if it's happening tomorrow night, for Christ's sake, why aren't you marshaling the forces to track this Burke woman down?*

What makes you think I'm not?

That's a question it gives me pleasure to answer. *Because you didn't put me on the case. You didn't even tell me such a thing was happening. You'd want my help.*

Williams says nothing. His mind is closed. He doesn't even glance my way.

That's the giveaway.

The muscles at the back of my neck bunch. "You *purposely* kept me in the dark about Belinda Burke?"

He shifts in the seat, his back straight, his eyes hooded.

"There are a lot of things I don't tell you, Anna. I can never be sure you won't go off half-cocked."

Like today.

He doesn't say it or think it, but it hangs in the air between us.

The implication is like a knife in the gut. "Are you saying you trust me to take care of scum like Fisher but you don't trust me to take part in something as important as finding a witch who may unleash a demon?"

His expression is unapologetic. He offers neither a denial nor an explanation.

His mind reaches out to mine and I feel something close around my thoughts like a noose drawing tight. *Now,* he says, *tell me what you know about Belinda Burke.*

I'm angry. Angry enough to close him out of my head. But if I do that, I won't get what I need from him. Information about this witch who threatened Culebra.

It doesn't take long to fill Williams in on what I saw in Beso de la Muerte. The discussion/fight that took place between Culebra and this Belinda Burke. The way she disappeared like a puff of smoke, to be followed minutes later by Culebra. The utter barrenness of the camp. The creepy sensation of being chased out of there by a malevolent spirit.

Nothing concrete.

Now it's his turn to tell me what he knows. I look to Williams for answers, but he's shaking his head.

"This is not good. Burke is a powerful witch, but teleportation is a new trick for her. She has tapped into a new source."

He's talking in riddles. "New source? What does that mean?"

"Witches derive their energy from the elements of nature. Earth, wind, fire. They are bound by them. Teleportation involves escaping the bonds of earth. It shouldn't be possible."

"You and I shouldn't be possible, but here we are. And I saw Culebra do the same thing, too."

Williams shakes his head. "If that's true, the situation

is even more serious than I thought. If Culebra and Burke are working together—"

"No way. I saw the way he looked when he was talking to her. And after, he was distracted. He sent me away. Said not to come back until it was safe." I'm replaying the scene in my head. "Then he disappeared. We were face-to-face. One minute he was there, the next, he was gone."

Williams doesn't buy it. "Then he tricked you somehow. He's a shape-shifter. He can't teleport. It's impossible unless Burke . . ."

It's there, unspoken. Gave him the magic—or used magic on him to transport him somewhere he didn't want to go.

Williams resolve is hard and unbreakable as concrete. I know that from past experience. Still, I have to try.

"What do you want me to do?"

He has his face turned away from me, his mind unreadable.

"Williams?" I prod. "What do you want me to do?"

At last he stirs, half turning in the seat to look at me. "Nothing."

"What do you mean, nothing?"

A flash of annoyance tightens his jaw. "I told you what you were going to do. Disappear. If not to Beso de la Muerte, then you pick another place. But it has to be away from here and it has to be tonight."

Now the annoyance is mine. "You're kidding, right? You're going after this all-powerful witch and you don't want me to help?"

"You can't help."

He says it without equivocation.

He says it like I have no say in the matter.

He says it like Max telling me to butt out of his investigation.

But Williams isn't Max and this isn't a human matter.

"Culebra is my friend," I whisper.

He remains unmoved.

I have to change that. All the aggravation and frustration

of the past two days sweeps over me, driving away any hesitation, any vestige of good sense. I launch myself at Williams with the ferocity of a tiger.

He doesn't see it coming. One minute he's sitting up in the seat, his resolve like a smug halo. The next, I have his throat in my hands and his body pinned beneath me. I feel Ortiz' startled reaction from the front seat. The car begins to slow.

Drive on.

He hesitates, glancing backward.

I put more steel in my voice. *Drive on, Ortiz.*

The pure heat of my fury convinces him. His foot presses the accelerator and the car resumes speed.

Good.

I've had a bitch of a week, and I'm really tired of arguing with men.

CHAPTER 22

WILLIAMS DOES NOT STRUGGLE. HIS MUSCLES go slack, his face clears of emotion—no anger, fear or surprise. He simply waits for me to recover my senses and let go of his throat.

He knows I will. I know I will, too. I just want his attention.

Culebra is my friend. I don't know what part he is being forced to play in this witch's scheme, but he is being forced and he needs my help.

You're sure he's being forced?

Yes.

Williams' eyes reflect skepticism. *Culebra is a shapeshifter with powers of his own. He is an old soul. Burke is a powerful witch, but a young one. She could not force him to do something he doesn't want to do.*

I don't accept that. I saw the way he looked at her. She has some kind of control over him.

Williams doesn't respond, but his thoughts are clear on the subject. He doesn't believe it.

I sit back, uncurl my fingers from around his throat. He slides back away from me and sits up, tugging at his collar.

You wonder why I call you impulsive?

He can call me anything he wants. As long as he understands that I intend to play a part in whatever he has planned for tomorrow night.

Williams is staring straight ahead. I may be more powerful physically than he is, something I still don't understand, but if he closes off his thoughts, I can't get inside his head. Unless I forcefully take his blood. Doing that would break the tenuous bond we've formed in the last couple of months. I'm not ready for that. There has to be another way.

I blow out a breath and work at the kinks in my neck with the palms of my hands. I temper the anger out of my head and replace it with contrite rationality. "I'm sorry. It's been a rough week. First Max, then David. The telephone calls. Now this—"

Williams swivels toward me. "What telephone calls?"

I'd forgotten that I hadn't mentioned the calls before. "Someone is harassing me. Or trying to. I think it's Foley, trying to get me to lead him to Max."

Open mouth, insert foot. I know as soon as those words are out of my mouth that I should have left that last part out. I'm glad I didn't say more because Williams jumps all over it.

"Then how do you know he isn't here in El Centro? That he didn't see what happened in that canyon?"

Jesus. I'm pretty sure he did more than see it.

My silence confirms Williams' suspicions. "Anna, you're keeping something else from me, aren't you? No matter. If there is a mortal following you, it's even more important that you get away."

Williams pauses and I see the thoughts churning behind those eyes even if I can't read them. Then his expression clears and he snaps his fingers. "You are going to Beso de la Muerte."

"What? I just told you . . ."

"That the place was deserted. That's what makes it perfect. Culebra is gone, but the protection spell will still be in place. No one can follow you there."

"I don't care about that. I want to find Culebra. He needs my help, I'm sure of it. This is ridiculous. You're doing this to keep me away from the witch thing. You know where they're going to be, don't you?"

When he refuses to answer, irritation boils up, once again washing over me like a tidal wave. I have an over-whelming urge to grab Williams again and shake him like a dog with a chew toy.

He senses it. He responds with red-hot anger that matches my own. "I let you get away with throwing your childish tantrum once today. I don't intend to let you do it again. I'm trying to help you whether you realize it or not."

He must send Ortiz a telepathic command because the car coasts to a stop. Williams opens the door and steps out. He turns around and leans inside. "You'll find money in the glove compartment and a suitcase in the trunk. I'll get a message to David. Something to the effect that you need to get away for a little while. After what happened between you, he shouldn't be surprised. Don't come home until I send for you."

He doesn't give me the chance to argue. Like every other man in my life lately, he's here one minute and gone the next.

CHAPTER 23

ORTIZ LEAVES WITH WILLIAMS. THEY CLIMB INTO another car parked a hundred feet or so down the road. I was wrong. Williams didn't tell Ortiz to stop. This was all prearranged.

I climb out of the backseat and slam the door. I have an overwhelming urge to shout something obscene at the departing car but what good would that do?

I slide into the driver's seat and reach over to open the glove box. There's an envelope inside. Ten hundred-dollar bills.

A thousand bucks to spend where? Certainly not in Beso de la Muerte.

I look into the glove box again. There's a cell phone. One of those disposable ones with the prepaid minutes. Sixty in this case. Williams wants to make sure I don't get chatty with anyone. Sneaky. Calls can't be traced, either. Just for kicks, I pull out the car registration. It's in the name of Anita Long. There's a California driver's license attached to it with a paper clip. My picture. Not my name. Anita Long.

He's thought of everything, hasn't he?

I don't even look in the backseat to confirm my next suspicion. My purse will be gone. Along with life as I know it and my real identity.

The engine is still idling. I turn it off and lean my head back against the seat.

Part of me understands why Williams wants me out of the way. But a bigger part knows there's more behind his concern than the fact that I exposed myself to mortals yet again. This vampire existence is still new to me. If I had *chosen* to become, if I were an orphan with no friends, if I were simply evil, I might be more inclined to go along with the rules about disengaging from mortal concern. Of course, if I were evil, I wouldn't be interested in becoming a real Watcher. I know it involves more than policing our community, which is all Williams is allowing me to do at this point. It involves doing what Williams has done, placing oneself in a position to offer the most protection to our human charges.

Because, when all is said and done, that's what mortals are. We're in a partnership, a symbiotic relationship. We need blood to survive and they need to be protected from the more aggressive of the supernatural species. Unfortunately, there are many of us whose sole purpose is to kill without remorse or discretion. There are bad seeds in every species.

What should I do now? I could go against Williams wishes and simply go home. What's he going to do? Kill me? Been there, done that. But Williams is my lifeline. Just as Culebra offers sustenance, Williams offers community. I need both. As David so eloquently pointed out, I've disconnected from humans in every way that's important. I purposely lied to my parents, told them that Trish was my brother's child, so that they would have her to care for when the time comes for me to dissappear from their lives. And Max? If we'd made love again, would I have resisted feeding from him, knowing it was *that* sensation he really craved?

Maybe Williams keeping me out of the witch thing is for my own good. He knows I have an affinity for Culebra. Perhaps he sees that as a disadvantage. Maybe he's afraid I'll do something rash and get us all in trouble.

Why would he ever think that?

Shit.

Maybe I'm thinking too much.

I can't do anything about David. I have no idea how to find Max. I'm tired and I still have the vestiges of a hangover from last night. Now that I'm alone and the adrenaline has stopped pumping, there's an annoying, dull ache behind my eyes. I want nothing more than to find a bed and get some sleep.

I crank over the engine.

If I try to make Beso de la Muerte tonight, I'll be on the road at least two hours. Too long for the way I feel to say nothing of the fact that once I get there, where will I sleep? The idea of curling up on the bar floor or trying to get comfortable in the backseat of this car is not appealing. I plan to cross the border at Mexicali, so it would make sense to spend the night in Calexico. It's only a short drive south from El Centro and there are a couple of truck stops offering big food and soft beds. Won't need the food, but a bed would be nice.

I release the emergency brake and coast onto the road. If Williams takes care of Belinda Burke tonight, Culebra may be there to greet me when I pull into Beso de la Muerte tomorrow. If not, I'll still have one day to come up with a plan. In any case, a search for Culebra would have to start in that town.

Within thirty minutes, I've found a place that looks like it might offer more beds than bugs. I visit a gasoline station washroom first, though, to scrub Alan's blood from my face. Can't walk into a motel office looking like a character from a horror flick. Evidently blood-spattered jeans aren't cause for alarm, though. The manager doesn't give my clothes a second look.

Once in my room, I open the suitcase Williams left for

me. I don't know what surprises me more, the very short, very see-through nylon nightie or the thong underwear. I dangle a red number by two fingers. This is how Williams sees me? Or did Ortiz do the shopping? Must be Ortiz. The bra is two cup sizes too large. Maybe his girlfriend did the shopping.

Lucky Ortiz.

I paw through the rest—jeans, a couple of T-shirts, a sweater. Not much. At least I can take comfort in the fact that he doesn't expect me to be gone too long.

But short time or no, I have no intention of wearing that nightie. I peel off my clothes and, after a long, hot shower, climb naked between cool, crisp sheets.

CHAPTER 24

I'T'S AMAZING WHAT SIX HOURS OF UNINTERRUPTED sleep can do. After a shower and clean clothes, I feel almost human.

Still pissed at Williams for dumping me out in the middle of nowhere, and still without any real idea of what I'm going to do, but almost human.

On my way out, I stop for a newspaper in the coffee shop. I'm curious how the press, especially the local press, is spinning what happened yesterday.

The guy behind the counter does a double take when he looks at me. Then he narrows his eyes and flips the paper over so I can see what he does.

The headline reads, "El Centro Woman Rescued in Palm Canyon Shoot-out." And there is a picture of Dan, Sylvie and me looking like deer caught in headlights.

A picture of me.

It's a grainy picture, but good enough so that even the counter man recognizes me.

I don't know which of us is more startled. This is the

first image I've seen of myself since becoming a vampire. In truth, I didn't know I could be captured on film. I assumed not, that it would somehow be tied to the casting no reflection thing.

Evidently, I was wrong because here I am, looking—what?

Thin. If the camera adds ten pounds, I'm downright skinny. But the muscles in my arms are lean, defined, and my shoulders look strong.

The counterman clears his throat, disturbing my analytical appraisal. He taps the newspaper with a forefinger. "It is you, isn't it?"

I see no reason to deny it. I nod.

He grins and hands me a pen. "Will you sign the paper for me?"

I start to laugh, but realize he's serious. This guy knows who I am now, autograph or not, so I scrawl my name under the caption. He grins wider. He reaches behind the counter and pulls out another copy of the newspaper. "Here." He thrusts it into my hand. "On the house."

He's looking around like he wants to announce my presence to the world. I slip away before he can.

Safe behind the wheel of the rental, I can't help but stare at the picture. My hair looks a little too long but nothing like it would if it grew naturally.

When I was human, it grew fast—really fast. I had a standing appointment for a haircut every four weeks. It's been months now, and from the picture, I'd gauge it to be maybe a half inch longer.

I touch my hair, run my fingers through it. The texture feels the same. Williams probably knows someone who specializes in cutting vamp hair. He does have his colored, after all. Or should I let it grow?

Weird how I never thought about it before. Or how I was going to handle getting a haircut. Can't go back to my salon with its wall-to-wall mirrors, that's for sure.

Wow. I'm amazed at the emotions stirred up by seeing

this picture, this image of the vampire Anna. I can't help staring at the face that's mine, but not quite. Something's changed. More than the hair.

The eyes.

My eyes.

Captured by the flash of the camera, they glitter like obsidian in a dark cave. Am I the only one who thinks they don't look quite human? The guy at the motel didn't seem put off. I wish I could see what he did when he looked at me.

Not that I miss mirrors. Vanity was never a concern of mine. In truth, I was never a girly-girl. I liked running with the boys. I liked short hair and jeans. I liked having a strong rather than voluptuous body.

I guess it's a good thing now, isn't it? I hold the picture up. Don't think vampire females come in voluptuous sizes.

I slap the paper down on the seat. I guess one way to keep track of my appearance is to have a picture taken once in a while. Another nugget to add to the list of *Helpful Suggestions to Aid in the Care and Feeding of Vampires*. A book I intend to write someday.

I have one more stop to make before heading for Mexico. Last night I noticed a hunting outfitters store at the edge of town. I pick up a sleeping bag, coffee pot, premeasured coffee packets, and a down-filled jacket. The best down-filled jacket. Not that I need it. Vampires don't feel air temperature the way human's do. I get it as a present for Trish. Why not? It's Williams' idea to get rid of me and Williams' money I'm spending.

This time, no one asks for my autograph. In fact, no one pays much attention to me at all except to take my cash and bag my purchases.

Fame truly is fleeting.

The border crossing at Mexicali is a much-abridged version of the one in San Diego. While not as many tourist-laden family sedans wait in lines to cross, there are almost as many commercial trucks. It's a slow process. And I have to remind myself that I'm going west on Highway 2 once I get into Mexico, not east the way I would if I were coming from home.

The drive is as uninteresting in this direction as it is from the other. The rental car is a sedan that practically drives itself. I figure it's going to take me about an hour or so to get to the dirt turnoff that leads to Beso de la Muerte. I wonder what I'm going to find when I get there.

I wish I could call Max. If he joined me, we could go after Foley together and make him take us to Martinez. We have leverage now. Alan's death. Even if he has a story about how he did it to protect Dan and Sylvie, he wouldn't be able to explain not coming forward.

And Foley is the one looking to collect a million dollar bounty. Max seems to have cut himself off from all his contacts—including me evidently. Something Foley obviously doesn't know. He must still think I can lead him to Max. Maybe all the angst I've suffered over breaking up with Max is moot. He's taken care of it for me. A quick call to my voice mail confirms my thinking. The only messages I have waiting are from David. Nothing from Max. But David has left ten of them, escalating from apologetic to frantic.

I delete them. Williams said he would call David and explain my absence. I'm happy to let him do it. I have no desire to speak to David, especially today. Gloria's restaurant opens tonight and I'm sure he'll be gushingly excited. I wonder if he even realizes how appropriate the date is. Today is Halloween. High holiday for witches.

Once on the dirt road, the rental demands more attention. It bucks and skitters, clearly not as comfortable with ruts and potholes as it was with asphalt. It takes both hands on the wheel to keep it centered.

It takes almost as much effort to ignore the fear building in my chest. Approaching Beso de la Muerte, I have an overwhelming urge to turn the car around and flee. The same creepy dread that immobilized me the day Culebra disappeared is back. Suddenly, staying at Avery's doesn't sound so bad. If I turned around now, I could be back there in—

I hit with a sickening crunch of metal on metal. The airbag deploys with an explosive rush of air and powder and noise, knocking my head back against the headrest with tremendous force. Then I'm ricocheting forward toward the steering wheel, bouncing off the rough textured airbag, the skin on my cheek flaying off with the impact. I have a fleeting thought that if my face hit the bag dead on, my nose would have been smashed flat.

Then, just as quickly, the bag deflates. The car's engine stalls and cuts out. I rock in the seat, holding my head in my hands, trying to collect my thoughts. When I open my eyes to see what the hell I hit, all I see through the shattered windshield is smoke curling from the ruined engine.

And?

A shadow, curling toward me like another wisp of smoke. Formless, faceless until a slit opens and a sound like distant thunder fills my head.

I have him. You can't help. Go back.

I climb out, legs shaking with the effort. Have who? Culebra?

But the apparition is gone. The only smoke is the black plume from the engine. I smell hot oil and gasoline. I have to hang on to the side of the car to propel myself forward. Where did it go? What did I hit? Eyes search, first the air, then the ground. I expect to see something—an animal, a deer maybe, fallen beneath the tires.

But there's nothing.

Nothing.

I hold out my hands, groping like a blind man to understand what could have caused the collision.

At first, I'm flailing at air. Then, I feel it.

I suck in a breath, laying both hands flat against—I don't know what—but it stopped my car as surely as any brick wall would have.

With one big difference.

This wall is invisible.

CHAPTER 25

AN INVISIBLE WALL? THE WITCH'S DOING? MUST be. I've made the trek into Beso de la Muerte on this very road a hundred times. I'm pretty sure I would have remembered if there had been a wall. I knew there was some kind of spell protecting the place, but this spell almost gave me a concussion.

Why is it here now? And why tell me that she has Culebra? If she thinks that will make me go away, she doesn't know me very well.

I slump back against the car. Smoke is still curling up from under the hood and both front tires are flat. The hood is folded back like an accordion. No sense in even trying to start the damned thing.

Resuming my blind mouse act, I feel my way to the right about a hundred feet from the car. The barrier stretches on. The same to the left. I stretch up on tiptoes, but can't feel a top to the thing, either. It's as smooth as plastic to the touch and about the same temperature as the air.

I return to the car and lean against the passenger side

door to review my options. If I call Williams, what are the chances he takes my call? I'd guess pretty slim. He may have even set this up. It's his style for sure. Strand me in the middle of nowhere to keep me out of trouble. I doubt even the special effects would be beyond him, although he'd know the hint of Culebra in trouble would be enough to spur me on to Beso de la Muerte, not discourage me from trying. No, this can't be Williams' doing.

I think David would come get me, providing I could pry him away from Gloria on her big day. But that would involve explaining what I'm doing out in the middle of a Mexican dirt road in a rental car that's just smashed into an invisible wall.

Call a tow truck? I doubt an American company would drive out here and a Mexican company would most likely hold the car for ransom if they'd even venture this far from Tijuana. 'Course, it would serve Williams right if he ended up having to pay for the car. It could get sticky for me, though, too, if it's discovered I'm carrying phony ID.

My headache comes roaring back.

There is one other person who might help. The only other shape-shifter I know besides Culebra. Daniel Frey. I reach for the phone and flip it open.

No service.

I stare at the screen in disbelief. No service? Is this Williams' idea of a joke? Send me into Mexico with a phone that doesn't work out here?

I shake the phone in frustration. It doesn't improve the situation. The message remains the same. No service. Shit. I've just spent half an hour trying to decide who best to call and it turns out, it doesn't matter. The fucking phone is no good.

I get out of the car and throw the piece of shit as far into the desert as I can.

Now what?

It's at least a thirty mile walk back to the border. As a vampire, I could do it and not break a sweat. The problem is I came here for a reason. Culebra. Of course, without a phone, I'm stuck out here with no transportation. Until I get to the saloon. I know Culebra has a landline and as far as I remember, he didn't take the time to have it disconnected before he disappeared.

I look in the direction I hurled the phone. Probably shouldn't have done that. If Culebra's phone is not working, I might have gone back toward the main road and caught a signal.

Good job, Anna.

I approach the wall again. This time I push at it as hard as I can with both hands. It's unyielding. I kick at it. Beat it. I even take a couple of steps back and run full force at it. I bounce off it like a damned tennis ball. I try to shimmy over, but it's slick as glass and I can't get a toe- or handhold. If I try to jump it without knowing how tall it is, I'm sure I'll end up on my ass in the dirt.

Frustrated and furious, I lean back against the wall and lower myself to the ground.

Think.

I need help. I need someone I can reach telepathically. I've never tried to summon anyone or anything using only my mind. I don't know if it's possible to reach out that way at all, let alone from a distance.

And yet . . .

A niggling thought tickles. Someone has reached out to me, though, many times. In fact, he pops into my head seemingly at will. Casper. He's pulled my butt from the fire twice before. The first time when I was captured by the Revengers and later, when Ryan, my niece's friend, was in trouble and I had no way to get to him. I don't know who or what he is. I just hear his voice in my head. I gave him the name Casper because he's like the friendly ghost in the comics.

Maybe I can work the magic in reverse. I haven't heard from him in weeks, since I started working for Williams, in fact, but what harm will it do to try?

I stand up and close my eyes.

Casper.

I open my eyes and tilt my head to listen. Nothing. I squeeze my eyes shut again and force everything out of my head.

Casper. Can you hear me?

Shit, with my luck, he's probably on vacation. I suck in a breath, concentrate harder.

Casper. Damn it, you have to hear me. I'm in trouble.

You don't look like you're in trouble.

The voice makes me jump. I didn't expect the summoning thing to really work. I smile.

Good. You heard me.

Of course I heard you. You were screaming in my head.

Well, I wasn't sure if you'd answer. You never did any of the other hundred times I called you.

You didn't need me the other hundred times. You just thought you did.

His sarcasm should trigger an angry response. But not now. I want him on my side. I gesture around. *Can you see where I am?*

Of course. I see what you see.

Then you see the problem.

You wrecked your car? You called me because you wrecked your car? You mistake me for a tow truck?

I should be so lucky. I swallow that smart-ass reply, modulate a little pleading into my voice. *Check it out. What did I hit?*

I let my eyes sweep the front of the car. Show him that the engine is smashed flat where it hit whatever the hell it hit. Show him that there's no natural, physical reason to explain the damage.

Hmmm.

Glory be. I think he gets it.

Looks like you hit a force field of some kind. Casper's voice reflects a spark of interest.

That's what I think, too. How do I get around it?

You don't. It's there to keep you out.

The way he says *you* grabs my attention. *Keep me out? Me, specifically?*

I "feel" Casper nodding. Can't explain how, just know that he is.

I need to get to Beso de la Muerte. If something erected this force field, there has to be a way to get rid of it.

No response at all from Casper this time.

Come on. Help me out here. If a spell made it, there must be an antispell to dissolve it.

There's a tingling in my head. As if Casper is arguing with himself about something. I take that as a good sign and wait.

Finally, he says, *There is no "antispell." Only those who erected such a barrier can destroy it.*

Those who erected it? You mean it took more than one?

Yes.

So, it wasn't Culebra then. As far as I know, he works alone in Beso de la Muerte. But what did Williams say about Belinda Burke and her coven?

I feel Casper's mind grab onto that thought and a shimmer of concordance ripples through me. He says, *Yes. A coven could accomplish such a thing as this.*

How do I get around it?

A pause. *Do you know how a witch gets her power?*

Williams said it was from the earth.

Yes. From the earth. Not of it.

And the difference is?

The barrier rests upon the earth. It is possible to get underneath.

I cast a doubtful eye toward the hard packed desert sand. *Not without a jackhammer and backhoe.*

Oh ye of little faith.

If you mean the kind that moves mountains, you're right. I'm fresh out.

There's another pause. *If I help you, Anna, you must understand, it will be the last time.*

My shoulders jump, not only from what he says but the way he's says it. Solemnly. A pronouncement from which there is no appeal. The same way Williams sounded when he said I had to disappear. *You mean forever?*

Yes.

But why?

Because to do this for you, I have to be with you. Once we share physical space, the bond between guardian and charge is broken.

Guardian and charge?

The relationship between you and I.

Like a guardian angel?

Casper chuckles. *An angel?*

It makes sense. You helped me when I was caught by the Revengers and again when Trish was in trouble. What happens if I need you in the future?

That is why you must decide now. You can leave this place. You don't need to go into Beso de la Muerte. You must realize that what you hope to accomplish may not be possible.

How does he know what I hope to accomplish? *I* don't even know that.

Yes, you do. You hope to help your friend Culebra and have time left over to save Max.

A thrill of alarm races up my spine. *Does Culebra need help? Does Max?*

You believe that they do.

He's right, of course. My mind races into overdrive. Max is god only knows where. Culebra may be here and under a definite time constraint.

Is Culebra close?

Casper doesn't answer.

Maybe he doesn't need to. The fact that this barrier is here can mean only one thing—whatever the coven has planned for tonight has something to do with Beso de la Muerte. Whether Culebra is a willing participant or not, he took great pains to empty his camp and scare me away. There could only be one reason. He planned to try to stop her. Unsuccessfully, from the message that accompanied my hitting that wall. If Belinda Burke is as powerful a force as Williams thinks, what chance did one shape-shifter have against her and a coven of witches determined to open a gate to the underworld? My instinct is telling me I need to get into Beso de la Muerte. Culebra is smart and resourceful. He may have left a clue there to help me find him.

That is your decision?

It is not surprising that Casper knows the answer before I do. *Yes.*

Instantly, the air around me swirls and draws away, like the sea receding from a beach at low tide. The sensation is accompanied by a rushing sound, loud, aggressive, hostile in its intensity. I put my head down, fighting the urge to cover my ears, then my eyes, as I'm assaulted by a blinding white light. A rip appears in the fabric of the desert and fills with the light. Then, just as quickly, the light and sound fade. When I raise my eyes again, I'm no longer alone.

I blink. *You're Casper?*

He sniffs. *That's not my name, you know. My name is Avatoar. And you don't have to look so surprised. What were you expecting?*

I don't know what I expected. I just know it's not what I see in front of me. Casper—or Avatoar—stands about three feet tall and has a bushy head of brilliant red hair. He has on a green jumpsuit that looks like it's made of silky parachute material. Perfect, I suppose, for jumping dimensions.

I know I'm staring but I was expecting Michael the Archangel and I got— *Are you a leprechaun?*

Again, he blows out an exasperated puff of air. *Where would you get that idea?*

Maybe from the slightly oversized head on the diminutive body. Since he doesn't react to that, I have to assume he's no longer in my head and I can take a few seconds to check him out. His face is wrinkled but not unattractive. He has round blue eyes and a strong chin. His body is well proportioned, just *small*.

His mouth is curved in a frown.

Finished gawking?

I blink again and nod.

Then we should get to work.

I wait expectantly for him to tell me what to do.

He puts a hand on my shoulders and pulls me down to a kneeling position so that we're eye to eye.

This will hurt a little. But not for long. Try to relax.

That, of course, causes the opposite reaction. My shoulders tense, my body becomes rigid. *What do you mean, this will hurt?*

He doesn't respond. Avatoar's eyes are fixed on a point somewhere in the distance, just over my shoulder. I try to swivel my head to see what he does, but his grip is tight and the pressure of his fingers just at the base of my neck holds me immobile.

Then the pain creeps up.

When it begins, my first impulse is to fight. I slash at his arms, but for a little guy, his grip is mighty. I can't break his hold and I can't escape the blistering heat. It starts at my feet and works its way up. My skin is on fire. I'm being drawn into some kind of whirling, white-hot vortex. I feel Avatoar's hands but when I open my eyes, all I see is a blur of space. It's a *Wizard of Oz* tornado but Dorothy never looked like she was experiencing this kind of pain. I open my mouth to scream, but the intensity of the gale forces the scream back down my throat.

I'm trapped, I'm powerless and I'm being burned alive.

CHAPTER 26

"ANNA. ANNA. WAKE UP."

Second time in as many days I've heard those words. This time, though, the voice is high-pitched and tinny. Like one of those munchkins in the *Wizard of Oz*.

Something shakes my shoulders. "Come on. It's over. Wake up."

I don't want to wake up. Wherever I am is quiet, peaceful. No pain. No noise. No light. No hunger. Over the rainbow?

"Am I in heaven?"

The laugh is loud. Rude, even.

I burrow deeper into whatever I'm lying on and refuse to open my eyes.

"You're crushing me. Get up."

Suddenly, I'm aware of movement. Beneath me. Something is squirming, trying to escape.

Oh my god. Am I back in that motel room in Santee? Have I done it again?

I pop one eye open, fight back a wave of nausea and spy an unfamiliar face with bright red hair.

I have done it again. This time with—what? This guy looks a little strange and the length of his body stops somewhere just below my waist.

I screwed a midget?

The nausea is stronger, forcing me to squeeze my eyes shut again. Still, the spinning continues. It's like the horrible, out of control feeling from a bad drunk just before you pass out—or throw up.

"Don't even think about it."

The voice screeches in my ear.

I jump up and away. A midget in a bright green jumpsuit stares at me. How did I get in that movie?

"Thank the gods."

"What?"

He frowns. "Will you snap out of it?" He waves a hand. "See where we are?"

I tear my eyes off the face of the munchkin long enough to sneak a look around.

We're in the middle of a dirt road. There's a car with a smashed front end—

A flash of recognition. The car? I touch my cheek. The skin feels rough, and it tingles.

A memory hovers just out of reach.

I shake my head. Concentrate.

The midget stirs. "Come on. I have places to go, things to do. I can't wait here all day."

"Listen, Casper—" That automatic response snaps everything into place.

It must show on my face because Casper—er, Avatoar—grins. "At last. Jeez, Anna. It doesn't usually take so long for a vamp to come back. You were really out of it."

I arch my back, working out a vicious kink. "I thought you said that would only hurt a little?"

He shrugs. "If I told you it would hurt like a son of a bitch, would you have agreed to try?"

His tone, his expression, his very words are certainly different from the rather ethereal character who used to tell me things like "don't forget who you are."

I raise an eyebrow. "Who are you and what have you done with the real Casper?"

He answers with a withering look.

I approach the front of the car. Cautiously. Don't want to bounce off the damned wall again. A tentative probe confirms that, as I suspected, I'm now on the *other* side of the barrier.

There's a hole at my feet. Big enough for the two of us to have squeezed through.

"Want to tell me how you did that?"

"Pretty obvious isn't it?"

I look from the hole to Avatoar. "You mean we tunneled under the barrier?"

He makes his hands flutter. "More like bored under."

That explains the heat and friction. "Why aren't my clothes torn or my skin?"

"I could protect us from some of the effects of the vortex. Unfortunately, not the pain."

"I noticed." I kick at the dirt. "Well, what now?"

Avatoar doesn't answer.

I turn around.

I'm alone.

I do a complete three sixty. Casper is nowhere in sight.

I'm not surprised or angry. He did his part. Got me where I needed to be. But—

I wave a hand at the sky. *Wait, Casper. I have a question for you.*

For a moment, there's no answer. Then, *Make it quick. I said I have places to go.*

How did you find out about me? In the beginning, with the Revengers?

Casper's laugh floats back to me like music on a summer breeze. *Jeez, Anna. I would have thought a smart cookie like you would've figured it out by now.*

Figured what out?

That the Watchers may not be the only game in town. Bye, Anna. And good luck.

CHAPTER 27

WELL. I DON'T KNOW WHAT KIND OF ANSWER I expected, but certainly not that one. Now, of course, I have a hundred other questions. The Watchers aren't the only game in town, huh? Casper may be gone but I'll certainly grill Williams about it when I get out of here.

I turn back to look at the car. I guess I'll have to burrow back to the car, gather the stuff I bought this morning to bring to Beso de la Muerte, and head for town.

I look down.

Avatoar isn't the only thing gone.

The hole is, too.

Shit.

I throw up my hands. "You could have left the hole."

I don't expect an answer and I'm not wasting time trying to make Avatoar come back. I believed him when he said I wouldn't be hearing from him again. I guess my probation period as a vampire is officially over. I'm sure when I have time to think about that, I'll miss Casper. But right now, I'm too busy being irritated with him. All the provisions I brought for this little foray are still locked in the trunk of a car I can no longer reach.

The sun is already low in the sky. Nothing to do now but make my way into Beso de la Muerte and see if Culebra left any clue about what's happened to him.

I start out at a jog, a pace designed to prevent my unprotected head from bouncing off any other obstacles that Burke might have thrown up. But this time, I get all the way into town with nothing to slow me down but the mounting desire to be running the other way. My feet tread relentlessly forward, but my head is yelling at me to turn around and get the hell out of here. The fact that darkness is falling adds to the escalating feeling of dread.

Once in sight, the street and its decrepit collection of rotting buildings looks even more run down than I last remembered. It's as if with Culebra and his "guests" gone, decomposition has accelerated. The boards on the dusty sidewalk creak an ominous warning as I approach the saloon. I have to force myself to push open the swinging doors and walk inside. The threat of something dark and evil makes every motion of my hand, every footstep, heavy with foreboding. It's right in front of me, floating just out of reach, a shadow promising the torment of a nightmare, the embodiment of one's worst fear. It's forcing itself into my head and under my skin. It's designed to raise the hackles on the back of my neck and bile in my throat.

It's beginning to piss me off.

I do a slow turn around the room. No light. No sound. But something is here. I exhale to steady my voice, calm my heart and say, "Okay, whatever you are. Save the theatrics for the paying customers. Either show yourself or leave me the hell alone."

There's a rustle from behind the bar.

Suddenly, my bravado wilts like a spring flower in the hot desert sun. My heart hammers with adrenaline-laced fear. What have I summoned?

The rustling grows louder, something gathering itself to

what? Attack? I hear a low, ominous growl. Shape-shifting perhaps into a monster fashioned from my very own nightmares?

Should I run? Even as the thought passes through my head, I know I can't. I'm rooted to the spot. I force myself to move, to approach the bar. I'll meet whatever is there head-on. I pick up a chair, hold it over my head. My reflexes seem to have reverted back to human speed. Fear has driven even the vampire away.

"Come out, you son of a bitch. I'm right here."

The rustle gets louder, concentrated almost. But the thing doesn't show itself.

A thought dawns. Maybe it's as frightened of me as I am of it.

Or maybe it wants me to think that. To let my guard down and approach even closer, exposing myself to the full brunt of its attack.

My head is starting to hurt again. I can't wait much longer if I'm going to find Culebra before the witching hour. I've come this far pretty much intact. I may as well go for broke.

My grip on the chair tightens. I open my mouth to let out a banshee yell. If nothing else, I'll scare the damned thing to death.

A head pokes over the top of the bar, a hand waves frantically. "Damn it, Anna. Give me a minute, will you. I'm trying to get my pants on."

The chair clatters to the floor. "Frey?"

He disappears again and I catch the brief, sibilant sound of the metal teeth on a zipper meshing together. Then he stands up and holds up both hands. "It's me, okay? Relax."

Relax? "What the hell are you doing here?"

Daniel Frey comes around the bar, shirtless, barefoot. And grins.

"Williams sent me. I've been waiting for you."

CHAPTER 28

WAITING FOR ME?
    I don't know which question to ask first, so I spew them all out. "How did you get here? How long have you been waiting? Why did Williams send you? What does he expect you to do?"

He picks up the chair I dropped, rights it and straddles it, leaning his arms on the back. "I got here the way any cat would, I padded on little panther feet. I've been here since last night. Wished Williams would have mentioned there was no food. Had to hunt and around here, pickin's are slim. Have you ever tried to eat coyote?" He pantomimes spitting something out of his mouth.

"Why are you here? What did Williams say?"

Frey shrugs. "Didn't give me any specific orders. Just told me to keep an eye on you."

"But how did you get past Culebra's wall?"

He grins. "Wall? What wall? Obviously whatever was in your way was constructed to keep humans and vampires out. Not animals."

"Where'd you get the clothes?"

He jabs a thumb toward the bar. "Found them right there in back. Don't know who left them but I wish whoever it was would have dropped off some real food, too. What I wouldn't give for a big juicy burger."

His answers are well rehearsed and glib. I'm not unhappy that it's Frey here instead of the faceless monsters I'd conjured up in my imagination, but something still isn't right.

"Were you trying to scare me when I was outside on the road just now?"

He frowns. "I don't know what you mean."

"Come on. Were you projecting some kind of malevolent energy?"

He shakes his head. "Malevolent energy? That's a little dramatic, isn't it? Sorry, Anna. You give me way to much credit. All *I* felt coming here was hunger and thirst. Still do. You didn't by any chance bring any groceries with you?"

I shake *my* head. "Vampire. I don't need groceries, remember?"

But I cross to the bar and look behind it. The cooler is still there. I open it, pull out a couple of bottles of beer, pop the tops and come back to Frey. "Here."

I know he doesn't really like beer, he once told me he was a wine man, but he accepts the bottle anyway and takes a swig. He drinks greedily, eyeing me. When he comes up for air, he says, "Aren't you joining me?"

After what happened two nights ago with Dan? I may never drink again. Instead of saying that, though, I make a sweeping gesture around the bar. "Why didn't you change into your human form before this? You would have at least had something to drink."

Frey finishes off the beer. "I wanted to be ready in case anyone besides you showed up. I figured the sight of a panther would discourage visitors." He hands me the first bottle and takes the second. "If you're not going to drink that . . ."

I hand it over. "Visitors? I told you there's an invisible

wall out there that pretty much takes care of discouraging visitors."

Frey raises an eyebrow. "And I told you, I didn't know anything about that."

I pull a chair close to him and sit down. He's chugging the second beer the same way he did the first. While I watch him drink, that something-isn't-right feeling comes roaring back. Only now, I know exactly what isn't right. "You said you've been here since last night?"

He nods.

"And Williams sent you to wait for me? Did he tell you why I'm here?"

"Probably because he wants you out of the way for some reason."

"You think?"

Frey is watching the play of emotion on my face. We no longer have the mind connection, I took care of that when I fed from him a few months ago, which broke the psychic link between us. But he has animal instincts and he picks up on my anger and confusion.

"Maybe he is trying to protect you," he says finally. "Rumors have been going around that something's about to stir up trouble in the supernatural community. Big trouble. Williams might want to keep you out of it."

"No 'might' about it." Irritation brings me to my feet, and I shove the damned chair out of my way. I wish it were Williams I was shoving. "He as much as told me the same thing just before he banished me with one sweep of his mighty hand. He didn't want me involved in the great witch hunt."

"Witch hunt? You know about that?"

He says it like he's surprised. "I take it *everyone* but me knew about it. Williams thinks I can't help. He thinks I'd be a liability. I can't believe he's forced me out here to stand on the sidelines while my friend is in danger."

"Maybe it's *because* your friend is in danger," Frey says quietly. "The witch has to be stopped at all costs. You are protective of those you love."

"You mean Culebra might have to be sacrificed for the greater good? That's bullshit and you know it. Williams thinks Culebra is a partner in what's about to happen. I know he's not." I start pacing. "I'm pretty sure the witch sent me a message. Right after I hit that damned wall. Said I couldn't help him and to go away."

As soon as I say that, something clicks in my brain. "Why would she try to scare me away from *here*?" I stop pacing and turn to look at Frey. "Where does Williams think this magical hell raising is going to happen?"

Frey looks unsure whether he should answer. I take a step toward him and glare. "You'd better tell me. I can do a lot of damage to that human body before you can make the change back to cat."

It's an empty threat and I'm sure Frey knows it, but it gives him the chance to respond without feeling as if he's betraying Williams. A threat from a vampire is a serious matter. "Arizona," he says. "We're pretty sure that Burke plans to raise the demon in Sedona where the power of the vortex will enhance her own magics." A pause. "But he may be wrong about that."

I shake a hand impatiently for him to go on.

"I did some prowling around in the desert last night. Came across what I thought was the usual Wiccan wannabes getting ready for their annual Halloween naked dance in the moonlight. Now I'm not so sure."

"Because?"

"Well, for one thing, to get to the place you have to travel underground. And there were guards. With guns. Williams has a lot of inside information, though, so he's probably right about Arizona." He lets his voice drop.

"But you're not sure?" I can't help but smile. Poor Williams. If Frey is right, he banished me to the one place I most need to be. Life's a bitch sometimes, isn't it?

Frey continues, frowning. "I think you should know that there is another reason Williams wants you here, out of the way."

Once again, he gets my full attention.

"Williams heard from that agent, Foley, yesterday morning. Martinez has Max."

My stomach lurches. "Williams told you that?"

Frey nods. "Foley also said that somehow, Martinez found out about you. Martinez is looking for you now. Foley wanted Williams to tell him where you'd gone so they could offer you protection. Then the story broke about El Centro. I think Williams wanted to be sure he got to you before Foley did. He doesn't trust him. He wanted to make sure you'd go somewhere safe."

And somewhere out of communication, obviously. I don't think I've ever been more angry with Williams. He kept the fact that Martinez has Max from me. Probably thought he was doing a good thing when I told him what I suspected about Foley tailing me. And I hadn't even filled him in on the other part—Max's conviction that Foley was now working with Martinez and my suspicion that it was Foley who shot Alan.

Shit. I need to talk to Williams now. But what to do about the witch? If she has Culebra . . . "If the witch is here, can we stop her?" I ask Frey. "You and I?"

He raises a shoulder. "It would be better if we had help."

"You mean Williams? Get him here?"

Frey nods. "Call him on your cell and . . ."

My cell is with Williams. The cell he gave me is stuck on a cactus somewhere in the middle of the desert. But I spy Culebra's phone on the counter and start toward it. When I lift the receiver, I get nothing. The phone's dead.

Frey reaches out a hand. "You do have your cell with you, right?"

From the look on my face, Frey divines the answer. "That's not good. This isn't something we should try on our own. The witch has some pretty serious mojo."

Serious mojo? This from an English teacher with a degree from Harvard?

Frey interprets *that* look, too. "All I'm saying is, we're going to need help. Maybe I can change back into panther mode and find Williams."

"Before midnight? And isn't he in Arizona?"

"I could make it to Balboa Park in a couple of hours. Someone there might be able to contact him. A chopper could get him here in an hour."

I glance at my watch. It's almost eight o'clock. Assuming Frey could do it, it's still cutting things too close. Could he get to a phone somewhere else in time? Where? And once he did, what would he do? Change back into human form and beg naked on the street for money to make the call?

"Damn it, Frey, what are we going to do? We can't let the witch open the gates to hell or whatever she has planned. And we certainly can't let her use Culebra to do it."

"So, you have another plan?"

"Not yet. But we made a pretty good team once before."

His brows draw together. "Against *humans*. This is different."

"Well, unless you come up with a better suggestion, we're going to have to try."

He crosses his arms and a tense, speculative expression settles on his face.

"What?" I ask.

"I'll help you. But, Anna, there's something else I should tell you. Now. Before we start out."

I can't imagine what else there could be. My own expression must reflect my impatience because his eyes slide away and focus somewhere over my shoulder.

Then he says, "We can't have sex when it's over."

I can't have heard him correctly. With all that's going on, *this* is what he has to tell me? I just stare at him, speechless.

Color floods his face. "I have a girlfriend now. She'd kill me."

I step close to him. "Are you kidding me? The witch will probably kill us."

"Well, just the same. I remember the last time. I took care of you when you needed it. I can't do that again."

He's talking about what happened when we went after

the men who hurt my niece. He offered himself, with sex and blood, and I took both. I had no choice. I pass a hand over my face and look into his dark eyes. "I promise to control myself, okay?"

Frey uncrosses his arms. "Are you sure you can?"

There's an uncomfortable minute while we both stare at each other. No, I'm not sure I can. But I will. I nod.

He accepts it and moves behind the bar. I hear the zipper again. He's taking off the jeans, presumably to shapeshift into animal form. And he's doing it behind the bar.

"I've seen you naked, Frey. I promised to control myself, didn't I?"

I get only a growl in response.

CHAPTER 29

FREY'S OTHER FORM IS PANTHER. WHEN HE SLINKS out from behind the bar, I marvel again at the strange creatures I've come in contact with since becoming vampire. Creatures I thought existed only in the pages of novels or on the big screen. Some are beautiful and inspire awe, like this sleek, man-sized cat full of grace and primitive power. Others, like Avery and Simon Fisher, were vampires who inspired fear and dread.

I'm still not sure where I fit in the continuum.

Frey approaches, alert, watchful. His eyes hold a spark of humanity though I know from seeing him in action that the cat is in full control. He looks at me, then moves to the door. I follow him outside.

I realize once we set off down the road that I should have asked him where we were going. But it's no problem for me to keep up. He trots ahead, muscles bunching and releasing under a pelt of dark fur. I follow, my own senses probing the night.

There's no moon. The sky is huge and black and filled with a million stars never seen in a city sky. I spy diamonds moving swiftly overhead, airplanes, and the slower moving pinpoints of light are satellites traveling around the earth in their solitary orbits.

I smell mesquite and dust and the decay of recent death. Animal. I wonder if it's the coyote Frey mentioned earlier. I see the outlines of cactus and rock and scrub oak. I also see the small creatures that slither or run away at our approach. Whether they're running from the panther or the vampire, I can't tell. Tonight they needn't fear either. I hear the calls of birds, the "ping" of bat radar, the single, lonely cry of a wolf somewhere far from us. It carries on the still, night air like an echo from another time.

I'm filled again with a sense of wonder. I've never let the animal inside me free to observe the world from this perspective. When the vampire is released, it's to feed or fight. This is a new experience. Exhilarating. Liberating. For the moment at least, I push worry for Max into a dark corner of my mind. Right next to anxiety over what will happen to Culebra if Frey is wrong.

Frey keeps going, deep into the desert, away from the road. He doesn't hesitate or falter but continues at the same pace until we're miles from the saloon. We hit no obstacles. I guess the witches did not expect anyone to approach from the heart of the desert. Approach what? I still don't know.

Lights appear on the horizon. And I hear other noises now, sounds of traffic and the acceleration and deceleration of airplane engines. We're nearing the Tijuana airport. But from the desert side. The lights of the city of Tijuana stretch beyond. Are we going into the city? Would the witch be planning to work her magic in the middle of a city?

Frey keeps going straight toward the airport. When we're about a half mile away, he veers toward an industrial park. Or what passes in Mexico as an industrial park. It's more like a landfill, but one dotted with junkyards, truck yards and small warehouses and workshops. The place floods with light when airplanes approach the runways, only to be plunged into darkness when they've passed overhead. It's like being in a time loop of accelerated sunrise and sunset, made all the more eerie because I detect nothing human here at all. Big trucks and small tractors crouch like cowering beasts. A dog barks inside one of the buildings but it's more a howl of loneliness than a growl of warning. The place feels utterly empty.

Frey trots up to one of the warehouses. He looks up at me. Then back toward the door.

Doesn't take a genius to understand what he wants. But before I open that door, I put an ear to it. I don't want to be surprised by a welcoming party. I detect nothing. No movement. No sound.

The door has an old-fashioned latch. It lifts with a touch. No lock. I half expect a siren or alarm to go off as I gently tug the wooden door open a fraction of an inch. When nothing happens, I pull it back wide enough for Frey and me to scramble inside.

The instant I pass over that threshold, I'm hit by a wave of fear as tangible and painful as a gunshot. It knocks me back, breathless, shaking, numb, pins me against the wall with invisible hands. Images fill my head. The essence of anything that has ever scared me, every nightmare, takes physical shape and hovers before me, ready to attack. Donaldson is there, the vampire who turned me, and Avery. Fisher, grinning and blood soaked, reaches out to pull me close to him. I feel his claws dig into my arms, his bared teeth snap at my throat. My blood spills over his hands.

These nightmares inflict pain.

I can't move. The rational part of my brain knows this isn't real. It can't be. Donaldson, Avery, Fisher are gone. I saw Donaldson and Avery disintegrate into dust, felt the last shudder as I drained the life from Fisher. This is not real. Still, the instinctive part of my brain screams to run. Get out before it's too late. My body tenses to take flight. I have no choice. If I'm to survive, I have to leave this place. Leave and never come back. If I'm to live.

"Anna. Where are you?"

A voice shouts from the void. It's far away. Too far away to help. Fisher and Avery press closer. Avery is smiling. His hands trace a path down my cheek, across my breast. I'm naked and where his fingers touch, my skin blackens and sloughs off. I try to slink away but I can't. The door to the warehouse swings open. A light shines in. Outside. I have to get outside. That's where I'll be safe.

My feet break free. I scream and whirl away from the nightmare. Move. Run.

A hand pulls me back.

No.

A voice. "Anna."

Over and over. Familiar. Coaxing.

But it can't save me. If I don't leave this place, I'll die. Avery tells me. Fisher and Donaldson. Get away. Save yourself.

I slash at the hand holding me. It doesn't let go. I snarl and bite down until I taste blood. Still, I'm held fast. Furious, the vampire erupts. Blindly, I seek the throat of the creature. I find it and rip until the blood washes over my tongue. I drink.

And at the first taste, I know.

The blood. The taste, the texture, the essence. I recognize it. I know this creature.

It doesn't matter.

I can't stop.

The voice doesn't scream or beg. It doesn't struggle or pull away. It's grown quiet and still. Waiting.

That is what stops me.

I burrow against its neck, but not to drink. To listen. To understand. And when I grow quiet, too, it puts its arms around me and holds me. Then it pulls me forward, and I'm falling.

Falling.

Into the void.

CHAPTER 30

I DON'T KNOW HOW FAR WE FALL. AT SOME POINT, the creature holding me lets go but I'm not afraid. The fear is gone. Suddenly, there's a crunch of flesh against concrete. Mine. Brutal pain where my shoulder makes contact. When I open my eyes, I'm lying on a cold, damp floor.

Relief that I'm no longer in the grip of terror washes over me. It's so dark, I think for an instant that my eyes are still shut. But I raise my hands and I can see them against the inky darkness. I press my fingertips together and raise them to my lips. I smell the blood, taste it in the back of my throat.

Frey. Where is he?

A tiny noise behind me brings me to my feet. I crouch and whirl around, ready to spring. The sound comes from something lying against a wall a few feet away. It's a moan, and it comes again. When I approach, the figure stirs and tries to sit up. I recognize him and rush to his side.

Frey is in his human form. He is naked and bleeding, from a wound to his arm and another at his throat.

Wounds I made.

I kneel at his side and offer my hand, not sure if he'll accept it or knock it away.

He reaches out and lets me help him into a sitting position.

"Are you very badly hurt?" I ask him.

He leans his back against the wall and stretches his legs out in front of him. "That will teach me to come between a vampire and her nightmares," he says.

"Did you see—?"

"Only your reaction. It wasn't difficult to fill in the blanks."

"You weren't affected?"

"I stayed in animal form until I realized you were in real trouble. As a panther, I was immune. When I changed, I felt the same horrors you did, but I managed to get you to the tunnel." He smiles. "I just wished I had had time to shape-shift back to the cat. It would have made the landing a hell of a lot easier."

I look around. "Where are we?"

Frey pushes himself up. He moves stiffly, stretching and testing each limb. He seems to have forgotten that he's naked. Not so long ago, he hid behind a bar to keep me from seeing the view I'm enjoying now. He catches me checking him out.

"Didn't know I'd be changing back before we got back to the bar," he grumbles. But he doesn't try to cover himself. "You really should stop staring."

Like there's anything else to look at. But I drag my eyes off Frey and do a slow turn. We're in some kind of tunnel. White tile walls. Cement floor. Recessed lighting. It has a familiar look.

"I've seen this before." I press my fingertips against my eyes. "I can't remember when, though. I think the fall has affected my memory."

Frey shakes his head. "I doubt you've ever been here. More likely, it looks familiar because the tunnels have been in the newspapers and on television. Not this particular tunnel, of course, or we wouldn't be standing here. But ones just like it. The desert between Tijuana and San Diego is riddled with them."

Of course. It was discovered a couple of years ago that drug runners had built an elaborate tunnel system running under the border. The media made a big deal out of it, but as fast as one tunnel was exposed and filled in, another sprang up seemingly overnight.

"Come on," Frey starts to move down the tunnel. "We'd better hurry."

I follow, whispering, "How did you find this?"

He doesn't slow down or look back at me. "Wasn't a lot to do while I waited for you to show up last night but prowl. I saw a car pull up outside the building. A woman and three men got out and went inside. No lights. No sound. When they didn't come back, I looked into a window. They had disappeared. So I changed and snuck in to look around."

"You were able to walk in?" The memory of being trapped in a living nightmare still looms fresh in my mind.

He raises both hands. "I don't know what to tell you. Last night I didn't feel anything like what we experienced a few minutes ago. In fact, I didn't feel or see anything at all, even in human form. I thought they must have gone out a back door. But then one of the men came back. Scared the shit out of me. I barely had time to hide. A trapdoor opened in the floor and this guy climbed out, went out to his car and drove away."

"Why do you think it has anything to do with the witch? These tunnels are used by drug dealers."

Frey gives me an impatient frown. "I did a little exploring after he left. Followed the tunnel until I reached the end. What I saw there had nothing to do with drugs. The woman who arrived in the car was watching a dozen or so men make something out of wood in a clearing not far from the end of the tunnel. An altar, I think. Of course, I didn't know then what it was for. I told you I thought it was a bunch of wannabes getting ready to dance their way into a sexual frenzy in honor of Halloween. It happens all the time out here in the desert."

He may still be right. I won't know for sure until I see if Belinda Burke is here.

"If the witch is using these tunnels," I reply, "whatever drug cartel dug them must be letting her—maybe she's giving them something in return. But if she is working with a cartel, why the glamour to keep people out? Why not just have guards with guns?"

"Last night, it was guards with guns," he says.

And yet now, tonight when the ritual is to take place, there are no guards. A primitive warning sounds in my brain. Does she know I'm here? Is it what she wants?

Frey raises a hand to his lips, and points, a signal that we're nearing the end of the tunnel. There's a staircase just ahead. He drops to one knee, lowers his head, and with an exhalation of breath, transforms back into the cat.

I've seen him make the change once before, but that time it was gradual. One shape morphing into another. This time, it's accomplished in the blink of an eye. A shudder racks his body, a cry becomes a growl, and the human Frey is gone. It must be painful to make the change so fast. The panther trembles a moment before gathering himself to make the ascent out of the tunnel.

I'm right behind him. It's a steep, slippery climb, on rough slabs of stone set into the concrete. I have to go slowly, Frey bounds up like—well, like a cat. There are about twenty steps leading into a darkened passageway. No lights here. We're guided by a strange sound, a litany sung in an unfamiliar language. And the scent of incense and burning mesquite.

We tread softly. I have a hand on the scruff of Frey's neck. I'm afraid what will happen if I'm plunged into another nightmare scape. Frey seems to sense it, because he presses closes to me as if for assurance. There's no doubt in my mind now that we're in the right place. Before we reach the triangle of light that marks the doorway, I lean down and whisper in his ear.

"If something happens to me, stop the witch. Don't let her hurt Culebra."

He pushes his head against my chest and makes a guttural noise.

Then I straighten up and lead the way outside.

CHAPTER 31

WHAT WE SEE THROUGH THE DOORWAY *IS* A scene from a nightmare. This time, though, it's not my own personal hell, but a tableau from an ancient book on witchcraft. A huge fire crackles and dances, sending sparks and laps of flame into the night. The reflection cast by the fire is the only light, making the darkness beyond dense and impenetrable. In the flickering shadows, an altar rises like a specter, and something that looks very much like a gallows. There is a form suspended on the scaffold, not hanging from a noose, but spread-eagle on a cross. It looks human. And it's very still.

Frey stops me from moving forward by taking my hand gently into his mouth. I'm so intent on trying to make sense of the scene, I almost blunder into the trap. A thin wire stretches ankle height across the door. We can't see what it would trip, but it doesn't matter. I step over while Frey leaps it with feline gracefulness.

The chanting comes from our right, out of sight behind an outcropping of rock. It's a melodious, ancient sound that reminds me of the old Catholic high mass. Latin, maybe, or Celtic. It's accompanied by an instrument with sweet, clear tones. A recorder.

Frey and I scramble across a bare expanse of ground to take shelter behind a rock. I don't know if we're in Mexico or have crossed into the United States. Most of these tunnels exit somewhere in the Otay Mesa area of San Diego County, but I haven't a clue how far we traveled.

I peek up from the rock, keeping as still as I can to avoid attracting attention. My breath catches in my throat when I recognize what is hanging from that cross. There are two bodies, back to back, lashed together. One, facing me, is a woman, her limp, naked body a pale, flickering silhouette in the firelight. I can't make out the other. I can't even tell whether the two are human, although I suspect they are.

Or if they are alive.

Where is Culebra?

The chanting becomes louder, more urgent. I glance at my watch—it's ten minutes before midnight. I'd lost track of time. We must have traveled much farther than I imagined.

I shift my gaze in the direction of the sound. Dozens of people form a hellish chorus, standing close together, dressed in long dark robes with the cowls pulled over their heads. They sway and moan the words, caught up in some demonic rapture.

A woman steps from the group, opens her robe, lets it fall to the ground. She has dark hair that sweeps forward to cover her face. Her naked body glows in the reflected light. When she turns toward the altar, I see it. On her right shoulder is a tattoo. A crimson skull with a rose. Belinda Burke.

At a signal from the witch, the others let their robes fall, too. Now, men and women, all stand naked. They intertwine hands and follow as she makes her way toward the altar. She alone climbs the steps. Still chanting, the others form a circle around the fire and the altar.

Belinda Burke looks down on her congregation. She raises a staff and they grow quiet.

"We have taken the first step," she says, her words infused with a dark energy that makes a shiver touch my spine. "The gathering is complete. The hour approaches. We will accomplish what no other coven has done before. We will summon the demon, Aswah, and he will be our servant. He will cleanse the earth of those who hide themselves among us, pretending to be human, pretending to do us no harm."

She gestures to the cross behind her. "We will seal this pact with the offerings. A human woman, to show Aswah what earthly pleasures await him. And the demon, shapeshifter, to remind him of his mission."

My body tenses as her words stab at my heart. *Culebra? Is it you?*

There is no answer from the motionless figure. How could this have happened? Culebra is powerful, possesses strong magic. How could he have let himself be trapped by a witch?

Burke is still talking, but I no longer listen. I've got to stop this. I feel Frey shift beside me, his eyes hold a question I can't yet answer.

Burke raises the staff again. The coven responds. The chanting is louder, more compelling, filled with the zealousness of renewed purpose. Burke's voice floats out over the others, intoning the summoning spell. The fire leaps higher as if in response to her words. The ground begins to shake beneath our feet.

It's two minutes to midnight. Think. What did Williams say? There is only an instant when the summoning can be completed, when the worlds of the living and dead overlap. We have to interrupt at that instant.

The fire parts, dividing itself to form a chasm in the pit. Burke's face is wild with desire, her voice shakes with emotion. She is caught up in a frenzy of excitement and joy. Her feelings reach out across the coven, sucking them in, increasing their own passion. I feel it, too. Watch in wonder at the power that springs forth from the gathering. I'm drawn in, thrilled by an almost sexual longing to be a part of what is happening. I stand up, ready to join them, ready to raise my voice in welcome to—

Frey snaps at me, biting down hard on my arm.

I jump at the pain, whirl to face my attacker.

Frey growls and snaps again.

Blood, my blood, runs freely down the length of my right arm. The sight and smell of it clears my head in an instant.

The minute hand of my watch sweeps toward midnight. Thirty seconds.

I start to run, across the ground, clearing the distance in a heartbeat. Frey is in front of me. He hesitates only a second and I point to the person closest to him, just yards away. He launches himself at the same time I throw all my weight against the circle, breaking the bond between outstretched hands. A lightning bolt of power passes through me and I stumble from the impact. Then it flows out of me and into the ground, and the chanting stops.

There is a roar. Animal-like and ferocious. I whirl toward the sound. The fire in the pit closes around something scrambling to escape. A huge creature, black, red eyes, sharp-tipped horns glistening. The mouth is open, screaming in rage and fear. Its eyes turn in my direction, its gaze burning into my soul, knowing, blaming me for what is happening. It reaches a clawlike hand toward me, to draw me into the pit. I feel myself moving forward. I dig in my heels, but I can't stop. It smiles, a ghastly grin that shows fangs and a forked tongue, and I know. It recognizes that I am vampire and it will have its revenge. I'm at the very edge of the pit. My clothes are burning, the heat singes my skin.

With an explosion of ash and flame, the fire collapses in on itself. The demon is drawn down, howling with frustration, back into the pit. I'm thrown to the ground with bone jarring force. The earth beneath our feet roils and stirs as if revolting against the demon it's being forced to take back. With one last violent shudder, it grows still.

I collapse back, relieved, and rest my head against the

ground while I collect my thoughts. We stopped the demon. Frey and I.

Where is Frey?

I push myself up on my elbows and look around.

I'm surrounded by an angry coven, pushing closer, their rage palpable as they close the circle around me.

"Vampire."

Burke's voice draws my eyes to the altar.

She's standing at the foot of the cross, a crossbow in her hand. At her feet, a still, dark form.

My heart leaps.

Frey.

She nudges him with her foot. But he doesn't move or make a sound. The bolt in his side says it all.

CHAPTER 32

FREY IS NOT MOVING, BUT HE'S ALIVE. I KNOW BE-
cause his form has not changed. He remains a panther.
When a shape-shifter dies he reverts to human form. I
can't remember whether it was Culebra or Frey who told
me this, but the important thing is, he's alive. But for how
long?

My gaze shifts to the witch. She holds the crossbow to
her shoulder, the bolt pointed at my chest. I'm fast, but can
I out run an arrow?

Muscles tense to try.

Burke smiles and shifts the crossbow. The bolt is
pointed now at Frey. "If you run, I shoot him again. Then I
kill the woman. Then I kill Culebra. It's your choice."

I relax, letting the energy drain out of my system like
water down a pipe. "What do you want?"

She gestures with the crossbow. "Join me."

I hold up my hands to indicate acquiescence and start
for the stage. The coven follows at my back, snapping and
growling like a pack of wild dogs. Their animosity shimmers around me, a black energy I can feel on my skin and

taste in my mouth like acid or vomit. They want nothing more than to tear me apart. Perhaps that's what the witch has in mind.

She's taller than I remember, her lean body glows in the moonless night. She's stands erect and unashamed, her nakedness a challenge. She watches me come up the steps, the crossbow pointed at my chest and held with a steady hand. She has a smile on her face as she motions for me to come closer.

"You are Anna Strong."

If she expects that I will react in shock that she knows my name, she is disappointed. After all, I know now the warning she so dramatically delivered when I'd crashed into her wall was aimed specifically at me. To achieve this very result.

"Do you know what you have interrupted here?"

We are face-to-face. Her expression is calm, untroubled. She speaks as if to a recalcitrant child. I think I'd prefer it if she screamed. This air of mild annoyance is definitely at odds with the powerful rage I feel from her followers watching us.

I gesture at the people below. "Looks like they've been stood up. I don't think they're very happy about that."

She looks down at them. "They are angry. Understandably. The opportunity to raise Aswah will not come again for a decade. What do you suppose they would do if I threw you to them?"

But she makes no move to do it. Her tone is lazy, indulgent, a woman who likes the sound of her own voice.

"Pretty good special effects, Burke," I snap back. "But a little over-the-top, don't you think?"

She raises her chin and smiles. "You know my name?"

I nod. "I saw your mug shot at SDPD the other day. It was a very unflattering picture. You look short with clothes on."

"Foley was right about you. He said you have a smart mouth."

For the first time, she says something that surprises me. "Foley knows about"—I wave a hand around—"this?"

"Why don't you ask him?"

From the shadow behind the cross steps a figure. He, too, is smiling and he holds out a hand as if we're meeting in the most mundane of social occasions.

Agent Foley drops his hand when he realizes I have no intention of shaking it. Instead he puts one hand on Belinda Burke's shoulder while taking the crossbow from her with the other. It remains pointed at my chest.

"Well, Anna. It's about damned time."

CHAPTER 33

"So, FOLEY?" I ASK. "DID YOU ARRANGE ALL THIS? You've been following me around for two days. If you wanted a date, all you had to do was ask."

Foley frowns. "Following you? What makes you think that?"

"Come on. Don't be coy. The telephone calls? The shooting in the canyon? I know it was you. Were you having fun?"

I remember what Frey said about Martinez having Max and wanting me. "Well, here we are." I turn to Burke and gesture to the unmoving, silent figures hanging from the cross. "Why not let them go? The demon is snacking on whatever they snack on in hell. You have no need to keep them."

Burke shrugs. "My followers will want to take their revenge on someone. It may as well be those two. Unless, of course, you are volunteering to take Culebra's place?"

I glance down at the mob. I sense only humans, full of venom and unrestrained fury, but no supernaturals among them. I know I'd have a better chance of surviving than a human or an injured or drugged shape-shifter. Culebra must be hurt or under the influence of a powerful spell. He has not reached out telepathically to me. And there is Frey. He is lying injured and bleeding at our feet, the arrow in his side rising and falling with each labored breath. He must get help soon. "Will you let the panther and the girl go, as well, if I agree?"

She frowns. "You aren't serious? Do you think you could survive against this crowd? Do you think they would allow your friends to walk away? Some of Aswah's followers have waited years for this night. You have ruined it. If I don't allow them their revenge here and now, they will not rest until they have tracked down the shape-shifters and the girl and destroyed them."

Foley interrupts with an abrupt guttural hiss. "I don't know what you two fruitcakes are talking about," he snaps. "But I've got what I want. I don't give a shit what happens to those two." He kicks at Frey. "And the panther? Isn't that overdoing it just a little, even for a drama queen like you?"

He's talking to Burke and I see her shoulders grow tight. But Frey makes a mewling noise at Foley's touch and that ignites a fire in my belly. "Don't touch him." It comes out in a growl.

Foley laughs. "Or you'll do what?" He centers the crossbow again, at my chest.

Burke stiffens beside him. "Be careful, Foley," she says. "Anna is . . ."

She doesn't have a chance to finish the sentence. In the next instant Foley finds out exactly what I am.

CHAPTER 34

WHEN I LUNGE, WHEN THE VAMPIRE LUNGES, Foley flinches. He's not prepared for the sight or sound of my fury. I'm at his throat, dimly aware of the danger of the crossbow in his hand, acutely aware that he is a threat to my friends, Frey at his feet, Culebra on the cross. I press my body against his, forcing the hand with the crossbow down between us. If he fires now it will be painful, but not deadly.

But Foley doesn't fire. In fact, he does nothing. His eyes are wide, staring, unbelieving. He can't seem to look away, makes no move to flee. He is rooted to the spot, terrified, confused. I remember what it was like, that first realization that what confronts you is a creature from a nightmare. It hasn't been that long. The paralyzing fear, the reeling mind, the body numb with shock.

It fills the vampire with power, wonder, lust. It makes taking a human easy.

I feel it now. I hear the voice—Anna's voice—telling me to be careful. Foley is human. If I kill him, if I feed from him, I will be changed. He is not a willing host. He is not feeling the pleasure that comes from *wanting*.

My heart is pounding, deafening in my ears. My body is on fire with the bloodlust. This overwhelming urge to kill a human overtook me once before—when I had Trish's tormentor by the throat. Frey stopped me then. I have to stop myself now.

Foley is limp in my arms. He's whimpering, making a sound much like the one Frey made moments before. Not of pain. This is the sound of surrender, of terror. My lips are at his throat, the rush of his blood makes them tingle with anticipation. I let my tongue rest lightly over the pulse point at the base of his jaw. His heart is hammering and I revel in the knowledge that he is mine for the taking.

A movement, small and inconsequential brings me back. Frey, squirming in pain at our feet. And a sound, the witch yelling.

I jerk my head back from Foley and whirl around.

Humans are coming up the stairs toward me. They clutch pieces of sharpened wood in their hands and their faces are masks of hatred. These humans know about vampires. They are not paralyzed by fear or wonder. With a swooping motion, I grab Frey. I glance over at the cross. I can't do anything for either the human or Culebra. I can only save Frey and myself.

Culebra, I scream silently, *I'm sorry.*

There is no answer.

The woman hangs alone on the cross. Culebra is gone.

CHAPTER 35

THE PANTHER'S BODY IS LIKE A CHILD'S IN MY arms. I leap off the altar and race for the darkness beyond. The humans, however full of hate, cannot keep up. I leave them behind with a howl of satisfaction.

I don't go to the tunnel. The witch knows the tunnel. It is her domain. I head out into the desert, following an instinct I didn't know I possessed. Back to Beso de la Muerte. I need to get the cat to shelter.

I race over the desert terrain with a sure footedness that surprises me. When we came this way before, Frey led and I followed. I don't know what instinct is at work now, but I surrender to it, let an inner guidance system direct my feet the way I had let Frey guide me earlier. In much less time than it took us to reach the tunnel, I'm racing down the dusty streets of Beso de la Muerte.

When I reach the saloon, animal instinct stops me from bursting through the doors. I don't know if Culebra is dead or if he has beaten me back here or if the witch awaits both of us inside. I lay Frey on the street, out of harm's way, and approach. My senses tingle with apprehension. I listen, not only with my ears, but with my entire body. My nerve endings are on fire. The skittering of bugs crawling across the floor and the hum of the wings of flying insects are sounds both distinct and identifiable. I listen harder—for mortal breathing and the pulse of a heartbeat. I probe for things nonhuman—vampire and shape-shifter. When I am sure I am alone, I sweep the cat into my arms once more and take him inside. I lay him gently on the floor and hunker down beside him.

The hammering of my heart, the rush of my blood, the desire to attack *something* is so intense, I actually consider going back to find the witch. Foley is human. The witch is something else. Without Frey's well-being to consider, I could stop her from harming my friends again. Permanently. Killing her, drinking from her, would be exquisite revenge for what she did to Culebra, to Frey.

The human Anna comes back slowly.

When she—when *I*—return, I have to close my eyes, clear my head until the shaking stops. I've felt it before, the dichotomy. I've fought against it. But tonight, when the vampire took over, Anna was gone. Rational thought gave way to instinct, and human emotion to an animal's drive for self-preservation. If Foley had fought, I would have killed him. I would have killed Burke or any of her coven if I'd gone back. I've been fooling myself to think my humanity was stronger than the creature that shares my body.

The guttural sound of an engine floats across the still night. A car approaching. The barrier must be down. Perhaps when Frey and I broke the circle, we broke the spell as well.

I lay Frey down carefully behind the bar and crouch there, too, to wait. It might be the witch and Foley. If it is, I'll be ready.

The car pulls to a stop right outside the saloon. Three doors slam, almost in unison. My mental probe detects nothing. Either three humans approach or these visitors have cloaked their own thoughts the same way I am cloaking mine.

I creep to the end of the bar, hidden in shadow, and peek around.

The doors swing open with a rustle of air.

Anna? Are you here?

I don't realize how tense I am until the sound of the familiar voice sends relief flooding through my body. I leap up.

Williams crosses the floor in a blur of motion almost too fast to see. He grips my arms and looks down at me.

His expression of concern is so intense, a ripple of fear replaces the relief. "What's wrong?"

He lets go of my arms and steps back, color flooding his face. Embarrassment? I wonder why. Because he guessed wrong about the witch and where she would be tonight or because I accomplished what he and his Watchers could not?

I let him read my thoughts, see the color deepen, feel chagrin replace discomfiture. But I don't push. Part of me is glad to see him. Part of me is furious with him. I let that come through, as well.

For the first time, I see who arrived with Williams. Ortiz and another. Not a vamp. But not human.

He steps forward. "Is Frey with you?"

He opens his mind. Shape-shifter.

Yes. And he's hurt. Can you help him?

He motions for me to lead him to Frey. I do. He bends down and places one hand on each side of the arrow.

I watch as he gently probes. He appears to be in his fifties, tall, broad shouldered, rangy muscle. His face is full of concern for Frey, his thoughts mirror that concern. Before I can ask what he intends to do, he has grasped the arrow and pulled it from Frey's body with one single, violent jerk of his hand.

Frey's body spasms. I jump toward the shape-shifter, a growl of rage erupting from deep inside. Williams grabs me from behind and spins me around.

Wait. Watch.

He turns me back so can I see.

I shake loose of his hands, still reeling from the surge of anger that would have had me at the shape-shifter's throat had Williams not stopped me. I take a step away from Williams. If I decide to attack again, I want to be out of his reach.

The shape-shifter is bent over Frey. He has placed his hands over the wound. Frey is still squirming, making a sound in his throat that is half cry, half growl. But he breathes. I see it. The rise of each inhalation and fall of each exhalation. In less than a minute, his breathing becomes less labored, his body quiets, Frey's keening sound dies away.

Only then does the shape-shifter lift his hands. They are red with Frey's blood. He falls back as if the healing has drained him. That's when I see it—a gash in his shirt and an open lesion corresponding to the wound in Frey's side. He closes his eyes and leans back against the bar. While I watch, the wound closes, the blood is absorbed back into his skin. The only indication that anything has happened at all is the rip in his shirt.

I switch my gaze to Williams. *Empath?*

He nods.

Like Sorrel? Can she heal, too?

Sorrel's gift is to heal the spirit. He gestures to the man now climbing slowly to his feet. *Stephen's gift is to heal the body. Each is distinct unto itself.*

When I look again at Frey, he has shifted back into human form. He shakes his head as if awakening from a particularly vivid nightmare. There's confusion and alarm in his expression and a kind of breathless anticipation as rational thought creeps back.

He struggles into a sitting position and looks around. Stephen says, *How do you feel?*

Although I can't hear Frey's response, I can read the relief and gratitude on his face. He reaches out a hand and Stephen grasps it, pulling Frey to his feet. Only then does Frey turn to me.

"You're all right?"

I nod. I want to throw my arms around him and express just how relieved I am that he is all right. But I don't want to embarrass either of us and I don't know how he would react. After all, he did tell me that he has a girlfriend now and he is standing here naked. Who knows what kind of reaction a near death experience might have on him if I press myself against him?

He's looking at me as if he reads my thoughts. He smiles and reaches down for that pair of jeans he'd left behind the bar. This time, though, he doesn't turn away or hide himself, just slips them on.

When he's zipped up, he comes around to join us. "What happened to the witch?"

The question is directed at me. I shake my head. "I don't know. I grabbed you and got out of there when the coven started getting restless."

Williams releases a breath. "I don't understand why she came here. It doesn't make sense. The very reason we didn't have a sentry in Mexico was because every one of our sources said she planned to raise the demon in Arizona, outside Sedona, where she could tap into the power of the vortex."

"Then what brought you here?" I ask.

"Avatoar." Williams lifts a shoulder. "He came to find me in Arizona. Told me about the barrier. Said it was definitely constructed by a coven."

"So you know Avatoar?"

He brushes the question aside with an impatient wave of the hand. "Obviously. Why do you think the coven would construct a barrier aimed to keep you out?"

"I don't think it was," I reply. "Not anymore. Burke knew that letting me know she had Culebra was the one sure way to get my attention. She wanted me here."

Frey frowns. "What do you mean? We stopped the demon. She almost succeeded in raising it. She wanted you to do that?"

"No. She wanted to raise the demon all right. She didn't think I could stop it. But you were hurt and didn't see what happened after."

He motions for me to go on.

I turn to Williams, anger flooding back. "There was another guest at Burke's party. Foley."

Williams' shoulders tense, his eyes grow watchful, wary.

You knew Martinez had Max. You said nothing yesterday. You sent me here.

Williams is standing so still I can hear the beat of his heart, the stirring of the hair on the back of his neck as he absorbs the enormity of my fury.

I don't know if I can forgive you for this.

Frey senses the heat of what is passing between Williams and me even if he can't read the message. He looks from one of us to the other as if hoping by that simple act to break the tension. When he doesn't, he asks, "Foley was there, too? Why?"

I look away from Williams.

"They were both waiting for someone else to show up at midnight. They were waiting for me."

"She's right."

The voice comes from the doorway.

Culebra is there, holding the woman from the cross in his arms. His face is battered with grief. "They wanted Anna," he whispers. "And because of me, this woman is dead and they almost got her."

CHAPTER 36

STEPHEN RUSHES FORWARD, HIS ARMS OUT-stretched to take the woman from Culebra.

But Culebra shakes his head and brushes past him. He lays the inert form on the bar. "It's too late for her." His words are harsh. "Something else I must accept responsibility for."

"How did you get away?" I ask.

Culebra raises his eyes, reluctantly, to meet mine. It seems to take a great deal of effort for him to wrest his mind from anything except the dead woman. "When you broke the circle, you broke the spell that bound me, as well. But it took some time for me to shake off the effects. The distraction you provided when you grabbed the panther gave me time to shape-shift and free myself. But it wasn't in time to save her." His voice drops. "Burke saw me. She got to her before I could change back and free her. Burke strangled her while I watched."

I've never seen Culebra like this. For the first time, I see that the "woman" who had been hanging from the cross is really no more than a girl. Thin, pale, sixteen or seventeen years old. "Who is she?"

He touches her hair gently. "A runaway. Burke picked her up on the street, promised her food and shelter. Instead, she became a sacrifice."

His distress is so acute, it's painful to feel. I open my mind to offer him solace but he swats it away.

I don't deserve your sympathy. All that has happened is because of my arrogance and conceit. I should have told you what the witch had planned instead of thinking I was strong enough to handle it on my own.

Williams interjects himself into the conversation. *You are right to blame yourself, shape-shifter. We could have stopped Burke if we had known.*

Williams' arrogance snaps my temper once again. *How would Culebra have known you would accept help? You certainly didn't from me. In fact, you sent me away.*

That was for a reason. You do not consider the ramifications of what you do.

Culebra emits a growl from deep in his throat. *Let me guess. Did Anna think it more important to protect me than stop the demon?*

Williams doesn't answer. He doesn't have to. His mind snaps shut with an almost audible click.

Culebra shakes his head. *And yet Anna is the one who stopped the witch. She does what must be done. I would accept her help far more readily than I would trust my well-being to you, vampire.*

The air is charged with energy. I'm caught in the middle of a supernatural clash of the titans. There's an undercurrent between the two that I want to question. Something both explosive and dangerous. But right now, Max's well-being is more important. I hold up a hand to break the tension.

We stopped the demon from rising, but Burke is still out there and so is Foley. Culebra, what happened after I left?

His eyes are locked on Williams but after a moment, he drags them away. *Foley left almost immediately. I don't think he understands what he witnessed. He was disoriented and angry. He blamed Burke for letting you get away.*

Whatever deal they struck is apparently void. I heard a car engine so I'm assuming he took off to find you. Maybe into Tijuana. Or maybe just back across the border.

And Burke?

She spent a little time with her followers, trying to calm them down. They knew nothing of Foley and were not pleased at the presence of an outsider. Burke offered no explanation. They demanded a sacrifice and to appease them, she took the girl. There was nothing I could do. Then they set fire to the altar and left. I just managed to get her body off the cross before the whole structure went up.

He grows quiet. His mind sinking again into a deep hole of black despair.

You did what you could, I tell him. *Burke killed this girl, you did not.*

This time he allows himself to take a little consolation from my words. But he lets me see that it is only because he has reached the decision to avenge her death. *Burke will pay with her own life for the taking of this innocent.*

I nod my understanding and pledge my help. *She almost killed a friend of mine, too.* This exchange occurs only between Culebra and myself. Williams is watching as if he knows we are sharing thoughts he is not privy to. His uneasiness shows.

But first, there is Foley to deal with. I turn on Williams. "You didn't tell me that Martinez has Max."

His eyes shift to Frey.

I don't let him get distracted. "Did Foley say how Martinez found Max?"

He shakes his head. "Only that Martinez set a trap and Max got caught in it."

"Then there can be only one explanation. Money. Foley was trying to collect a bounty Martinez put on Max. Originally, he may have planned to kidnap me to draw Max out. If Martinez captured Max on his own, Foley would have no claim on the money. Martinez wanted Max because he thinks it's Max's fault his family was killed. I may be the revenge Martinez is seeking for the death of his own family."

"But how would he know where to look for you tonight?"

I shake my head. "I don't know. He thinks I'm human. Even after I turned, he didn't believe what he was seeing. And he thought the demon was sleight of hand, special effects to wow Burke's followers. How could he have connected me with that?"

"Burke saw you here with me." Culebra replies. "That day you came to feed. I think the better question would be how Burke and Foley managed to get together. Unless she has a connection to Martinez that we know nothing about."

Williams and Culebra both look to me for the answer. Trouble is, I don't know. Max has never mentioned magic in his dealings with Martinez. And it's not a subject I'd be likely to bring up. I shrug and let them know.

Williams shifts restlessly from one foot to the other. "Well, I don't see that there is anything more we can do here tonight. I need to get back. Anna, do you want to come with us?"

Before I answer, I look at Culebra. He nods that I should go, that he will be in touch soon.

Still, I'm uneasy at the thought that Culebra might go after Burke on his own. Only when he assures me that he will not attempt it, do I agree to leave.

Besides, he adds, *there are many I sent away who need to be called back. I jeopardized their safety as well as my own. I have much to make up for.*

That Williams picks up on. *We'd better go before your compadres start reappearing.* His tone is mocking. *I'm sure I'd recognize one or two. Probably on that same poster that features Burke back at my headquarters.*

Culebra's reply is equally curt. *Probably.*

Frey decides to go back the way he came to Beso de la Muerte—in animal form. Stephen asks if Frey would like company.

I have so few opportunities to run free, he says. *There is no moon tonight. We can make it to town before daylight.*

Frey agrees and they shed their clothes, leaving them in

a pile that I pick up and promise to deliver to Frey in a day or two. They make the transition with an almost gleeful abandon. Stephen's other form is wolf and the two waste no time, disappearing into the darkness beyond the saloon, the wolf's bay of farewell hanging on the air long after they are out of sight.

For a moment, I envy their freedom.

Williams motions to me that it is time to go. He says nothing to Culebra. Ortiz is just about to precede us out the door when he stops, head tilted.

"A car," he says.

I hear it, too, approaching fast. There is only one narrow road in and out of Beso de la Muerte. The tension level ratchets up a notch. It's a very good bet whoever or whatever is on its way in is not a friend. The unspoken consensus between us is that it's better to stay our ground and meet the stranger on familiar turf than try to beat him out of town.

Williams and Ortiz take positions beside the bar, Culebra in front of it. I step near the door and off to the side, ready to fling myself at the intruder if necessary.

With an intense single-mindedness, we listen as the car nears. It stops outside the saloon and a door opens. There is a pause, as if the driver is deciding on a course of action. Then footsteps echo on the wooden planks and the saloon door swings open.

Foley steps inside. He is neither alarmed nor apparently surprised at seeing San Diego's chief of police standing in the middle of the ruins of a ghost town saloon. His gaze sweeps in a lazy arc to take us all in.

When he spies me, he smiles. "Well," he says, turning back to Williams, "you do keep the strangest company."

Foley's air of self-assured nonchalance takes some swallowing. I feel the hair stir on the back of my neck, a flush of rage sends adrenaline pumping. I want nothing more than to ravage that smile off his face. He acts as if he doesn't see the dead woman lying in front of him on the bar or the man beside her who hung on a cross over his head not an hour ago. Instead, he stares at Williams with the defiant posture of one who believes he is in control.

Surprisingly, Williams lets him get away with it.

Instead of attacking, Williams meets Foley's gaze with a frown. "What are you doing here, Agent Foley?" he asks, his tone reflecting only mild curiosity.

Foley's smile never waivers. "I could ask you the same." He waves a hand. "But I will tell you. I came for Anna."

"In an official capacity?"

He shrugs. "If it needs to be. I came to ask for her help, but I can make it less pleasant if I have to."

"You have no authority in Mexico, Agent Foley."

"Neither have you."

God. Another pissing contest. They're so busy marking their territories, they forget that the object of the conversation is standing right here. "Would you like to tell *me* what it is you want?"

Both Foley and Williams turn abruptly in my direction.

I deliberately step between them. "What do you want?"

"It's not so much what I want," he replies. "It's what I can give you."

I raise an eyebrow. "I can hardly wait to hear this. What can you give me, Foley?"

"Max," he says. "I can give you Max."

CHAPTER 37

"YOU HAVE MAX?" I SHAKE MY HEAD AT FOLEY. "Right. And you called Burke a drama queen?"

He starts to open his jacket, but, as one, Culebra, Williams, Ortiz and I all take a menacing step toward him. His hand freezes. "Easy. I have something I want to show Anna, that's all."

Williams motions for him to go ahead. "Slowly."

He continues in theatrical slow motion to reach into an inside jacket pocket. What he pulls out is a picture. He holds it out to me.

I take it from his outstretched hand and turn it over. The image is dark, as if taken inside a dimly lit room. But the central figure is clear. It's Max. He's bound and gagged and lying on a bed. His eyes are open. Not fixed in death, but staring, aware. There is a newspaper on his chest. Yesterday's *San Diego Union-Tribune*.

I swallow back panic and the rising tide of anger. I raise my eyes to Foley. "Where is he?"

Foley shrugs. "I really don't know."

I take another step toward him. "You just said you had him."

He holds his ground. "Well, in point of fact, Martinez has him."

"So you admit it? You're working for Martinez?"

He looks around. "No use denying it. There's nothing any of you can do about it." He focuses on me again. "But if you agree to come with me, Martinez promises to set Max free."

Williams moves so that he is between Foley and me. "What kind of game are you playing? Why would Martinez want Anna? Max is the one he thinks betrayed him."

"Can't answer that one, either."

But I can. Martinez is seeking payback for what happened to his family. I know there is no chance that he will free Max with or without me. I know Foley knows this, as well. But I have a decided advantage in this game. I open my thoughts to Williams.

I will go with him.

Williams' shoulders bunch. *No. I won't permit it.*

YOU won't permit it? That he would even say that to me has my skin crawling with disgust. *There is nothing for you to permit.*

Think, Anna. It's a trick. Max is already dead. You know that.

But there is a chance that he is not. I'm willing to take it. I can take care of myself. I doubt Martinez has supernaturals on his payroll.

Culebra's voice interrupts. *I can help. I can follow Anna as my other self.*

Williams snorts. *Rattlesnake? How do you propose to follow them in that form?*

Tire treads. Dirt roads. I have done it before.

And what if Foley crosses the border? Takes paved roads? What then?

I call upon other animals. I have many friends in this part of the world.

Williams is unmoved. *No.*

It is not your decision. My voice cuts into the dialogue. *I will go with Foley. Culebra will do what he can. I am not afraid.*

During this exchange, Foley shifts impatiently from one foot to the other. He does not know what is passing between the three of us. I suppose he thinks I'm debating just how far I'm willing to go for a man I supposedly love.

His next words confirm my thoughts. "I knew you wouldn't go for it. I told Martinez. You are a selfish bitch. Max is only one of a string of lovers. He's not important enough to you to risk your own skin."

I slap his face so hard he loses his balance and falls backward, landing on his ass in an unceremonious heap. He's back on his feet in an instant though, and his hand dips again into his jacket.

I grab it and twist. "You want my cooperation?" I snarl. "Better treat me with a little more respect."

He tries to pull free but I bend his hand backward at the wrist while removing the gun from the clip on his hip. I toss it to Williams.

When he has it, I release Foley. He doesn't know whether to rub his bruised cheek or to nurse his aching wrist. His ego prevents him from doing either. He glares at me in furious rage but doesn't say anything.

Smart.

Williams' thoughts are furious, too, aimed not at Foley, though, but at Culebra and at me. *You are intent on doing this?*

Yes. If Foley makes it back, be sure he never gets a chance to spend all his blood money.

Williams doesn't yield the intensity of his disapproval, but he does nod.

I glance at Culebra who nods, too, that he is ready.

I blow out a ragged breath. "Okay, Foley. You've got me. Let's go."

Foley stares at me in disbelief. "You'll come?"

He's so obviously surprised, I can't help but laugh. "You are a moron, you know that? If you didn't think I'd come, why all this?" I wave a hand. "You exposed yourself to a police chief and a deputy. What did you think would happen if I refused? You could go back home and we'd pretend nothing happened?"

His eyes shift away.

"Oh," I answer for him. "I get it. Martinez will pay more for a live Anna than a dead one. You didn't get Max, so I'm the consolation prize. Explains what happened in Palm Canyon."

His expression hardens and I know I'm right. I look over at Williams. "Better start making the case against this idiot for the shooting in Palm Canyon as soon as you get back to San Diego. Not that I expect Foley is planning to cross the border again. Not under his real name anyway."

But Foley's face shows no emotion except a deepening frown of growing impatience. "Are you going to shut up anytime soon? I'd like to get out of this dump."

The temptation is strong to whack him again. But he's right. The sooner we get on the road, the sooner I can do something for Max. I don't bother to say anything else to Williams or Culebra. It's all been said. I motion for Foley to lead the way and he does, casting one hesitant glance backward to assure himself Williams is not going to stop us. When he's confident that the way is clear, his back straightens, his walk becomes a swagger and his face takes on an expression of smug calculation.

He thinks he's won.

He has another think coming.

CHAPTER 38

FOLEY IS DRIVING A BIG SUV, SHINY BLACK IN THE diffused light of approaching dawn. The windows are tinted. He doesn't bother to see if I'm actually going to get in. He leaves me to open the passenger door while he crosses confidently to the driver's side.

When I'm inside, he cranks over the engine and pulls away. For the first few miles, he keeps a close watch on the rearview mirror. As we get farther from Beso de la Muerte and no headlights reflect in the mirror from a tail, he relaxes a bit in the seat. He glances over at me. "Guess you aren't worth much to your friends. They aren't even trying to follow."

I ignore the remark. "Where are we going?"

He just smiles.

I settle back in the seat. "So, how did you and Burke get together anyway?"

A sideways glance. "Mutual friend."

"Ah. Martinez, right? He has some interest in the black arts does he?"

Foley chuckles. "I think it's crap. But he and his crazy

mother believe in that stuff. After I told him you'd dissappeared from San Diego for real yesterday, he said Burke knew she could find you—could 'summon' you because she had some friend of yours. He paid Burke a shitload of money to lure you to that freak show. He really wants you bad." A smirk touches his mouth. "It worked. I'll give them that."

"You don't have a clue, do you?"

He snorts. "About what?"

"You think last night was all pyrotechnics and special effects. If Burke had succeeded, you would have been demon food. It almost would have been worth it."

He laughs. "Yeah. Right. I do have one question for you, though. What were *you* on? Speed? Angel dust? You got scary looking for a minute. And strong. And you beat it out of there so fast I couldn't even catch you in the car. Lucky Burke knew where to find you."

Yeah. Lucky.

I put my head back and close my eyes. It will give me such great pleasure to show Foley how really scary I can be.

I wonder if Culebra can track the car the way he said. But it doesn't really matter. I'm on my way to Max. The only thing I ask is that he still be alive when I get there.

We stay on the main road for a mile or two from Beso de la Muerte. Even pass the wreck of my rental car. But not too far after that, Foley yanks the wheel sharply to the left, cranks into four-wheel drive, and we off-road it into the desert.

I turn an inquisitive eye toward him. "Where *are* we going?"

He keeps his eyes on the road. "You'll see soon enough."

He has both hands firmly on the wheel, fighting the car whose name, TrailBlazer, was not meant to be taken literally. I brace myself with one hand on the dashboard and the other on the door to keep my head from hitting the roof. Even the seat belt does little to lessen the pounding. The only good thing is that if Culebra really is following, these tracks will be easy to spot.

"Now that we're alone," I say, my voice bouncing along with the bucking car, "you can come clean. You have been following me, haven't you?"

Foley glances at me. "I told you. I haven't been following you. Why the hell would I? I didn't know Martinez was gonna want me to bring your ass in 'til yesterday."

"I don't believe you. You wanted Max. You thought I'd lead you to him."

He shakes his head. "I actually believed you when you said you hadn't been in touch with him. Are you telling me you were lying? What a surprise. Anyway, right after I left you, I got a message from Martinez. He told me Max was on his way to Mexico. He was waiting for him to cross the border. Bad luck for me that he got to him first." He snickers. "But we made another deal."

I don't have to ask for whom. But Max was with me for an hour or so after my meeting with Foley. How did Martinez know where he was headed? Guilt tightens my shoulders. If I hadn't left when I did, I might have known what Max had planned. Or could have kept him with me.

Have I done anything right the last few days? It doesn't feel like it now.

A dust cloud rises from the rim of a hollow ahead of us. Suddenly monotonous desert sounds, the chatter of insects, the cries of animals and birds, are drowned out by the din of a helicopter engine.

I glance over at Foley. "Martinez has spared no expense, has he?"

Foley grunts a reply. "Don't know why he bothered. He should just let me shoot you and be done with it."

"And Max? You'd let him shoot Max, too?"

He shrugs. "He knew the risks."

His nonchalance about Max's fate—the fate of a fellow law enforcement officer no less—quickens my anger, but I hold it in check. Foley will feel the force of it soon enough.

The helicopter is a small one, painted a gunmetal gray.

The rotor turns in a whirl of speed that kicks up dirt and sends it spiraling into the air. I can see the pilot at the controls, head turned to watch our approach. The sun has not yet risen fully in the sky, but his eyes are shielded by the requisite Ray-Ban Aviators favored by pilots—I glance over at Foley—and evidently, Feds. He's wearing an identical pair.

Foley pulls to a stop beside the copter. He looks at me. "Are you going to make this easy?" he asks.

"And if I don't?"

He reaches across me to open the glove compartment and pulls from it a small leather case. He unzips it and tilts it so I can see what's inside. A syringe, filled with a pale gold substance. "I doubt you'll have as much fun with this as you did with whatever the hell it was you took last night," he says. "But I guarantee it'll get you on that copter."

I push his hand away. "You still don't get it, do you? I'm getting on that copter because I want to. Because of Max."

He doesn't look convinced. He slips the case into the pocket of his jacket with a "just in case" expression. I shake my head and beat him out of the car.

The pilot has climbed down and is standing beside the copter. He sports an impatient frown behind those sunglasses, the air of one who is not happy to have been kept waiting. He says something to Foley in Spanish, in clipped tones.

"Relax, compadre," Foley replies in English. "We're here. Let's go."

He gives me a needless little shove and the pilot smiles. I let him get away with it. I even let him manhandle me through the narrow door and into a seat. His puts one hand on my chest to hold me in place while he secures the harness. The pilot watches from his place at the controls and Foley, knowing he is watching, lets his hands wander over my breasts and down between my legs.

"Want to be sure you're secure," he says, yanking the belt tight. "Wouldn't want you to have an accident, would we?"

That brings a bubble of laughter from the pilot. He understands English. I file that away for future reference. He snaps his own harness into place and turns his attention to the controls. Foley slips on a headset identical to the pilot's and they begin to chatter back and forth in Spanish. He doesn't offer me a headset.

The helicopter rises in a tornado of dust. The pilot clears the hollow and banks sharply to the south. Doesn't surprise me that we're headed farther into Mexico. I look down at the ground. Unless Culebra can enlist the help of a bird or two, I'm on my own.

We fly over desert, mostly, and the occasional village. My bet is we are not headed for the coast or any crowded tourist destination. We're flying low. A little too low for my taste. I can see coyotes scramble on the ground as we roar past. Avoiding radar detection maybe? If that's even a consideration. Money can buy anything in Mexico, including invisibility.

After fifteen minutes or so, we approach a hilly, forested area. The copter slows. I don't see any place to land until we come up over a rise and there, beneath us is a valley. I see no roads going in or out, only a compound tucked so completely into the folds of the hillside, I'd bet it's hidden from any view except ours—a bird's-eye view. I search the surrounding terrain. You'd really have to know where to look to spy this even from the air. Have to give it to Martinez. Perfect setup for a drug dealer.

As we get closer, more details snap into relief. Buff-colored buildings with red-tile roofs, three that I can see, and a wall that stretches all the way around them.

While we're still a good distance above ground, I search for a road. Or for anything that looks as if it could be used by ground transportation. With a sinking feeling, I realize there's nothing. Which means getting Max and I out of here might prove to be tricky. And that whatever happens, I'd better protect this asshole pilot.

The copter heads for the pad nearest the larger of the buildings. The pilot brings it down smoothly, touching ground with just the slightest of bumps. He glances back at me, expecting what? A round of applause for the smooth landing?

I ignore the look and busy myself getting out of the harness. Foley has already freed himself and jumped down. He motions for me to come on with an impatient snap of his fingers. I congratulate myself for not grabbing those fingers and snapping them off.

I jump down and look around. No Martinez. No armed guards. No welcoming committee of any kind.

My face must reflect surprise because Foley says, "What were you expecting? Banditos with automatic rifles?" He waves a hand. "Look around. Where would you go if you even attempted to escape? That's the beauty of this place. Only one way in and one way out. Come on. Martinez is most anxious to meet you."

We landed in front of a hangar. Inside are two small prop planes and a second, larger helicopter. The pilot heads into the hangar while Foley steers me to the right, toward the second of the buildings I saw from the air.

As we approach, I realize this might be a residence. There is a courtyard leading to oversized carved oak doors. Water cascades in a melodious tumble from a three-tier stone fountain. Hibiscus and jasmine climb up the walls in a riot of glorious color. It looks like something out of *Architectural Digest*.

Whoever said crime doesn't pay never saw this place. Or didn't deal drugs.

Foley steps in front of me and knocks on the door.

We wait. The seconds tick by and I start to think Foley has dragged me to the wrong place. Just when I'm ready to call him a fuckup and tear the truth out of him, the door swings open.

A small Hispanic woman smiles a greeting at Foley. She is wearing an ankle length black dress over which is tied a spotless white apron. Her dark hair is salted with gray and gathered back into a braid that reaches down the middle of her back. She looks to be midfifties maybe and her compact little body, while sporting an extra twenty pounds or so, is well muscled and not the least bit flabby. She looks like she can take care of herself.

She and Foley exchange greetings in Spanish. When her dark eyes turn to me, they spark with something that looks very much like anger. The corners of her mouth turn down in a tight frown and the comment she spits out does not sound flattering.

I look to Foley for an explanation.

"Your reputation precedes you," he says. "She knows you are the whore of the man who killed Martinez' family. She looks forward to hearing your death screams."

I don't know how embellished Foley's interpretation of her remarks are, but such an ugly sentiment coming from the mouth of this pleasant-looking woman sends a chill down my spine. Obviously, when the time comes, I can expect no help from her.

She turns away abruptly, starts down a hallway.

Foley puts a hand at the small of my back, but I move after her before he can push. The interior of the house is cool and dim, insulated by thick walls of whitewashed plaster. She leads us through rooms with tile floors and heavily curtained windows. She moves quickly and with purpose, giving me only the briefest impressions of plush furniture, shiny wood, and gilt framed pictures. I make mental notes to mark the rooms we pass through. If I have to get Max out of here in a hurry, I don't want to get lost. The house is big.

And we seem to be going straight through it to the back, ending up in a kitchen the size of the entire first floor of my house. A big steel refrigerator and a restaurant-sized stove look like they belong in here, a rich person's kitchen. Only an arsenal of automatic weapons displayed in a gun case near the back door strikes the wrong chord.

There are two people, an elderly man and woman, chopping vegetables at a granite counter. The two don't look up or say a word as we pass. Neither does our hostess, ignoring them as she heads for a row of cabinets lining the back wall. She reaches for a canister on the first shelf, but instead of picking it up, she yanks it forward. There is a mechanical whir and the entire middle section of the cabinets moves silently forward.

An entryway appears.

And through it, a staircase.

She stands aside with a grim smile and motions me ahead.

I'm so startled by the setup that this time Foley manages to move faster than I do and he pushes me toward the stairs. I stumble forward. The woman does not come with us. When Foley and I are on the stairs, I hear the mechanism once more and turn to see the cabinets realigning themselves. They snap into position with an audible click and we are plunged into darkness. I almost stumble once more but catch myself. Foley is right behind me and I feel him pause on the stairs while my eyes adjust to the darkness and assume he is waiting for his to do the same. But in a moment, track lighting from above and below blinks on. Miniature incandescent bulbs glow softly along the bottom of each stair step and a fixture on the ceiling lights our way.

That's what Foley was waiting for. With a grunt, he prods me onward.

The stairs are thick wood, uncarpeted, and our footfalls echo in the narrow passageway. There is no handrail. The staircase is steep. I count twenty steps before we come to a landing. There is a door. I put my hand out to open it, and Foley swats it away.

"Careful," he says. "Want to get your head blown off?"

I don't bother to remark on the irony of that statement, seeing as how I imagine that's precisely what Martinez has planned for me.

Foley steps around me. There is a button to the right of the doorknob. Foley pushes it. Two short, two long pulses that translate into muffled buzzes just barely audible on this side. The door must be thick. After a moment, there is a click and the door opens.

Martinez is there to meet us.

CHAPTER 39

I'D SEEN MARTINEZ ONCE BEFORE, SEVERAL months ago, but only at night and from a distance. He'd been wearing a suit then and my impression was of a large, thick-bodied man. Not my impression now. Martinez has lost weight—a lot of it. His scarecrow frame is clad in an open-neck polo shirt hanging loose over jeans. He's barefoot. His dark hair is unkempt, longer than I remembered, curling around the collar of his shirt. It's limp with the oily texture of hair that hasn't been washed in a while.

And it frames a face ravaged by sorrow and madness.

I've seen the look before. On a vampire, not a human. But the effect is the same. I feel my muscles tense, constrict as a rush of adrenaline prepares for a fight.

But Martinez doesn't attack. He doesn't move, doesn't acknowledge Foley's presence.

He stares at me, eyes hollow and devoid of life. His hands hang at his sides, one holds a small black box. A light blinks red. Some kind of detonator? He's so utterly still, it's unnerving. I'm relieved when Foley breaks the intolerable silence.

"Well," he says. "Here she is. When can I get out of here?"

His voice sparks light in Martinez' eyes, drags him back from whatever pit he'd lost himself in. He places the box on the floor beside the door and the red light blinks to green. He glances at Foley with a look that reminds me of the flicker of a snake's tongue before a strike—quick, decisive, deadly. If I were Foley, I'd be getting out now.

But, of course, Foley is not that smart.

"I did what you told me to. She's alive. I'd like my money now. I've got to make plans. The San Diego PD will be on my trail. Can't go back across the border. Your pilot can take me to Mexico City, though, right? I've got a fake passport. I'll go south from there . . ."

He's rambling on, nervously, just now understanding what he sees on Martinez' face, a man teetering on the knife-edge of reason. Foley backs toward the doorway, hands outstretched in front of him, a vain attempt to ward off whatever Martinez might hurl at him.

Martinez' right hand moves slowly. Foley watches as if mesmerized as it drifts toward the small of his back, reaches beneath the shirt and produces a small gun. Only when the gun is pointed at him does Foley react.

He grabs me and swings me around to shield his own body. "Go ahead," he says. "Shoot. But Max isn't here to watch, is he? Wasn't that the object of this stupid setup? Make Max suffer the way you did? Make him watch while you torture the woman he loves? If you still want that, you're going to have to let me walk out of here. Give me my money and arrange for the pilot to fly me out. Anna will be with me until we get to the chopper. Then I'll let her go and you can have your fun. Do we have a deal?"

All the while he's talking, I'm trying to look behind Martinez, to see if I can spot where Max might be hidden. There are two more doors, one on each side of a narrow hall, but they are both closed. The good thing is that there doesn't seem to be any other guards. I can easily take care of Martinez and Foley. The hard part will be getting Max past that woman downstairs if he's hurt and unable to walk. I have a feeling she knows how to use those guns.

All this passes through my head while Foley is trying to manhandle me backward toward the stairs. Martinez still hasn't said a word. He has the gun pointed at my midsection. It won't kill me if he shoots, but it will hurt. Better to let him take care of Foley, one less bad guy I have to worry about.

I slump forward, letting my body go limp. Foley tries to lower himself with me, scrambling to regain a hold and hoist me up. He can't. My dead weight is too much. He lets me go and stands up, surrendering with upturned hands.

Martinez doesn't hesitate. He fires once. A neat round hole blooms in Foley's forehead.

CHAPTER 40

MY FIRST THOUGHT IS: GOOD, ONE DOWN.
Then: I'm glad the bastard is dead. I would have liked to make him explain about what happened in the desert, though. I figure he was afraid Sylvie's ex was going to kill me and he'd be robbed of his extra blood money.

A moot point now.

Martinez rolls Foley away from me. He reaches down and yanks me to my feet, his hands like steel bands on my arms. He's stronger than he looks. When he sees that I've regained my balance, he lets me go.

"Where's Max?" I ask.

A ghastly smile like a skull's rictus touches the corners of his mouth. He turns me toward the door on the left and pushes me forward.

"First," he says, "you must see why you have been brought here."

It's the first time I've heard his voice—gravelly, low pitched. He speaks perfect English, with a barely detectable accent. But this time, the tone is different. It's as scary as his eyes, full of venom and suppressed rage. He is a coil winding tighter with each passing moment. When that energy is released, it will flatten everything in its path.

He steps around to grasp the door handle. Even before the door swings open, though, I know what's inside.

The smell tells me.

Decaying flesh. Blood, long past flowing. Death.

I've smelled it before.

He blocks my way until he is inside. He wants to watch my reaction.

I steel myself. When he steps aside, I force myself to look.

There are four bodies on cots. A woman, three children. The woman looks to be in her midthirties. The children are stair steps, a boy about ten, a girl about eight, another boy, maybe six. I smell formaldehyde. Not professional embalming, the stink of decay is strong. But the bodies have been washed and dressed so the ravages inflicted on them are unseen. Except for the solitary bullet holes in each of their foreheads.

Max is not among them. A little thrill of relief races down my spine.

Martinez is staring at me. He misinterprets the shudder. "You are right to tremble. You see what they did to my family?" He steps to the woman, touches her swollen face with his fingertips. "I was to bring them here. They would have been safe. But I was betrayed before I could. Traitors in my own organization betrayed me." His eyes find mine. "Your friend betrayed me. He brought them to my home. And *this* is the result."

He circles the cots. "They were rounded up like animals. They were brought outside and shot down like dogs in the street. Shot in the head so there could be no open casket, the final desecration. They were left to rot in the sun."

The obvious question—where were you when all this was happening?—I leave unasked for now. I remember Max saying something about a shoot-out. Could Martinez have been inside hiding while his family was being murdered?

I meet his eyes. "Where's Max?" I ask again.

He recoils as if I've slapped him. "That's all you have to say? You stand here in front of my butchered family and show no remorse? Your only thoughts are for the *cabrón* that made this happen?"

I shake my head. "What happened to your family is inexcusable. I am sorry for them. But you deal in death. Drugs kill thousands of women and children every year. It is hard for me to feel anything for you."

I know I risk his wrath, but I keep my words measured and unemotional. He is close to losing control. I need him to take me to Max first. For all I know, he's rigged this door to blow just like the one at the head of the stairs.

My detached tone works the way I'd hoped. With visible effort, he straightens up, his face clears. For a moment I see the man as he must have been when he was in command. His expression stern, his spine stiff. He pushes past me without a word and I follow.

We're at the door across the hall when the buzzer sounds from the stairway. Martinez turns abruptly and goes to answer it. He picks up that little black box, depresses a switch and pulls the door open.

It's the woman who led us inside. The apron is gone and in her hands, she holds one of the rifles from the cabinet in the kitchen. She doesn't look so pleasant now. She freezes, the rifle pointed at Martinez. He nods that it's all right and she lowers it to her side.

She ignores Foley's body as if it was invisible, stepping over it with as little regard as might be paid a sleeping dog. His death is neither shocking to her nor obviously unexpected. She walks past Martinez and stops in front of me.

She says something to Martinez, pointing at me. Her tone is a combination of relief and anticipation, as if she's happy I'm still alive.

Martinez joins us at the closed door. "I would not do this without you," he says. He gestures toward me. "Speak English so she can understand."

She moves her eyes away from me long enough to nod

up at Martinez. In heavily accented English, she says, "I was afraid when I heard the shot . . ."

He flicks his hand. "The man Foley grew tiresome."

He reaches for the doorknob and lets the door swing open. "You wanted Max," he says to me. "Here he is."

CHAPTER 41

MAX IS SITTING UP ON A COT, BACK AGAINST THE wall, legs straight out in front. He is neither bound nor gagged. He's wearing slacks and an open-neck white polo. He has socks on but no shoes. When the door opens, his head swivels toward the sound. He looks at me, at Martinez, but nothing registers on his face. His eyes are blank.

My skin turns cold at his complete lack of recognition. I approach the bed. Touch his forehead with the palm of my hand. His skin is clammy, sheeted with sweat, feverish. There is no reaction to my touch.

I round on Martinez. "What's wrong with him? What have you done?"

He shrugs. "I have only eased his pain."

"Pain?" I whirl back to Max, eyes searching his face, hands passing gently over his chest, his arms, down his legs. When I touch his right ankle, he groans and winces away. Carefully, I roll up his pant leg. The ankle is swollen and discolored and twisted to an unnatural angle.

"Martinez, you are making this so easy," I say under my breath.

He and the woman step into the room. "What did you say?" he says.

The woman pushes impatiently past him. "We are wasting time," she snaps. "I want to see her writhe in pain. I want to hear her screams. I want this man to bear witness." She pulls a syringe from her pocket. "Give him this. Now. It will bring him back."

Martinez takes the syringe from the woman, shoves me aside, and plunges the needle into Max's arm. Quicker than I would have thought possible, Max's eyes clear. In rapid succession, his expression flashes relief at seeing me, uncertainty at how I happened to be here, horror as memory floods back. Then the pain hits, and pain becomes the center of his reality. He groans and falls back against the wall.

A flash of something silver catches the corner of my eye. Pain, white-hot and searing, races up my arm. I turn in time to see the woman, face contorted with rage, slash at me a second time with a knife. I reach out a hand and stop hers in midair. Her look of astonishment would be amusing if I wasn't so angry. I back her up against Martinez. He, too, is stunned at my lightning-fast reaction.

I twist the woman's arm until she drops the knife. Then I keep twisting. "Who are you?" It comes out like a hiss.

She has recovered herself. She isn't cowed and she shows no reaction to the pain. She merely leans into me to relieve the pressure. Her expression is defiant. She leans in close to whisper, "Burke was right about you. You are vampire."

Her eyes glisten with eagerness and some of the same madness I saw reflected in Martinez. "What relationship do you have with the witch Burke? Are you one of her followers?"

She laughs. "No. I am not one of those children. And Burke is not a witch." She lifts her chin defiantly. "You cannot begin to imagine what she is."

"Then why don't you tell me." Impatience is bringing the animal in me to the surface. I feel the quickening of my blood, the lust to rip answers from this smug woman. I bring my face close to hers, let her read my eyes, see the fury building.

Martinez breaks the spell. He grabs the woman by the arm and yanks her back. "This is not what we brought her here for. Did you forget?"

For an instant, I think she is going to strike out at him. So intense is the hatred in her face, it makes me wonder what their relationship really is. Obviously, she is not the servant I first imagined.

I put as much scorn as I can into my words. "Who is this woman who looks at you with such contempt?"

Maybe not the most prudent thing to say. They both whirl toward me and the animosity directed toward each other is now aimed at me.

Max groans and the three of us turn to the cot. I take his hand. "Max."

He looks up at me, eyes clouded with pain. "How did you get here? Why did you come?"

I sit on the edge of the cot, easing myself down carefully to avoid his injured leg. "Foley brought me. I came for you."

"Foley?" The first spark of real life, anger flares in his eyes. "Where is he?"

I glance up at Martinez. "He took care of Foley. He's dead."

"Anna."

There is so much sorrow, recrimination and regret in the way Max says my name, I'm overwhelmed by it. Still, I put steel in my own voice when I say, "We'll be all right, Max. I promise."

Martinez laughs. "Yes, you'll be all right, Max." He turns away from us. "Marta, are you ready to end this?"

Marta. Somehow the name fits. Harsh, unmelodious. A name befitting the malevolent spirit that radiates from the woman.

She is watching me as if reading my thoughts. She nods. "Yes, *mijo*, I am ready."

She uses a Spanish term of endearment. Are she and Martinez related?

She pulls me from the cot. I let her. I'm ready to end this, too. My only concern is what will happen when Max sees what I become. For a fleeting moment, I wish they'd left him drugged and unresponsive.

But there is no turning back now.

CHAPTER 42

I'VE GIVEN NO THOUGHT TO HOW I'LL OVERCOME Martinez and the woman, Marta. I am vampire. I am stronger, faster and deadlier than any human. I stand quietly and wait, curious to see what they have planned.

Marta pulls another syringe from her pocket. She holds it up to the light and turns it this way and that, as if in a bizarre show of respect for the substance in her hand.

"This," she says, "is very special. It is my own invention. A drug that immobilizes muscle but enhances the senses. Pleasure. Pain. Exquisitely enhanced. Your body will not be able to respond, but you will feel every cut of the razor, be aware of the blood draining from your body, experience life slowly slipping away. And when you are dead, we will do the same to Max. But his suffering will be greater because he will have watched his beloved die in unspeakable agony and have been powerless to help."

Max stirs and tries to push himself off the cot. "You have me," he says. "Let Anna go. She had nothing to do with this."

Martinez shoves him back, places a hand on his broken ankle and leans into it.

Max groans, writhing with the pain, sweat beads on his face.

His agony unleashes the beast. Martinez is oblivious to the change. He is completely focused on the pain he sees in Max's face. He is drinking it in, smiling in satisfaction. He turns only at the sound, the howl that comes from an unknown place deep inside me. This much rage, this much pure hatred, is more than I can control. It overwhelms me, pushes the human Anna down into a place so deep, she's gone. Utterly.

I spring at Martinez before he has a chance to react. I throw him to the floor, clawing at his face, ripping at his neck with my teeth. Blood sprays from torn arteries, soaking us both. I hear Marta scream, but it's from far, far away. I feel a sharp prick. Marta is beside me. I swat her hand away, pull the syringe from my arm, lunge again at Martinez. I lock him against my body and use teeth and hands to tear at his flesh. I'm beyond wanting to drink. I want to rip his head off his body. My jaw locks on his neck. His mouth is open, his lips move, but if he's screaming, the sound is blocked by the roar of my own blood. It boils in my veins, colors the whole world crimson. It's all I feel, all I taste. Blood. Hot. Red.

His blood.

My blood.

Then.

Nothing.

CHAPTER 43

A T FIRST, I THINK I'M ASLEEP. A DEEP SLEEP. ONE from which I'm not ready to awaken.

But something is crawling into my consciousness, willing me, commanding me, to come back.

My senses respond slowly. Taste and smell are first. I'm assailed by the rich, metallic scent of fresh blood. I taste it, too, in the back of my throat.

I lick my lips.

I don't open my eyes. I'm not ready. I listen, though. It's quiet. Beyond quiet. No sound at all. No insect or animal noises. No human stirrings.

Deadly quiet.

I try to move. My body is heavy and unresponsive. I'm lying down. Whatever I'm lying on is rough textured and smells of—what? The outdoors. Slightly gamy. Like a camping blanket that's been stored unwashed in a musty attic.

How do I know that smell?

A memory flashes. My brother and I on a camping trip. Too many years ago to count. Another lifetime.

Where am I?

Open your eyes.

I think the command comes from inside my head. But I don't want to open my eyes. I'm not ready. I'm afraid.

What am I afraid of?

"Anna, open your eyes."

The voice makes me jump. I cringe away and raise my hand to cover my eyes.

Another's hand snatches it away.

"Open your eyes, vampire."

A female voice. Cold. Unsympathetic.

"Very well. This will bring you back."

A sharp prick. Pressure as a plunger is depressed. Something snakes into my bloodstream, trailing an icy finger. I feel it move, invade my system, awaken every nerve ending, reach into my brain and gnaw at me until I can't fight it anymore.

I'm yanked screaming back into consciousness.

CHAPTER 44

A WOMAN IS LOOKING DOWN AT ME.
    She's smiling.

She'd be pleasant looking if it weren't for the blood that mats her hair and streaks her face.

Blood? Whose blood?

Why can't I remember?

A memory cuts like a strobe light into my head. It pulses in black-and-white relief. A body. Ravaged. Torn. Blood everywhere.

Instinctively, I raise my hands. They are flaked with dried blood. My nails are embedded with tissue.

The groan starts deep in my gut and spews forth in a wail of despair.

What have I done?

Why can't I remember?

CHAPTER 45

WHEN I OPEN MY EYES AGAIN, I REMEMBER.
Everything.

Marta is no longer standing over me.

I look around.

I'm in a room identical to Max's. I'm on a cot, lying on a torn, rough-textured blanket. A sheet has been thrown over me. I'm naked beneath it.

I don't know where I am in the house. I thought there were only two rooms on the landing. But I'm alone here. And there is no blood on the white tile walls, none on the cement floor. After what I did to Martinez, there would be blood.

Unless.

I pull myself into a sitting position, groaning with the effort. My limbs are in revolt.

But I have to sit up to look around. There is a drain in the middle of the floor. And from it wafts the scent of pine and bleach. And underlying it all, blood.

The sheet falls away, and I see that the room is not the only thing that has been cleaned. There is no blood on my body, on my hands. My nails have been scrubbed. The same slightly antiseptic smell of soap wafts up when I raise my hands to rub at my eyes. The wound on my arm from Marta's blade has a dressing covering it. I rip it off. There is only a flush of color where the knife penetrated my flesh.

Confusion clouds my thoughts.

If this is the same room, where is Max?

Max.

A tremor passes through me.

Where is he? What have they done to him? Why did I let this happen? I should have attacked Martinez the moment I saw him at the door. I should have had a plan. I let the fact that I am vampire lull me into thinking I could handle anything a human could throw at me. I was wrong. It may have cost Max his life.

I swing my legs over the side of the cot and push myself off. Marta has left me nothing to cover my nakedness. I tear the sheet into two pieces and knot the smaller portion around my body. It falls just to my knees allowing me the freedom to move without tripping over the ends.

I'll need to be able to move.

I start for the door. I expect I'll have to break it down, and I'm surprised when the knob turns in my hand. Cautiously, I let it swing open.

The corridor is dark and empty. And quiet. I pull the door shut behind me.

I cross to the other side and put an ear to that door to see if I detect any sound. There is none. Again, the knob turns in my hand and the door opens.

The cots are lined up as before. But the bodies of Martinez' family are gone. Three other bodies are laid out.

I tiptoe from one to the other.

Foley.

Martinez.

Max.

I touch Max's face, too full of anguish to do anything else. When my fingers brush his lips, I realize with a jolt that he is warm. I rub the tears out of my eyes to examine him more closely. His color is good, flushed even. I push my ears against his chest. There is a heartbeat. Slow. Regular. His chest rises and falls in measured, controlled breaths. He is asleep. Drugged again?

But alive.

It sparks my resolve.

I move to Martinez. There is no doubt that he is dead. His throat has been torn open. His head is cocked back at an unusual angle, shattered vertebrae visible through the wound. Delicate streamers of shredded skin are all that hold skull to shoulders. The connection is tenuous. I don't know how anyone managed to lift him onto this cot without the connection being severed. His skin is pale, his eyes closed, his mouth open in a silent scream.

I view him with detached coldness. I know it was I who inflicted the damage. But he was going to kill me. He was going to kill and torture Max. I used the weapons I had at my disposal. Teeth and my vampire nature. I feel no remorse.

My glance falls on Foley. Martinez killed him with a gun he had under his shirt. I slip a hand beneath Martinez' body. The gun is no longer there. I'm sure Marta thought to take it before leaving me alone to find the bodies.

Because I'm also sure this is part of her plan.

I need to be smart this time. Decide how to handle her when she comes back. I can't kill her outright. I'll need her to help me get Max out of here. To bring him around when we're in the chopper.

The chopper. A memory surfaces. Before we got out of the car in the desert, Foley threatened to drug me if I was uncooperative. Is the syringe still in his jacket?

A sound in the corridor distracts me. The door to the landing is opening. I'm at Foley's cot in two strides. I yank at his jacket, searching first one pocket, then the other. My fingers close around the leather case just as footsteps approach the door across the hall. I open the case, tuck the syringe into a fold of the sheet at my breasts, and slip the case back into Foley's pocket. I hear the click of tumblers falling, the quiet opening and closing of the door across the hall and know.

Marta is now right outside my door.

CHAPTER 46

I'M TREMBLING. WHETHER FROM STRESS AND FA-
tigue or the effects of whatever drug I've been given or
from anticipation, I can't tell. I only know it takes conscious effort to keep my hands still. I finally press them
against my sides.

Marta is cautious about opening the door.

She is a smart woman.

When the knob finally turns, I prepare to throw myself
out of the way just in case she comes in blasting.

But she doesn't. Her hands are empty and hang at her
sides. She has cleaned the blood off her body, too, and is
dressed in a simple black skirt and white peasant blouse.
Her hair is wet and hangs straight down her back. She is
barefoot.

Her eyes glance behind me.

"You have seen that Max is alive."

I nod.

"It is my gift to you."

I narrow my eyes. "Gift?"

She nods, too. "I could have killed him. I could have

killed you, too, while you slept. But I did not. It was a show of good faith."

She's not making any sense. I gesture toward Martinez. "I did that to your friend. Why would you want to show me good faith?"

She brushes past me and stands beside Martinez' cot. She places a hand gently on his shoulder. "As soon as I saw the two of you fighting, I knew how it would turn out. I tried to stop it. I plunged the needle into your arm, but the drug was no match for the strength of your rage. It took too long to work and when it finally did, it was too late for my son."

"Martinez was your son?"

Tears slide down her cheeks. "I tried to make him drink. I took your arm where I had cut it and pressed it against his lips. If he had only swallowed. Just one drop. He would be as you are."

I'm staring at her now in disbelief. "You tried to make him drink my blood? You tried to make him a vampire?"

She turns slowly. "I tried to save him. It's what any mother would have done. Your attack was too savage. He died in my arms. Now I exact the penalty for his death. For his murder. And you will pay it because I hold the life of one you love in my hands."

When she faces me, she has something in her hand. Another syringe. She holds it in front of me. "This is not like the others. This is poison. If I inject Max with this, he will die screaming."

She backs toward Max's cot. "You move quickly. I have seen it. But not, I think, quickly enough to prevent me from injecting Max. It takes only a tiny amount, a pinprick of the needle, and Max will die."

I take a step toward her. "Is this the gift you spoke of? You saved Max and me so that you could kill him while I watch?"

She smiles and lowers the syringe so that it rests on Max's chest. "Oh no. The gift is your lives. You and Max will be allowed to live. You will be flown to safety and I pledge no harm will befall you. What happened here will be forgotten."

"And what do you get in exchange for this generosity?"

The smile this time is humorless and touches only the corners of her mouth. "Immortality," she says. "You will make me vampire."

CHAPTER 47

My LIPS PULL BACK TO BARE MY TEETH. I POINT to her son. "You saw me do that. And you want to be like me?"

She blows out a disdainful breath. "Like you? Never. You are undisciplined and willful. A spoiled child. I would use the power wisely."

I look around. "How? To take over where your son left off? Is that your plan? Become the czarina of the drug world? Don't you know your empire is in ashes? Max saw to that."

She glances at Max, her fingers tighten on the syringe. In that moment, I know that she has no intention of letting Max go.

I don't wait for her to draw another breath. I lunge, hitting her body away from the cot and slamming her into the wall. The attack catches her off guard and the syringe falls from her hand and skitters under Max's cot.

With an oath, she scrambles to her feet. She pulls a knife out of a pocket in her skirt. She doesn't threaten me with it, though, but holds it to her own wrist.

"You will do as I ask," she growls. "Or you and Max will die here. Without me, the others downstairs will kill you on sight. And even if you make it past them, the pilot has his orders. He is watching the house. If you approach without me, he will take off and leave you here. You have seen how well hidden we are."

She presses the blade against her skin. "There is no telephone. No radio with which you can contact the outside world. This house will become your mausoleum. In a few weeks, the jungle will reclaim it's own. Your bodies—our bodies—will never be found. It will be as if we never existed."

She speaks in a slow, measured cadence. Her eyes bore into mine. She does not fear what she describes. She is accepting of whatever fate befalls her. Her grip on the knife tightens and before I can stop her, she draws it across her wrist.

Blood spurts and begins to drip in a steady stream onto the floor.

She watches it with a detached frown. "Can you resist?" she asks, holding the arm toward me. "Blood. I offer it to you in exchange for eternal life. I want you to take me. For him."

Her eyes shift to her son. I wonder why she didn't take my blood while I was out. Does she think the vampire has to be conscious, has to will the change?

It hardly matters now. While her attention is on her son, I make my move. I dive for her, hitting her low, trying my best to ignore the call of her blood, its texture and smell. I fight the animal inside and refuse to let it surface. I need to keep my wits about me.

"You are a crazy bitch," I scream, hooking an arm around her waist and dragging her to the floor.

She fights me, pushing the arm at my face. It takes me a moment to realize she's manipulating the knife in her other hand, trying to distract me with bloodlust while she positions herself to plunge the knife into my arm. She is still intent on mingling our blood. I refused to do it her way, now she will try another.

I jump away from her before she can cut me. She is snarling like an enraged beast, howling with frustration and anger. She moves toward me, swinging the knife in front of her in wide arcs, hoping to get close enough to slash my skin.

I don't let her. The human Anna is still in control despite the siren call of blood. I avoid the point of the knife and step inside, grabbing at her uninjured wrist and forcing it back. I swing her around and pin her against the wall.

Her will is strong. She doesn't drop the knife. She fights until she's broken free and whirls again to face me. This time, she grasps the knife as if to throw it.

"This is getting old, Marta," I snap. I reach into the folds of the sheet and withdraw the syringe. "Go ahead, throw the damned thing. You'll miss and I'll stick you with this."

Tears of rage stain her cheeks. She pulls back her arm and flings the knife in my direction. I sidestep it easily and before the clatter of the knife hitting the floor dies away, I've plunged Foley's needle into her arm.

CHAPTER 48

I HAVE NO IDEA WHAT TO EXPECT SO I STAND BACK to watch. Marta's face undergoes the transition from anger to astonishment to utter vacuity. When I am sure she will no longer attempt to bite or gouge me, I step close to her and lower her to a seated position against the wall.

The blood is still flowing freely from her wrist, but it's not arterial blood. I can tell the difference. Whether by chance or on purpose, she did not cut deep enough. I tear at the hem of the sheet wrapped around me and bind her wrist. The cloth quickly soaks through. I tear another piece and fashion a tourniquet above her elbow. I don't care if she lives or dies, but she controls the pilot and those two downstairs. She is going to help me get Max out of this house.

The tourniquet seems to work. Blood no longer flows in a steady stream but rather drips from the cloth into a desultory pattern on the floor. Now that the immediate danger is past, the proximity of this much blood makes me tremble. It's all I can do to keep from lapping at it as it falls. But I don't. Instead, I move away to avoid temptation.

Marta's eyes follow me as I cross the room, but her body remains motionless. Her head lolls against the tiled wall as if too heavy for her slender neck. She opens and closes her mouth and I wonder if she's trying to tell me something. I don't intend to get close enough, though, to find out.

Max is my chief concern now. He hasn't moved since I've been in the room. He's breathing; I can see that. I bend over him and gently tap his cheeks with my fingertips. There is no response. I slap a little harder. His breath catches the tiniest bit, then settles back into the same deep, regular pattern. He could be asleep or comatose. But unless I can bring him around, getting us out of here is going to be a problem. I can carry Max or Marta, but not both.

Marta makes a small sobbing sound. When I turn around, she's on her hands and knees, trying to get her legs under her.

Okay. If she can walk out under her own steam, there will be only Max to worry about. It makes sense that the drug intended for me would not render me completely helpless. Foley was going to use it to get me on that chopper and I doubt he planned to carry me. He just wasn't in that kind of shape.

I grab Marta under her arms and haul her to her feet. She slumps against the wall but remains standing.

"Can you talk?"

She groans an unintelligible answer, but it's enough to make me realize she understood the question.

"Okay. Here's what's going to happen. We"—I gesture to Max and then to her and me—"are going to walk downstairs together. Is there anyone in the house besides the couple I saw earlier?"

She shakes her head.

"Will they give us trouble?"

Another abrupt shake of her head.

"Do I believe you?" This time, I shake my head. She looks at me in confusion, but I forge ahead. "When we get outside, we'll go directly to the hangar. Is the pilot still here?"

This time I get a nod.

"Does he know why Max and I were brought here?"

She waits a second too long to shake her head.

Great. That means I can expect no cooperation from him unless Marta makes it happen. How do I convince her to do that?

I take her bandaged wrist in my hand and squeeze. She whimpers in pain and winces away, her expression clouded and confused. She may understand a lot of *what* is happening, but she doesn't seem to remember exactly *why*. Maybe I can use that to my advantage.

"You've had an accident, Marta. We'll need the pilot to fly us to a hospital. We're going to have to let him see that you are badly hurt and in need of urgent medical attention. Are you ready to do that?"

She gives me a nod but before she does, there is an instant when I see something flash in her eyes. Awareness. Craftiness. She's shaking off the effects of the drugs but she doesn't want me to know.

Too late.

It occurs to me that she may have one or two more of those magic syringes in the pockets of her skirt—or another knife. Since I'm sure she has no intention of letting Max or me go, I doubt I'll find anything to help him. But maybe something to use against her when the time comes.

I move quickly, before she "awakens" even more. I hold both her hands in one of mine. With my free hand, I pass it over the contours of her body, even lifting the hem of her skirt to skim her thighs and between her legs. I dip my hand into the pockets of her skirt and lift the curtain of hair that falls to the middle of her back. I find nothing. Her eyes follow my hand but she doesn't try to pull away. She's quiet and resigned.

It makes me very nervous.

I want to bind her hands. But if I did, how would that look to the pilot and her friends downstairs? The ruse is only going to work if they think Marta is in control.

It's now or never.

I pick Max up and turn away from the cot.

A sound like static over a telephone line interposes itself in my head.

I almost drop Max, I'm so startled.

I listen closely.

The sound comes again. Only this time, the static is a garbled message. Gibberish. As if someone is trying to say something but the connection between brain and speech has been disrupted.

Or severed.

My stomach churns.

I lay Max back down and take a step toward the cot where Martinez' body is resting. Martinez' eyes are open. His head, barely connected by strings of flesh to his body, is stirring.

I think I'm going to be sick.

I look at Marta. She is watching, too, with another of those appalling smiles on her face. And I know. Her son did ingest enough of my blood to become vampire.

Marta lied.

CHAPTER 49

I DON'T THINK I'VE EVER FELT SUCH DISGUST FOR any creature, human or otherwise. Martinez either *did* drink at Marta's urging, or there was blood transference through our injuries. With such devastating injuries, though, she could not have been sure that it would work. That's why she tried to make me turn her.

In any case, I can't leave him like this. Vampires have great powers of healing, but a nearly severed head reunited with a body? And what kind of vampire would an infamous drug lord make? I have to kill him—really kill him—before it gets any worse.

I rub my hands over my face in an effort to clear my head. I've killed rogues. But up until now, they have had at least a fighting chance. This will be like murdering a baby.

Almost instantly, cold, hard reality chases that thought out of my head. Martinez is not a baby. He was a killer in life. He will be a killer in death, too. Worse, because should he survive with vampire powers, he would be practically indestructible.

I feel Marta's eyes on me. She is watching to see what I

will do. I have no doubt she will try to stop me if she regains greater mobility. I have to do this now.

This room is furnished only with the metal cots. The room across the hall held nothing more, either. What can I use to inflict the second death? There is no wood to use for a stake.

My eyes fall on Marta's knife.

As soon as I bend to pick it up, she begins moaning. She tries to take a step toward me, but her legs aren't quite strong enough. She stumbles and falls to her hands and knees.

Should I push her out of the room? She's as despicable as her son, but forcing her to watch as his body disintegrates into dust seems harsh even to me.

I don't give her a chance to make any other attempts to communicate. I drop the knife, pick her up and carry her through the door to the room on the other side. She squirms in my arms like an angry child. I deposit her on the cot, and tear another strip off the piece of sheet I'd left there. I tie her good hand to the leg of the cot. I doubt she can untie it with her wounded arm and she certainly isn't strong enough to pull the cot through the door.

Her guttural moans follow me as I step back into the hall and pull the door shut.

I have to steel myself to go back to Martinez. If I could call up the animal, this would be easier. But it's a human decision I'm making and the human Anna has to handle it.

My hand shakes as I turn the doorknob. The knife is where I dropped it when I took Marta out of the room. I pick it up and approach Martinez, praying that he does not realize what I'm about to do. I remember that Avery, the vampire doctor who treated me when I was first attacked, seemed to be able to read my thoughts from the very first. I know I must do this, but inflicting terror first seems unnecessarily cruel.

Martinez' eyes are still open. They are focused on a point to my left. Quickly, before I lose my nerve, I move behind his cot, raise the knife and sever the tendrils of skin that hold his head on his shoulders. The head separates from the body, his eyes roll back. He projects a sigh that remains in my head long after the body has disintegrated into dust.

"Anna."

This time the voice is definitely outside my head.

I whirl toward the sound.

Max has raised himself up on his elbows. He is awake, suddenly, completely. His face is contorted with confusion and something else.

Fear.

His eyes are on the cot that until seconds ago, held Martinez' body. They shift away finally, to catch and hold mine.

"God, Anna," he whispers, voice raw and choked with undisguised horror. "What did you do? What have you become?"

CHAPTER 50

MY FIRST IMPULSE, TO THROW MY ARMS around Max in relief, is stifled by the expression on his face. He's afraid. I see it, I smell it. I don't know how to alleviate that fear so I do what I always do when cornered.

I crack wise.

"What did I do? I think I saved your ass."

There's no smile. The lines around his mouth harden, shift from being afraid of me to something worse, revulsion.

"What are you?" he asks again.

I think he knows the answer, or suspects it. He's spent enough time at Beso de la Muerte. When I don't reply, he lets his head drop back onto the cot. "I don't believe this," he says.

His voice breaks and with it, something deep inside me shifts. I know my relationship with Max is over. Vanished into dust with that stroke of the knife as utterly as Martinez' body.

Why do I feel such despair? Haven't I known all along

there was no other possible outcome? Wasn't I prepared to break it off with him as soon as I could? I know now that even if I had told Max at the beginning, his reaction today has shown me that he wouldn't have accepted what I am. How could he?

There's a shuffling sound from across the hall. It snaps my attention back. There'll be plenty of time to wallow in misery when we're safe.

"Can you stand up?"

Max heard the noise, too. He's looking at the door and for an instant, the old Max is back. He looks like a cop again. He draws himself into a sitting position, stretching limbs, testing. When he tries to straighten his right leg, the pain hits.

"Your ankle looks broken." I step close and put out a hand to roll up his pant leg.

He starts to cringe away. I know it's not from fear that I'll hurt the wound on his leg. He doesn't want me to touch him.

"Damn it, Max. We've got to get out of here. That bitch Marta is going to give us trouble if we don't move fast. She's drugged now, but she's coming out of it. We don't have time to waste."

In an instant, he's weighed and accepted the validity of what I've said. "We need to make a splint." He looks around the room. "The legs of one of these cots. Can you break one off?"

Easily. The cot comes apart in my hands as if it were made of papier-mâché. Ripping the canvas into shreds to make a binding acts as a welcome release to the pent-up emotions surging in my gut.

I wish it worked as well on Max. He watches the display of strength and the cloud of disbelief descends once again.

"Will you let me help you with the splint?"

He nods but his expression is wary.

I approach the cot. He rolls up his pant leg. The ankle is swollen and bent. "I'll need to straighten your ankle. It's going to hurt."

For the second time, a little of the old Max, my Max, surfaces. "You couldn't have thought to do this while I was out?"

It brings a smile to my lips. "I was a little preoccupied."

And before the words have dissipated between us, I've placed my hands on both sides of the injury and snapped the ankle back into place. No sense in giving him warning.

He gasps and cries out, his body convulsing with the pain. Sweat beads his forehead but this time, when I reach out to smooth his hair, he doesn't pull back.

"Good job," he rasps. "Glad I didn't see it coming."

The way he's looking at me, I'm not sure whether he's referring to what I just did, or something else.

I use three of the metal legs of the cot and canvas strips to fasten a splint. The fourth leg I hand him to use as a makeshift crutch. It's too short to be of much help, really, but in a pinch, it could serve as an effective weapon.

He hefts it, understanding my thought process without my having to say a word.

And he isn't even a vampire.

"Can you stand?"

He shifts his body to the edge of the cot and gingerly swings his legs to the floor. Sweat drips again from his face when he tries to place weight on both feet. But he is able to stand and hobble slowly on his own.

"What kind of welcoming party can we expect?" he asks.

I tell him what Marta told me. Then ask, "Are there really only those two downstairs and a pilot in this compound?"

He nods. "I don't doubt it. Martinez built this place as a safe house. Even his most trusted confederates don't know about it. You saw that from the air, it's practically invisible. He was arrogant enough to think he and his family could hide out here for months, maybe years, and surface later to reclaim his empire. Might have worked, too, if his family hadn't been killed."

There's a yell from across the hall. Marta. She's found her voice.

I hitch an arm under Max's shoulder. "Let's get her before they hear her downstairs. Don't know about you, but I'm ready to get the hell out of here."

CHAPTER 51

MARTA IS STANDING BY THE DOOR WHEN WE push it open. She remains tethered to the cot, but she has regained enough strength to pull it to the door with her.

"What have you done?"

She is whispering, but her eyes are clear and she's standing upright and under her own power. I imagine she'd been trying to get free of the cloth binding and would have if she'd had more time.

She looks from Max to me. "What have you done to my son, vampire?" she asks again.

I feel Max flinch at my side. If he'd been unsure before, Marta's words confirm what he'd witnessed. To his credit, though, he croaks an incredulous laugh and says, "You're even crazier than your son. Come on, Marta. Let's get you help before somebody throws your ass in a padded cell and tosses away the key."

Marta begins to shake with rage. She rips at the bandage covering her wrist. "We'll see who is crazy. When she smells the blood, she will turn. Your only hope is to help me. Cut me loose and together, we can kill her. She is an animal. She murdered my son."

I grab her injured wrist and stop her frenzied attempt to free herself. "Max was awake when I attacked Martinez, remember? He knows what happened. I stopped your son from killing him."

She grows still, keeping her eyes downcast. When she speaks again, it's in a hoarse whisper. "What will you do now?"

I release my grip and stand back. "That's a good girl. The way I see it, you can walk Max and me downstairs and out to the hangar, tell the pilot to fly us back to San Diego, or to the border if he doesn't have clearance, and we'll be out of your hair just like that. He'll come back for you and you can do whatever you want. I think I'd lay low for a while, though. I imagine there's going to be a fierce battle over who takes over your son's operation. What's left of it, that is."

She looks up at Max. "You did this to us. You should be made to pay."

"Now that's the attitude that could get you in trouble, Marta," I snap back before Max can. "You are not exactly in a position to bargain."

"But you are?" The fire is back in her eyes. "Pedro and Lila downstairs will kill you both if I but give the word. And my pilot—*my* pilot—would sooner kill himself than do something contrary to my orders. I can keep you both here until we all die of old age."

"Or boredom," I cut in. "I don't think you want to test your theory, Marta. I don't think you want to die in this shit hole, even if it is a nice shit hole. And look at it this way, if you let us out of here now, you and your witch friend can have another go at me. Otherwise, you know fucking well I'll outlive the lot of you and one way or the other, I'll get out. Vampires are crafty that way."

"Witch friend?" Max asks. "There's a witch involved, too?" His tone implies incredulity coupled with the shock of recognition that if vampires exist, witches probably do, too.

"Long story," I reply. "I can fill you in later." I turn my attention back to Marta. "So, what's it going to be?"

She takes a moment to consider. She's sunk into a sitting position on the cot, her hair a dark curtain shielding her face. I don't like that. I can't see her eyes.

I take her chin in my hand and turn her face not too gently toward mine. "Don't think too hard. You really only have one choice."

She wants to bite my hand, I see it reflected in the rage behind her eyes. I step back, mindful that she may yet try to orchestrate a mingling of our blood. The fact that I stepped out of reach makes her smile.

"You are not so brave as you let on. But you make a good point. Burke will be able to find you. She is much more powerful than you know. Together she and I will bring you to your knees."

"Blah, blah, blah. This is getting tiresome. Are we going now or what?"

Marta's decision shows first on her face, a grim smile of acceptance. She rises from the cot and gestures to the sheet binding her. I step around, keeping the cot between us, rip loose the tie, and use it to secure both her hands behind her back.

"Can you navigate the stairs on your own?" I ask Max.

He nods and I keep a firm grip on Marta's wrists as we start into the hall.

Marta stops outside the closed door facing us. "I want to see my son," she says quietly.

Just as quietly, I reply, "Dust to dust, Marta."

A single tear rolls down her cheek. She opens her mouth and I expect another round of recriminations and threats. Instead, she draws a deep breath, squares her shoulders and leads us without a word toward the stairs.

CHAPTER 52

MAX STOPS ME BEFORE I OPEN THE DOOR TO the stairs. "Where's the trip to the detonator?" he asks.

I'd forgotten about that little black box. It's no longer on this side of the door. When I look to Marta, she seems disappointed that Max remembered. I guess after all that posturing, she planned to blow us up anyway.

"Good try. Where is it?"

Her mouth draws into a thin line. She looks like a child being force-fed spinach. I take the cot leg from Max's hand and whack her across the back. Not too hard. Just enough to get her attention.

Her breath releases in a little huff. Her legs buckle but she remains on her feet. The second time I hit her, it's with a little more force. This time, she actually does fall to her knees.

"All right," she spits the words like venom. "The box is downstairs, in the kitchen. Lila has orders to open the door only at my instruction."

It's a good plan. If Max and I made it out alone, we'd be

blown to smithereens when we tried to get out downstairs. "How are you to contact them?"

"An intercom at the bottom of the stairs."

"Then how about I open this door and you go out first?"

She sniffs as though I've given her another example of my cowardice. Like I care. I have no intention of letting Max or myself fall into another of her traps. I twist open the doorknob gently and step away, at the same time, pushing Marta into the doorway.

She stumbles out, but nothing blows up and nobody starts shooting at us from the bottom of the stairs.

Hooray. One for the good guys.

I follow her, keeping a grip on her hands. It's slow going with Max. He has to hop down each stair on his one good leg and the jarring of that motion on his broken ankle makes him bite his lips to keep from crying out with pain. I offer him my shoulder to lean on, but he waves me off. He knows we can't risk Marta getting away from us.

At last we make it to the bottom. The intercom is to the left. I yank her hands to get Marta's attention. "You have one chance to do this. You're going through the door first. So if you want to live to torture me another day, you'd best not fuck this up."

She must find that good enough motivation because she says simply. "Press one-oh-two on the pad."

I reach up and do it. I hear a buzz on the other side, then a female voice in Spanish says, *"Quién es?"*

Marta replies. *"Señora Martinez. Lila, abra la puerta."*

I look over at Max. He looks wary. "Open the door, that's it?"

Marta sniffs. "What did you expect? A secret password? You Americans watch too much television."

Max shrugs but to be on the safe side, I gesture that he should join me as I step as far out of the doorway as I can. It's not much protection, there's only about six inches on each side. But in a moment, the mechanism that controls the cabinets whirls to life and the opening appears before us. I tense, waiting for an attack.

But nothing happens. In fact, Lila has stepped away, as if *she's* afraid of the same thing. When she sees her mistress, though, she rushes to her with a torrent of rapid-fire Spanish that sounds laden with concern.

I let Max take care of interpreting. He knows my Spanish is limited. If there's cause for alarm, he'll let me know.

I look around the kitchen. Pedro is not in sight. Marta is focused on calming Lila. No one is paying attention to me. I cross to the gun cabinet quickly and quietly, and pull it open. There's an arsenal in here, ranging from automatic rifles to a little silver-plated Derringer. That's the gun I pick. Easily concealed and we won't be engaging in anything but close combat. I snatch up a box of ammunition, too.

Marta and Lila are still deep in conversation. I slip the gun and ammo to Max and he puts it into a pocket in his slacks. Then I gather up the other guns, throw them into a heap behind the cabinets, and tug the canister. When the door is secured, I snap the thing off and toss it away. To check for a second control, I sweep the other canisters off the counter with the back of my hand. They scatter and fall to the floor with a shower of coffee, sugar and flour. There are other guns around here, I'm sure, but at least these are out of commission.

All the while, Max listens, his head cocked, to catch the harried conversation between Marta and her servant. Lila has untied Marta's hands and is examining her wound with an anxious frown. She leads Marta to the sink and gently holds her wrist under cold running water. She reaches above the sink for a bottle and bandages. Before she goes any further, I stop her with a sharp voice.

"Lila, you can tend to her later. After we're gone, right, Marta?"

Lila doesn't understand what I've said so Max repeats it in Spanish. She starts to protest but Marta waves her off and, wrapping a towel around her wrist, turns to us.

"By all means, let's get this over with. The sooner you've gone, the sooner I can contact Belinda. Get all the rest you can, vampire, because as soon as my pilot comes back, we'll be after you."

Thanks for the warning. But I'm still not sure we won't walk out of this house and into a trap. "Max, ask Lila where Pedro is."

He does and repeats her answer. "He's with the pilot, in the hangar."

"Are they waiting for us?"

This time, Marta answers before Max can relay the question. "He's helping the pilot. They're doing maintenance on the helicopter. Wouldn't want you to have an accident, now would we?"

"Is it ready to fly?" I ask.

She starts for a telephone but I'm beside her before she walks the two steps that take her to the instrument. "Don't try anything."

She sniffs and brushes my hand off her arm. She lifts the receiver, speaks into it.

When I look at Max, he nods. "She's asking if the copter is ready."

There's a pause while she listens, then she replaces the receiver and turns to us. "It's ready."

I gesture to Marta and Lila. "Then let's go."

At first, Lila acts like she's not going to come with us. But I'm not leaving her alone in this kitchen. She might take it upon herself to call Pedro and say something to upset our plan.

When I give her a shove, Marta says, "Leave her alone." She turns to the woman, *"Lila, venga con nosotros."*

Head down, Lila falls into step behind her mistress.

Max and I let them lead the way outside. The fresh air and sunshine come as a welcome relief after being cooped up in that hellhole for the last—what? I've lost track of time. When I turn my face to the sun, Max looks at me with a raised eyebrow.

"It's a myth," I explain. "The sun thing."

He nods as if I've just explained what makes grass

green or the sky blue. Like it's a perfectly normal answer to a perfectly normal question.

Maybe there's hope for us yet.

It's painful to watch Max hobble along. I keep an arm on his elbow, both for support and to be able to snatch that little gun out of his pocket if the need arises. Marta's done nothing to indicate that she knows we have it, so at least we have one small element of surprise.

The door to the hangar is open. As we approach, Marta calls out and the pilot appears. He looks shocked to see Max and me. Marta says something that must put him at ease because the anxious look is replaced with a curious frown. Max listens and nods to me. "She's instructing the pilot to fly us to Tijuana. She says he's to come back immediately."

So far, so good. The pilot returns to the hangar and in a moment, he and Pedro roll the helicopter onto the pad. The pilot dons his flight helmet and sunglasses. He climbs aboard and fires up the engine. Marta and Lila stand quietly behind us while we wait for the copter to warm up.

The hair on the back of my neck is stirring. This is too easy. I turn to warn Max that something doesn't feel right and I catch a flash out of the corner of my eye.

Lila has stepped close to Max. From somewhere in the folds of her voluminous skirt, she has drawn a gun, the twin, it looks like, to the one I slipped Max.

She presses it into his back and says something that's lost to me in the roar of the helicopter engine. When I look over at Marta, she is signaling the pilot. The helicopter abruptly grows silent.

For once, I wish my instincts had been wrong.

CHAPTER 53

MARTA TAKES THE GUN OUT OF LILA'S HAND. "Did you think I would let you go that easily?"

Exasperation makes me want to tackle her this very minute, but she's got the gun pressed into Max's spine. As quick as I am, I can't be sure I could knock her away before she pulled that trigger.

The pilot has joined us. He, too, has a gun in his hand. His is bigger. A .45.

I release my impatience in a sigh. "I thought we had a deal, Marta."

She laughs. Not pleasantly. "Oh, we did. But I've come up with a better one. I kill Max and lock you away until the hunger is more than you can bear. Then you may reconsider what I asked of you before."

Max, testing, takes a tiny step forward and turns to me. "What does she want?"

Marta closes the gap between them at once, keeping her gun in contact with Max's back.

She's not taking any chances. I shrug. "Simple. She wants me to make her vampire."

His brows shoot up. "Why would she want that?"

Marta shoves at him in a pique of impatience. "Ask me yourself," she growls.

Max stumbles, fights to regain his balance, tough with the broken ankle. But with the effort, he moves just far enough way from Marta to allow an attack. Marta realizes her mistake almost instantly, but I'm on her before she can correct it. I wrench the gun out of her hand and her injured wrist behind her back. I'm about to leverage the hold when the pilot's gun barks once.

I yank her around in front of me.

The pilot has his gun to Max's head. "The first one was to get your attention. The second will blow your friend's head off if you don't let her go."

His English is heavily accented but very good. He has Max with an arm around his throat. I'm about to release Marta, when Max sends me a look that coupled with a tiny shake of his head, gives me cause to reconsider. He has one hand in the pocket of his jacket; I see his fingers maneuvering the gun.

So does Marta. She starts to yell a warning. I snap her neck with one hand.

The pilot's mouth falls open in shock. But it's momentary. His fingers tighten on the trigger. Max slumps into him and in that same moment, fires the Derringer through the fabric of his pocket.

The pilot staggers backward, looking down at his midsection in disbelief.

The Derringer is a .22 and even a contact gut shot is very rarely fatal. The pilot raises the .45. Max whirls around, the gun now out, and follows up quickly with a round to the head.

That does it. The pilot goes down like a rock.

Lila and Pedro are screaming. I toss Marta's body toward them and scramble to pick up Lila's gun and the pilot's .45.

It's not until the adrenaline has stopped pumping that the reality of the situation hits.

"Max," I yelp. "You *killed* the pilot. How the fuck are we going to get out of here?"

For the first time, I get a *real* smile out of Max. "How do you think," he says. "We fly."

"You know how to fly a helicopter?"

"Don't sound so shocked."

"But you never told me you could fly a helicopter."

"You never told me you were a vampire. I think your secret trumps mine."

We hold this conversation as we make our way toward the helicopter. Max pauses at the hatch. "What do we do about those two?"

I turn back to look at Lila and Pedro. They are prostate with grief over Marta's death. Lila is on the ground, holding Marta and rocking her body as if it were a child's. Pedro is standing over them both, tears streaming down his face. Neither looks in our direction.

"Leave them."

If the coldness of my reply fazes Max, he doesn't show it. He doesn't argue, either. He merely reaches into the copter and picks up the pilot's helmet.

He hands me one, too, and a leather jacket that was slung onto one of the rear seats. I look at it for a minute.

He raises an eyebrow. "You're dressed in a torn sheet."

I'd forgotten all about it. I slip on the jacket and zip it up. It falls to above my knees. I reach underneath and pull the sheet out and drop it on the ground.

I help Max climb aboard. I take the seat beside him in front. He fires up the engine and the rotors spring to life. In a few minutes, we're in the air.

I don't bother to look back.

CHAPTER 54

IT'S TOO QUIET. MAX IS CONCENTRATING UNNECES-
sarily hard on the controls and I on the view outside the
windshield. I know why. There's a lot Max and I have to
discuss, I feel the tension like a third passenger. But I think
we're afraid to begin. Afraid of the questions, afraid of the
answers.

Max radios ahead once we're in the air and asks to be
patched through to SDPD. He hands me the radio when the
connection is made and Williams takes my call. I tell him
only that we're on our way to Tijuana. He says he'll dis-
patch a car for us and rings off. Abruptly. No questions
about how we are, no demand for details.

And there's something in the tone of his voice—
concern, uneasiness—that makes me wonder what it is he
isn't telling me. Something about Culebra, maybe? Or
Burke?

The silence between Max and me is becoming oppres-
sive. When I can stand it no longer, I turn to Max. "How
did you end up at Martinez'? Was it Foley?"

He shakes his head. "Martinez got a message to me

right after you left to meet David. Through a contact in Mexico. Said he wanted to meet."

"And you went? Just like that?"

He pauses, looks over at me. "Of course not. He said he knew about you. That if I didn't come, he'd put out a hit on you. *That* we can blame on Foley. Of course, it backfired on him. He never thought Martinez would use the information he was feeding him to come after me himself."

"But he did."

"Sent the helicopter to pick me up at the border. When Foley found out that Martinez had me, he went ballistic. Came to the compound and demanded to be paid. By this time, though, Martinez had come up with his new plan. Seemed killing me wasn't going to be enough. He wanted to make sure I felt the same pain he did. By killing someone close to me. By killing you."

"I knew Foley was following me. He could have picked me up a dozen times. Why did he choose Burke's little shindig? What connection did he have with witchcraft?"

Max shrugs. "I don't think he did. Marta came up with the plan to lure you to some sort of black magic ritual. And she knew Burke had a connection with Culebra." His voice takes on a cautious tone. "Of course, I knew you had a connection to Culebra, too. I just didn't know what kind of connection until now."

His tone is heavy with meaning. I wait for him to ask the questions he must want to. But when he doesn't, I break the silence by asking, "What happened to your ankle?"

"Broke it the first day I was there. Trying to escape. Fell down those fucking stairs. Don't remember much else after that. Foley kept me drugged up until I came to and you were there."

I'm doing a little mental calculation. "And you're sure it was Foley with you?"

He nods. "Yeah. I'm pretty sure he was there the whole time. Why?"

It's clear now why Williams sounded strange on the phone. He knows my anonymous caller wasn't Foley. It couldn't have been. He was too busy torturing Max to be following me around.

So who the hell was it who made the calls? And shot Alan? And why wouldn't Williams have told me when he had me on the radio?

"Anna?"

Max's voice pulls me back.

"What's wrong?"

I see no use in holding back. "Remember when I told you I thought Foley might be following me? That he was trying to get me to lead him to you?"

He nods. "What about it?"

"Well, the calls continued. From what you just said, it couldn't have been Foley. But somebody *was* following me. He even shot a guy I was fighting."

"A guy you were fighting? As in apprehending?"

"Kind of. Anyway, that's not important. What is important is each time he contacted me he said something like, 'tell your boyfriend.' That's why I was so sure it was Foley. I thought he was talking about you."

I feel Max bristle. "And he wasn't? How many boyfriends do you have?"

"Max, you're missing the point. If the caller wasn't Foley and you aren't the *boyfriend* he was referring to, who is? Williams sounded really strange on the radio. I've got a bad feeling."

He asks in a quiet voice, "You think it might be David?"

I nod. "He's the only other man I know that I'm seen with on a regular basis." I, of course, leave off the nonhuman species. No need to go into that with Max.

"Any idea who you've so thoroughly pissed off recently that he'd go after you like this?"

"No." It's true. Tuturo and Guzman were captured with very little trouble. The thing that happened with Alan was unexpected and spur of the moment. It doesn't make sense.

"We'll be at the airport in a few minutes," Max is saying. "If Williams is there, we'll get the answers."

He says *we'll* get answers. It's oddly reassuring. I had the feeling the moment this helicopter touched down would be the last moment I spent with Max.

CHAPTER 55

M AX AND I HARDLY SAY TWO MORE WORDS TO
each other the rest of the flight. But it's not awkward, the way it was when we first took off. It's strange that
we should be united in our concern over a man Max barely
knows.

When the copter touches down, it's met with a contin-
gent of police vehicles, Mexican and American. I don't
know what Williams told the Federales to allow American
access, but whatever it was, it worked. We're whisked away
first into a terminal building where Max is questioned
briefly by Mexican officials, then their DEA counterparts.
He gives them coordinates to Martinez' jungle compound.
I'm allowed to stay with him though no one directs questions to me.

There is a Mexican female officer who, seeing my
wardrobe predicament, produces a pair of jeans and a T-shirt
from somewhere, along with, even more remarkably, underwear that actually fits. I accept them gratefully and duck into
a restroom to change. When I come out, she hands me a pair
of huaraches. The sandals have obviously been worn, but

anything's better than going home barefoot. I slip them on and offer her the jacket in exchange. She takes it.

Because he is hurt, Max is released fairly quickly. He declares his intention to seek medical aid in the United States, and within an hour, we're bundled into the back of a SDPD car.

Williams has not come to meet us.

Ortiz is the driver of the black-and-white. He waits for us to get settled in the back before turning in the seat to greet us. He glances with concern at Max's splinted ankle. "Are you in much pain?" he asks.

Max shakes his head. "I'm fine. Have you heard anything about Anna's partner, David? Does he know she's okay?"

Ortiz raises an eyebrow and looks at me. *How does he know?*

The question confirms my worst suspicions. "Did something happen to David?" I reply bluntly and out loud. "Tell us. Quickly."

Ortiz frowns. "I am sorry to be the one to tell you," he says. "But something did happen while you were gone. David is dead."

CHAPTER 56

MAX GRABS MY HAND AND SQUEEZES. "JESUS, Anna. I'm so sorry."

I'm staring at Ortiz. This isn't right. David dead? Williams would never have sent Ortiz or anyone else to relay that news. He, better than anyone, knows what I went through to save David's life when Avery attacked him. He knows how important David is to me.

You are lying. Why?

Ortiz shifts uneasily in the seat and reaches to put the car in gear.

I stop him by grabbing the back of his neck. *Tell me the truth.*

Max reacts to this with a sharp intake of breath. "Anna, what are you doing?"

Ortiz pulls against my grip. I work my fingers tight around his throat. He manages to gasp, *No one else is to know.*

I release him. "Max is my friend. He can be trusted." I deliberately say it out loud. Max's eyes are wide with shock. He's trying to figure out what Ortiz did to set me off. I don't want to shock him further by admitting that Officer Ortiz is a vampire, too, and we can communicate without using our voices.

Better to bluff.

"I had a feeling he wasn't telling us the truth. He's going to take us to David now."

I avoid looking at Max when I say it. It's bad enough to feel his confusion—it's thick in the air—I don't have to see it, too. The silence is, once again, no longer comfortable between us.

Ortiz is silent, too. I don't attempt to apologize. He lied about David. Even if he'd had orders to do so in front of Max, he could have told me the truth telepathically.

Our ride ends at County General Hospital in Hillcrest.

Not the thing to inspire my confidence.

The moment I pass through the doors, I'm assaulted by the smell and feel of the place. Blood and desperation. My stomach begins to churn. I was brought here to recover from the attack of the vampire who sired me. Even after all these months, the memories are painful and intense. The doctor who treated me, Avery. All that happened after.

"Anna?"

Max's voice penetrates the veil.

I look up at him, realizing then, that I had come to a stop just inside the doors. His eyes are questioning.

"Are you all right?"

I shake off the fog of despair that descended so rapidly and without warning and release a breath. "Yes. Do you want to go to emergency while I check on David? You have to have that ankle attended to."

He waves off the suggestion. At the same time, I realize that someone has given him a pair of crutches. I don't know when that happened. It must have been while I was lost in my own black trip down memory lane.

Ortiz follows us inside and hands me a slip of paper. David's room number. "He's registered as Richard Smith," he says. He points us toward the elevator and when I turn to thank him, he's already headed for the door. His stride is stiff, angry.

I don't care.

The elevator whisks us up seven floors and when the doors slide open, we find ourselves in a critical care unit. Once again, that queasy feeling returns. David may not be dead, but he must be hurt pretty badly to be here.

A placard near the elevator declares that all visitors must check in at the nurse's station. When we do, Max is questioned about his own condition and if he should be on his feet. He is blunt in his insistence that he is all right. A nurse is just as insistent that he use a wheelchair and it's only after she refuses to point us to David's room, that he reluctantly agrees.

I wait through this exchange with an uncharacteristic patience. I am afraid. Afraid to see what has been done to David. Afraid to acknowledge that I must accept responsibility for whatever it is.

I left him alone.

When Max is in the chair, we are allowed to proceed down the hall.

Room 718.

The door is closed. There's a uniformed cop sitting on a metal chair. He's got a radio and at our approach, he stands and motions us to the door. "Williams says it's okay for you to go in."

I peek through the glass window.

Relief surges through me like a rush of adrenaline.

He's sitting up in bed.

No tubes. No life monitoring equipment.

I peer into the corners of the room.

No Gloria.

Hallelujah.

David is alone and breathing on his own. How bad can it be?

CHAPTER 57

I HAVE MY HAND ON THE DOORKNOB WHEN MAX stops me by placing his hand over mine.

"Does he know?" he asks.

It takes a beat or two for me to connect the dots. "Oh. Does David know about *me*?" I shake my head. "No. You are the only one who knows."

The only human who knows, that is. But I don't want to complicate things.

He doesn't look as if he believes me. "Look, Max, I know you have questions. I'm sorry. I'll try to answer them in time."

He's looking in at David now. He nods. "You're right. I'll wait. I think I deserve some answers, though."

"And you'll get them. I promise. Can we go in?"

He lets his hand drop. I take that as a "yes" and push at the door.

I make sure Max's chair clears the door before rushing around him to do something I've only done once before in our acquaintance. I hug David. A hug meant to convey relief, apology and remorse.

Not that David realizes any of that.

He merely accepts the hug as a gesture from a friend without comment before extricating himself gingerly from my clinging arms.

"Careful," he warns. He points in the direction of his left shoulder. "Stitches."

I jump back. "God. Sorry. What happened? What's with the cop outside?"

But David is looking at Max. "The better question is what happened to you two? Max, you look worse than I feel."

Max waves the comment off with the back of his hand. "Long story. Anna has been worried sick since we heard about you. Better fill her in."

I pull a chair up to David's bedside and sit my butt down. "Tell us."

David frowns down at me. "First, I owe you an apology."

"An apology?"

He nods. "I should have told you something days ago. I don't know why I didn't. It's not like you can't take care of yourself."

My brief flirtation with patience comes to a screeching halt. "Damn it—" I almost say his name. I have to bite it off at the last minute. "Get on with it. What happened?"

He smiles at the outburst. "Glad to see you aren't treating me with kid gloves just because I happen to be in the hospital with a gunshot wound."

I start to jump up and he waves me back down. "Okay, okay. I got shot. Two days ago. High-powered rifle. Another inch to the left and I'd be dead. But I must have a guardian angel because nothing vital was hit and I woke up to find myself here. The docs say I'll be fine."

"You're sure?"

He nods.

"Then why all the subterfuge?"

"Williams' idea," he says. "Before the shooting, I'd been getting calls. Somebody threatening to do me bodily harm. But after each call, the guy would say, 'tell your girl-friend.' "

My shoulders jump.

David sees it. Again, he misunderstands. "I know. I should have told you. But I thought he was referring to Gloria. So naturally, I assumed it was some kind of public-ity stunt. Especially with the opening of the restaurant and all. I even made Gloria double the security for that night. But then I got shot before the opening." He lifts his good shoulder in a half shrug. "I'm no closer to figuring out what it's all about now than I was before. But I should have told you what was happening. You could have been with me when I was shot. Hell, you might have taken the bullet instead of me. I had no right to keep something so impor-tant from you."

Max is looking at me. I feel it. He's waiting for me to take that cue. When I don't right away, he makes a sound in his throat. "I'm going to leave you two," he says. "I think it's time I get this ankle tended to." He reaches out a hand and David takes it. "Glad it's not more serious," he says. His gaze fixes on me. "See you later, Anna?"

I avoid his eyes but nod. I'm not anxious to admit to David that I, too, have been keeping secrets. Lots of them.

Max wheels himself out of the room. When the door has swished to a close behind him, David says quietly, "I really am sorry, Anna. I jumped on you for the way things have been between us, and I'm the one who hasn't been honest."

Again, my cue to jump in. Again, I find myself holding back. Why?

I reach up and smooth a bit of the sheet. A delaying tactic.

To declare David dead is pretty dramatic. How is Williams going to explain when David miraculously reap-pears? I can't help but feel he did it not to protect David but to protect me. There's one way to find out.

"So Williams has you here because he thinks the guy might take another shot at you?"

"Or you."

I hate being right about this.

"Must have made a big splash in the papers, though. Local jock killed. How was it handled? Was there a funeral?"

He shakes his head. "Small private service. I'm not the headliner you seem to think."

"No, but Gloria sure is. I assume she knows you're alive."

I expect a big smile and some lame explanation that she's spent the last two days fretting and crying at his bedside.

Instead, he frowns and his shoulders bunch.

"She knows. But she hasn't been here since the shooting."

That reply is so unexpected, my hand freezes on the sheet. I'm ready to yell, good riddance, but the expression on his face is too full of pain for me to actually say it out loud.

Doesn't mean I'm about to let the opportunity slip by without some comment, though.

I resume my sheet fluffing. "That's a surprise. Is she in protective custody? I can't imagine she'd pass off a photo op as juicy as mourning at your graveside."

David grabs my hand. "You can stop now. For whatever reason, Gloria isn't here. I don't expect her to show up anytime soon. Can we get back to the important topic? Someone was out to get me and if Gloria isn't the 'girl-friend' this guy is referring to, there's only one other woman I spend any time with."

"Me."

He nods. "You."

This is like an echo of the conversation I had with Max. But it also triggers a memory, a bad memory. The incident that landed me in Palm Canyon to begin with. I blow out a breath. "Is that why you said what you did after the Guzman thing?"

He looks glum.

"You wanted me out of the way in case that guy came

after you." I let a beat go by before asking, "You weren't really planning a move to L.A., were you?"

He doesn't say anything. He doesn't need to. Jesus. I hitch my chair closer to the bed. It's time I replaced some of his guilt with a much healthier emotion—anger. "You are probably going to want to shoot *me* when you hear what I have to say."

He gives me an inquisitive half smile and gestures for me to go on.

"I've been getting calls, too."

The smile morphs into an incredulous frown.

"I know. I know. I should have told you. But I thought it was someone trying to trick me into leading him to Max. It wasn't until—" I stop myself. Do I want to get into the witch thing and Foley and Martinez and all that happened in Mexico?

No. I backtrack with a sharp intake of breath. "Anyway, I realized that wasn't the case. And when Max and I were talking about it, the same thing dawned on us that dawned on you. Whoever is doing this thought *you* were my boyfriend. It wasn't about Max at all."

He leans his head back against the headboard. "Anyone take a shot at you?"

I think back to what happened in the desert. Another subject best kept for later. "No."

David drums his fingers on the bedclothes. "What about that incident in Palm Canyon?"

So much for that. "You saw the paper." Not a question.

He nods and adds sharply, "Right before you disappeared. Called you a hero for going to the aid of that woman when her maniac husband attacked her. The big mystery, though, was who shot that maniac husband."

He pauses, waits for me to say something. When I don't, he continues, sounding peeved. "I must have called Williams a dozen times when I heard what you'd been involved in. All he would say was you were all right and needed a little time away. He made it sound like it was my fault."

He stops suddenly, inhales deeply, as if struck by a sharp pain.

I touch his arm. "Are you okay?"

He lets the breath out through his nose, inhales again. His right hand reaches for his shoulder.

"David?" I whisper it, realize my mistake, flinch. I glance around the room like an idiot. Who the hell could be eavesdropping on us here?

He shakes his head. "I'm all right. Chest gets tight when I get . . ."

He doesn't complete the thought. I can fill in any number of words: exasperated, angry, frustrated, confused. I know because I can see it all on his face.

I start to stand up. "Maybe I should go."

He grabs my hand. "Sit down."

I don't want to upset him any more than I already have so I do.

When his face clears of the pain, I ask, "Did forensics compare the bullets?"

He nods. And his next words confirm what I already suspect.

"The bullet that killed that guy in Palm Canyon is a match to the one they took out of me."

CHAPTER 58

IT WAS SO MUCH EASIER WHEN I THOUGHT MY—
our stalker was Foley.

"Has Williams been any help?"

David nods. "He's been here every day. He has his men running the bullets through every database in the country hoping something pops up. Whoever this guy is, it's doubtful this is his first foray into criminal activity."

The door opens and the same nurse who insisted Max use a wheelchair approaches the bed. "Time to rest, Mr. Smith." She turns that steely gaze on me. "Your visitor can come back tomorrow."

She says it in a tone that brooks no argument. She even holds out an arm as if to usher me from the room. I bend close. "I'll be back tomorrow morning, Dick."

He shakes his head, smiling.

The nurse follows me out. "You are Ms. Long?" she asks.

I almost say no until I remember. That was the name on the phony ID Williams gave me when he sent me to Beso de la Muerte. "Yes."

She walks back to her desk and picks up a piece of paper. "There's a message for you."

A message? For Anita Long? It can only be from one person.

Williams. He's booked me a room at the Kona Kai Resort on Shelter Island. He says he'll meet me there in an hour.

I glance at the time stamp on the message. It came in thirty minutes ago.

I thank the nurse and ask about Max. She tells me he's been admitted. The doctors want to keep him under observation. Make sure there are no complications from his untreated broken ankle. She offers to get his room number for me, but I think it best if I leave Max alone, at least for the night.

The Kona Kai. Obviously, Williams doesn't think it safe for me to go home. Frankly, I'm too tired to argue. I could jog to Shelter Island from here. It's downhill all the way. But again, fatigue, emotional and physical, is taking its toll. The last few days have been hell.

When I ask where I can get a cab, the nurse directs me to the concierge desk in the lobby downstairs.

Hospitals have concierge desks?

Who knew? A rack of pamphlets offering services for everything from theater tickets to maid service almost obscures the tiny, white-haired volunteer seated behind the desk. She's dressed in a candy-striper smock and her pink-tinted glasses make her look like a Kewpie doll. She's so cute, I can't help but smile.

She's as efficient as she is cute. But it's not until she's secured the cab and it's pulling up in front that I realize, I have no money to pay for it.

She seems to read something on my face because she turns the telephone on the counter to face me. "Feel free," she says.

I thank her and dial Williams cell. He picks up.

"I'll meet you in front of the hotel," he replies when I explain my predicament. His voice is tentative, as if he expected something different from me than a request for cash.

He has a right to be cautious. He has a lot to answer for. Beso de la Muerte, and all that happened after.

CHAPTER 59

THE KONA KAI RESORT IS PRIVATE, PRICEY AND EX-clusive. The compound consists of a yacht club, a restaurant, a nightclub and a hotel. Figures Williams would be a member.

He is standing under the portico in front of the hotel when we pull up. He's leaning against a raised flowerbed, smoking a cigar, dressed in khaki slacks and a dark blue designer polo shirt. He has brown loafers on his feet that look like they might be Gucci. No uniform, no cop car in sight so he's here in an unofficial capacity. He looks like he fits right in with the yachting crowd. And he looks relaxed.

At least until he sees me getting out of the cab.

He tosses the cigar into the flowerbed and hurries to pay the driver. He doesn't say a thing to me until the car has pulled away.

Then Williams does something he's never done before.

He hugs me.

The gesture is unexpected. My body stiffens and my shoulders actually jump at the contact. He lets me go almost immediately and stands back.

"I am glad to see that you are well," he says.

I make it a point to look around. "Are you talking to me?"

He isn't letting me read his thoughts but I do get a flash that he doesn't appreciate the humor. He takes a card key out of his pocket. "Let's go up to your room. You must be tired."

I am, so I agree with a bob of my head. He leads the way through the lobby and directly to the elevators. Obviously he has taken care of registering. He uses the key to access the top floor of the hotel. The top floor.

When the doors slide open, he gestures to the left. A few steps down the hall, he stops in front of a set of double wooden doors with a brass placard that reads, "Presidential Suite."

He uses the card key to open the door and stands back to let me pass in first.

Instead, I take a step back. "The Presidential Suite? What is this?"

"You've been through a lot," he says. "I thought you could use a little pampering."

I push by him and stop right inside the door. There is a huge living room with a fireplace, fresh flowers on every surface, and three connecting doors leading off to what I assume are the bedrooms. There is a sliding glass door that overlooks the yacht club basin. It's open. In the late afternoon haze, the lights of the city across the bay are beginning to wink on.

"How many people are you expecting?" I ask, more than a little peeved. "If this is your idea of an apology for what happened with Max and Culebra, they should be the ones staying here, not me."

Williams' face gives nothing away. He is a very old vampire, who I doubt has ever apologized for anything. He isn't about to say the words even if an apology is what this elaborate gesture is all about.

I'm too tired to call him on it. Right now, a bath and a bed are all I want. It's been a long thirty-six hours since we parted company in Beso de la Muerte. I let him pick that out of my weary brain and he places the hotel key on a glass coffee table the size of Montana.

Do you require sustenance? He asks. *I have someone on call.*

His formality with me is foreign and strange. If I had more energy, I might care why.

As it is, I simply shake my head.

He leaves me without another thought or word. Once he's gone, I check out the bedrooms and pick out the one I like best. It has a huge round bed with about a hundred silk throw pillows scattered at the head. When I sweep them off and pull back the comforter, I find black satin sheets.

I wonder which president inspired *this* decor.

CHAPTER 60

I SLEEP FOR TWELVE HOURS. AT LEAST, THAT'S WHAT the clock tells me when I open my eyes. Then I panic because I don't remember where I am. The slick sheets, the smell of roses, the sun pouring through unfamiliar windows. I'm disoriented. The last time I opened my eyes after sleeping in an unfamiliar room, a blood splattered Marta was standing over me.

I sit straight up in bed, heart pounding. I'm alone this time. In a much nicer room. A huge bed. Furniture polished and gleaming. A vase of red roses on the nightstand beside me.

Slowly, awareness creeps back. I remember. The hospital. David. Williams.

I sink back onto the pillow. In the last week I've awakened almost every morning hungover, drugged or disoriented. It's a wonder I have a healthy brain cell left.

The message light is flashing on the bedside phone.

I don't have to guess who it is. I listen to Williams' voice, asking that I meet him at the hospital at ten. It's eight thirty now. I have time for another soak in that Jacuzzi tub.

I DON'T HAVE TO WORRY ABOUT CAB FARE. WILLIAMS left me money as well as my purse and clothes—outfits to hold me at least a week. I found both last night as I was preparing for bed. This time, I have no doubt that Williams did the shopping. Instead of jeans, tailored linen slacks, silk blouses and a blazer were hung on padded hangers in the closet. Even a pair of leather loafers that are butter soft and my size. I guess he didn't want my lack of style to embarrass him in front of his yacht club friends.

I fill the oversized tub to the brim and pour in bath salts. Like last night, soaking in a tub of perfumed water and lavishly applying the spa products set out on the bathroom counter, help to soothe away the horrors of Martinez and his mother. I won't soon forget what happened, but with these simple luxuries, I'm getting more comfortable again in my own skin.

When I appear at the door to David's room at ten, I'm surprised to see Max there. He's in a wheelchair, his ankle elevated. It's in a cast, but in spite of that, he looks rested and healthy. He's clean shaven and dressed in a hospital gown. There are two nurses in the room, too. Laughing and fluffing blankets and pillows as if that alone will guarantee quick recovery. I can't blame them. Between Max and David, the nurses must think they've died and gone to heaven to have two such handsome men to fuss over.

I'm glad I'm not a patient on this floor.

There's a break in the frivolity when I ease the door open. The nurses excuse themselves and leave. Max and David don't seem as excited to see me as they are disappointed to be losing their groupies.

I decide to take the high road and pretend I don't notice. "Williams isn't here yet?"

David gestures toward the phone. "He called a few minutes ago. Said he'd be a little late."

I turn to Max. "You look good this morning."

He gives me a once-over. "So do you. Real clothes. Have I ever seen you in anything but jeans before?"

I smile. "How's the ankle?"

He lifts it a little off the elevated platform. "Good. The break was clean. It's going to take time to heal; ankles evidently do. But the doctor commented on the fact that it had been properly set and splinted. He sends his regards to you."

David looks surprised. "Anna, you set his ankle?"

That launches us into what happened in Mexico. I let Max do the talking. He tells David a story that sounds credible because he purposely omits the incredible parts. To sum it up, Foley lured Max and me to Mexico where Martinez killed him. Max and I escaped and somehow Martinez and his pilot ended up dead, too. Max flew us to safety and when we got back to San Diego, we found out about David.

End of story.

No mention of vampires. No mention of how I decapitated Martinez or snapped Marta's neck with one hand. Max takes credit for the killings without actually saying so and I let him.

He finishes at the same time Williams makes his appearance.

He's in full cop mode today, even dressed in his uniform and carrying a leather attaché case. He makes no attempt to communicate with me telepathically. With him, another uniform, a street cop, takes up a position outside David's room.

"Another guard?" I ask. "For David or Max?"

"Neither," he replies, looking at me for the first time. "This guard is for you."

CHAPTER 61

T O SAY THAT I WAS NOT EXPECTING THAT ANSWER
is an understatement. He knows me better than to think
I'd accept a guard. Instead of shrieking at him, though, I
exercise uncharacteristic restraint by asking quietly, "Why
would I need a guard?"

Max frowns in concern. "Is it because of what happened
in Mexico? Has Anna been threatened by one of Martinez'
gang?"

I realize he hasn't heard David's story. When I look at
Williams, he's shaking his head.

"No. This has nothing to do with Mexico. We know
who killed Alan Rothman in Palm Canyon and who shot
David." He places the attaché case on the foot of David's
bed and opens it. He withdraws a half dozen pieces of paper and hands half of them to me and the others to David.
"Recognize this guy?"

The three sketches he hands me are artists' renderings
of a man in his late thirties, early forties. In each portrait,
the hair and beards are different, but the eyes and basic
facial structure are the same. In the first, the man is clean

shaven and dressed in a sports coat, shirt and tie. In the second he has a scruffy beard and wears a T-shirt. In the third, his head is shaved and he has an earring in his left ear. David and I exchange sketches. Again, different hair color, style and wardrobe, but definitely the same man.

I hand them back to Williams with a shake of my head. "I don't think I've ever seen this guy before."

"Who is he?" David asks.

Williams gathers the sketches. "The Ghost."

My internal alarm system shrieks. *Ghost? A real ghost?*

Williams allows a bubble of laughter to escape before realizing how inappropriate that will seem to Max and David. He tries to stifle it but not quickly enough. Max and David are staring at him.

He covers his mouth with his hand and fakes a cough. *Not a real ghost,* he says sharply. *There are no such things as ghosts.*

Like I'm supposed to know that.

He drops his hand and his features have rearranged themselves into a properly somber expression. "He's called The Ghost because we don't know who he is or where he comes from. The Feds suspect he's responsible for two dozen contract hits, maybe more. But ballistics matched the bullets from the Palm Canyon killing and David's shooting to others on file."

David asks the obvious question before I have a chance to. "A contract killer? Why would he be after Anna and me?"

"That question I think I can answer." Williams pulls a folded newspaper out of his case. "Have either of you seen this?"

He hands it to me and I hold it so that David and I can look at it together. There's a small article circled in the middle of the page. It's from the local paper and dated four days ago.

INMATE FOUND SLAIN IN JAIL CELL

Anthony (Tony) Tuturo was found dead in his jail cell early yesterday morning. Tuturo was being held pending extradition to New York where he was facing charges of extortion and grand theft. He was stabbed in the chest. No motive has been cited for the killing and no suspects have been named.

David and I finish reading at the same time. He says, "I didn't see this article. But what does his death have to do with a hit man? Or with Anna and me? All we did was pick him up on an outstanding warrant."

"Tuturo was to be extradited to New York," Williams replies. "Where he'd made a deal with the Feds. A deal that involved implicating a high-ranking government official in some kind of shady arms deal. That's when we believe a contract went out on him. Tuturo heard about it, panicked and ran. You picked him up on his way to Canada. When he was killed in jail, that effectively rendered the contract void. I suspect our Ghost friend was not happy about that. He was out a lot of money. I figure he decided to take his revenge on the two people who denied him a kill and a payday."

I start to wonder out loud why this Ghost didn't just kill me in Palm Canyon. Then I remember his last call. He wants to *enjoy* it. Must mean he intends to get up close and personal. Instead of sharing that, I say, "So, let me get this straight. David and I are the targets of a contract killer pissed off because we got his guy before he did?"

Williams nods. "It's the only thing we can figure out."

"So what do we do now?"

Williams smiles. "We set a trap."

It's not hard to figure out who the bait will be. David, after all, is already "dead."

Max jumps in before I can say anything. "You aren't seriously considering using Anna as bait to catch this guy."

He says that with great concern in his voice. And knowing what he does about me, that means a lot. Of course, he may not really understand what being a vampire is all about but I'm touched by the effort anyway.

I put a hand on his arm. "It's okay, Max. Chief Williams

wouldn't put me in any real danger. I'm sure he has a plan, don't you?"

My gaze shifts to him. He has his arms crossed over his chest. "A good one I think. Reporters have been waiting to speak with Anna since the Palm Canyon incident. We're going to give them the chance. Tomorrow. At a press conference. At that time, Anna is going to say that she's been vacationing in Mexico and didn't hear about the death of her partner. She'll let it slip that she's going to his resting place in Mt. Hope Cemetery to pay her respects."

Max shoots me a look. "What Palm Canyon thing?" he asks.

But before I answer, David asks, "Mt. Hope? Why Mt. Hope?"

Williams says, "Mt. Hope is perfect for what we have in mind. Hilly. Lots of big trees. We'll have the place staked out. When Anna shows, we're betting the killer will, too."

It's a good plan. I nod that I accept.

"The press will get the details tonight. Anna, watch the news. You're about to make headlines again."

Now Max is staring. "What do you mean Anna is about to make headlines *again*?"

"I got involved in a domestic violence thing, Max. No big deal but the papers got hold of the story."

David and Williams are frowning at me. Max sees it and grumbles, "Why do I think it was a big deal?"

When no one jumps on that, he continues. "Well, I don't like it. If this guy is as dangerous as you think, how do you plan to keep the press away from the cemetery? Innocent people could get hurt."

"They may be waiting for Anna at the cemetery," Williams answers. "But we'll have police there, too. And Anna will make it clear that she wants to visit David's grave site alone. We have thought this out, Max."

Still, he doesn't look convinced. "I want to go with her."

I put a hand on his arm. "In a wheelchair? I appreciate your concern, but that's not practical. Besides, you know I can take care of myself."

Williams picks up on something in my tone and he immediately sends me a mental demand to explain. I ignore it, countering with a demand of my own. "I think my friends and I deserve a little peace today, don't you, Chief Williams?"

He is clearly taken aback by the dismissal. He frowns. *I thought we would spend the day together. I want to know more about what happened in Mexico.*

I'm not sure whether he means what happened with Burke or what happened with Martinez and Foley. In any case, my response is the same. *Not today.*

Suddenly, I'm bone tired—tired of explaining and defending myself, tired of fighting.

I just want to be by myself.

Williams seems to detect a shift in whatever mental vibe I'm sending out. My actual thoughts are shielded, but he's picking up on something.

Anna?

Without a word, I pick myself up and walk out the door.

CHAPTER 62

I'S NOT HARD TO LOSE THE TAIL.
   I can't believe Williams actually assigned a mortal to watch me, but I guess he figured if I wasn't with him, I'd be spending the day in the hospital with Max and David.

   I take off down Sixth Avenue on foot. Straight down to the city, where I lose myself in the midday shopping crowd. From there I follow Broadway to the waterfront and head for Seaport Village. When I'm sure no one has spotted me, I hail a cab.

   I have the driver drop me off in front of Mission Café. It's crowded as usual, and I simply walk in and straight through to the rear. I take the alley and wait until I can lose myself in a group at a crosswalk to scoot across Mission and head for home.

   I use the back entrance, through the garage. The code lets me into the garage and the spare key I keep hidden behind a tool chest lets me into the house.

   Only when the door is closed and locked behind me do I breathe a sigh of relief.

Then I change into my own clothes—a sweat suit and socks—and climb into my own bed.

I unplug the telephone because I'm sure it will dawn on Williams eventually that I might have come home. If he has a clue about me, he won't send a cop to check or come himself. I'm fairly sure he knows me well enough by now to realize what a mistake that would be.

For the first time in a week, I have no one to answer to, no one to fight, no one to save. I don't have to guard my thoughts. I pull the covers up around my neck and cry. My simple life has gotten so complicated. I don't know how to make things right.

I only know I've got to make some changes.

CHAPTER 63

THE TIME I SPEND ALONE HELPS CLARIFY MY THINK-ing. In the last week, I fought with David, almost lost Culebra, revealed myself as a vampire to Max. I was betrayed by Williams, not overtly, but by omission, which is just as bad. It's time to make some changes in my life. And I know what the first one will be.

So when I show up at the press conference, I have every intention of telling Williams what I've decided. The opportunity never presents itself. He's late and the reporters don't give us a moment alone. Then he's called away, and I'm left to take a radio car to the hospital. When I get there, Max and David are together in David's room just as they were twenty-four hours before. It's a déjà vu moment except that this time, there's relief on their faces when they see me.

Neither says anything about my disappearing act yesterday.

"Williams will be here in a little while," I say. "He's going to take me to the cemetery."

Max says quietly, "Are you all right?"

"Yes. I'm fine."

David glances at the clock, then picks up the TV remote. "They'll be reporting the story about you on the nine o'clock news."

I take a seat beside his bed and we watch. I pretend to be interested in the cheerful banter between the cheerful newscasters. After fifteen or so minutes, the story about El Centro, my return from Mexico and David's death is broadcast. While they talk, the network flashes a picture of me that I don't recognize. Then I realize it's from a newspaper article written two years ago about David and I. I look different, softer, and I'm smiling. No wonder I didn't recognize it. When the taped segment from this morning is run, it's like watching a stranger. I answer the questions from the reporters soberly and with a complete lack of animation. I look like a robot. It reflects the way I feel.

When it's over, David clicks off the television.

Max and David give up trying to draw me into their conversation. Good thing. The topic is international soccer and evidently, David favors Italy, while Max thinks Argentina has a shot at the next World Cup. The two men seem to find this of major importance. I've never heard David talk about soccer before except to denigrate it when someone calls it "football." I'd find the passion they are displaying amusing if I could work up enough emotion to care.

When Williams shows up, he tries to reach into my head. I don't let him. I want to wait until this is over to tell him my plans. He begins to review what's going to happen this morning, and I listen with dispassionate interest. He's upbeat and optimistic, even predicting that I'll be back with David and Max by lunchtime.

There's a car waiting downstairs and Williams climbs into the backseat beside me. I expect Ortiz to be driving, but it's a cop I don't recognize. He's human. Williams is treating this as a normal police exercise.

Which, of course, it is.

Except for the fact that the target of this particular exercise, me, is not normal.

Williams has given up trying to communicate with me telepathically. Once we're on the road, he clears his throat in a way to make sure he has my attention and says, "You know what you're to do?"

"We get to the cemetery. I tell the media I want privacy. The car takes me to the grave site. I get out, walk to the grave and wait for The Ghost to shoot me. Did I miss anything?"

He stiffens beside me. "You are not going to be shot. We have sharpshooters covering every angle. They've been in position since early this morning. They may even have the guy by the time we get there. You are not going to be in any danger."

He doesn't mention the "vampires can't be killed by bullets" thing. I suppose that's for our driver's benefit.

We reach the highway turnoff. The driver takes it and steers toward the cemetery. As predicted, there are a half dozen media vans waiting at the entrance. I climb out and Williams joins me. He holds up a hand and the reporters gather around us. Williams signals for them to be quiet. He makes a few remarks about hoping they'll respect my privacy and I echo that sentiment and promise to talk to them when I return. Tears are streaming down my cheeks. I don't know when I started to cry or why.

Williams walks me back to the car. He opens the door and I slide inside. Concern shadows his eyes. "Anna, are you sure you're all right?"

The tears are what have him alarmed. I wipe at my cheeks with the back of my hand and cover with a sarcastic "Good touch, don't you think?"

I'm not sure he buys the sentiment but the attitude is familiar enough to spark relief. "I'll see you back here when it's over," he says. "I'll make sure no one follows you."

He closes the door, taps the roof with the palm of his hand, and the car whispers away from the curb.

Showtime.

CHAPTER 64

I HATE CEMETERIES ALMOST AS MUCH AS I HATE hospitals, even one as beautifully manicured and landscaped as Mt. Hope. The reason is as obvious as the marble tributes we pass. Symbols of man's mortality. Since becoming vampire, all I've thought about is how different my reality has become. Being here emphasizes the difference in a tangible way. I'll see my parents in a place like this, even Trish and her children's children, and I'll go on until an accident or a Revenger ends it. Then, my body will disappear, just like Avery's, and there will be nothing, not a marker, not a name on a wall, nothing to note my having been here at all.

Despair, almost too painful to endure, floods over me. My brother is buried here, on the other side of the cemetery. The desire to jump out of the car and flee is strong. Somehow for a vampire to be here is a desecration of holy ground.

The car is slowing. I look out to see that we've crested the top of a gentle rise. There are trees here, big, old trees. Trees that predate men claiming the area as a repository for their dead. Mt. Hope dates back to the early California Mission days, and this is the oldest part of the cemetery. I understand why Williams chose it. Tall box hedges surround the perimeter and though I can't see what's behind them, I know it's where the police wait. I feel eyes on me.

The cop in front asks if he should come with me. He doesn't turn around to look at me when he speaks, but his eyes are focused on scanning the area. I figure he's probably a member of SWAT, too, which would explain why Williams chose him to accompany me.

I tell him no and climb out of the car. As quickly as it descended, the despair lifts. There's nothing now. No panic, no alarm, no heightened sense of danger. The quiet within is as complete as the quiet that surrounds me on the hilltop. Only the occasional whisper of wind in the treetops breaks the spell. Maybe it's the spirit of my brother come to offer solace. I've learned in the last few months that anything is possible.

Williams showed me on a map which grave site was supposed to be David's. The earth is freshly tilled and covered with sod. No stone has been erected and I wonder idly whose grave he commandeered for our purposes. Would the family have had to give permission?

I start toward the grave. Nothing happens, no one steps from behind one of the huge tree trunks to confront me. No shots ring out. Williams had thought to bring flowers for me to put on the grave and I have them in my hand. In the bag on my shoulder is a gun. If all goes as planned, I won't have to use it. Any minute now, I should hear the scuffle as the police apprehend our "Ghost" character and the charade will be over. David can reclaim his life and we can try to sort out all that's gone wrong between us. I realize I want that most of all.

The simplicity of it astounds me. I know what I want. I want to go back to chasing bad guys. Human bad guys. Williams doesn't know it yet, but my rogue hunting days are over. Killing is getting too easy. The Watchers will have to get along without me.

I'm at the grave site now and getting antsy. How long do I have to stand here? I stoop to place the flowers at the foot of the grave. I remain in that position for a couple of minutes, surreptitiously looking around.

Nothing. No movement. No sound. I can't stay here forever. Irritated, I straighten up. Williams' great plan is a bust. For all we know, The Ghost is long gone, satisfied that claiming one of us was enough. I turn on my heels and head for the car. Now what? What's David going to do now? Christ, what was Williams thinking when he put this stupid plan into effect?

The cop is still seated behind the wheel of the car when I get in and slam the door closed. "Let's get out of here," I snap.

This time, he turns in the seat to look at me. His cap is pulled low on his forehead and his blond hair is cut short and just touches the collar of his uniform. He has a neatly trimmed moustache the same color as his hair.

He smiles and his eyes give him away.

CHAPTER 65

M ANY THOUGHTS PASS THROUGH MY HEAD SI-
multaneously. I wonder how he managed to pull
this off, how remarkably different he looks with just a
change of hair style and color, how long he's known that
David was alive.

The smile on his face broadens. "Welcome back, Anna,"
The Ghost says. "I've been waiting for you."

"I'll bet. So what happens now?"

He reaches across the seat and snags my bag with one
hand. "We go back to the hospital. I know a back way out
of this place, a service road. It will take a while for the police to figure out that Elvis has left the building. By that
time, I'll have finished what I set out to do. The next time
you and your partner visit this place, the circumstances
will be different."

He says it like I should tremble at his words. But he
doesn't wait to see if I am. He is confident that it could be
no other way. He is used to inspiring fear. So, he turns
away from me and starts the engine.

I have a number of options open to me. I can jump out

of the car now, signal the police, and let them take care of him. I can reach across the seat and snap his neck the way I did Marta's. I can let him think he's won and allow him a few more minutes to gloat before I show him what fear really is.

He adjusts the rearview mirror to keep me in sight. It doesn't work, of course, and he gives up finally, mumbling that the damned mirror must be broken. He tells me to move over to the right side of the seat so he can see me as he drives.

"Would you like me to get into the front seat with you? You could keep a closer eye on me that way."

He reacts with surprise to the way I address him. He pulls the car over and reaches over the seat to backhand me. My head snaps back, and blood flows from a cut on my lip. I smile and touch the cut with my tongue, let the blood pool and lick at it. "Is that the best you can do?"

He doesn't answer. He's looking at me, wondering why I'm not acting the way he expects. His eyes don't reflect real curiosity, there'd have to be some shred of humanity for that. Idle, bored speculation is the most he can muster. "Do you know who I am?"

I laugh. "A not very good hit man who let a couple of bounty hunters walk off with his prize."

And the minute I say that, I remember. I snap my fingers. "Of course. San Francisco. You were in the bar. The silk suit. You followed David and Tuturo outside."

A muscle at the corner of his mouth twitches. "It shouldn't have happened. He was mine."

"Evidently not. Evidently David appealed to him more than you did."

"Stupid fag," he snaps. "I spent the entire night watching those perverts, waiting for Tony to leave so I could follow him, and your partner walks in and waltzes him right out. It was sickening. I should have killed them both in the bar."

"I guess you should have. Ruined your reputation so I hear."

That gets a snicker. "No one, especially not a couple of amateurs from this pathetic town, is going to trash my reputation. Christ, even the police chief wasn't smart enough to recognize his own driver."

"How'd you pull that off anyway?"

"Thank SWAT. All those cops walking around in armor and headgear. Cops who think they're untouchable because they carry big guns. Won't they be surprised when they return to headquarters and find one of their fellow officers with his throat cut, stuffed in his own locker? Serves the arrogant bastards right."

Well, I guess I won't have to kill him after all. He's signed his own death warrant and all I have to do now is deliver him up.

"Well, you've certainly thought of everything," I say cheerfully. "Made my day, in fact. Now, we can do this the easy way or the hard way. Your choice."

He shakes his head, frowning. "What the hell are you talking about? What choice?"

I guess that means we do it the hard way. I punch him with my fist so hard and so fast, his nose caves, his eyes close, the back of his head bounces off the steering wheel and he's out before his brain registers that he's been hit.

Man, that felt good. Not bad for an amateur.

AFTERWORD

THE INCREDULITY IN WILLIAMS' VOICE WHEN I radio that I've got The Ghost and the look on his face when he approaches the car and sees him unconscious against the steering wheel bring a smile to my face each time I think of them.

But what follows over the next two days is not funny.

Williams is mortified that he hadn't bothered to ask for identification when the unfamiliar officer presented himself as his driver. But why would he? He was in the basement of his very own police department among a swarm of officers, not all of whom he could be expected to know personally.

Compounding the humiliation is guilt because a police officer was killed. There are questions from the press, from the officer's family, from the mayor and members of the city council. No one except those involved in the operation knew about The Ghost. The press is outraged that they were tricked into thinking David was dead. Now, the way Williams handled the situation is put under a spotlight and his every decision examined. The spotlight is not a comfortable place for an old-soul vampire to be.

I almost feel sorry for him. But while he is busy defending his choices, I am free to make some of my own. He leaves me a telephone message that he won't be going back to the park for a while. The press is hounding him and while he doesn't come out and say it, I know he can't take a chance that a reporter might see him disappearing through a magic doorway into an invisible underground facility. On top of everything else, *that* would be hard to explain.

Receiving the message is a relief. I'd already decided I'd had enough of the Watchers. Telling Williams that, though, is not going to be easy. I feel as if I've been granted a reprieve, even if it's only temporary.

After the capture of The Ghost, I returned to the hospital to welcome David back to the land of the living. Once the story got out, he had reporters camped at his bedside, too, until the hospital administration put a stop to it. Max and I were the only visitors allowed in to see him.

Then, Max left the hospital. He left without seeing me. I guess it's just as well. He knows what I am. I thought for a fleeting moment he might accept it. Since he didn't bother to say good-bye, I guess he doesn't.

I went back to the Kona Kai once, to return the clothes. I kept the shoes though. Seemed like a just reward. Maybe I should have checked out, too, but Williams can afford to pay for the room. I just want to put this last week behind me.

Seven days. It's hard to believe all that's happened in a little over one week. I know I should go see Culebra. Make sure he doesn't try to go after Burke alone. I never found out what happened when he tried to follow me, either. Considering we took off in a helicopter, I can't imagine he got very far.

But for a few days, I decide to cling only to the human side of my nature. I visit David at the hospital every day and we actually laugh again and talk the way we used to. There's no more discussion of dissolving our partnership.

And no Gloria. I still can't believe it. I try now and again to bring up the subject, but he insists he doesn't know where she is or why she hasn't come to the hospital. He is curt and abrupt when he talks about it, but I see the sadness in his eyes. I hope I get the opportunity to make the selfish bitch pay for his pain. I look forward to it.

Today David is being released from the hospital. I plan to pick him up and bring him to the loft. I've decided to stay with him a few days, mindful that I'll have to avoid mirrors and be careful around the windows at night.

Next week, my family returns from Europe. I can't wait to see them. I've been so busy taking care of the vampire Anna, that I almost lost track of the human.

I don't intend for that to happen again.

The Watcher is the third in Jeanne C. Stein's Anna Strong, Vampire series, following *The Becoming* and *Blood Drive*. Though Jeanne now lives in Colorado, San Diego will always be home. She is currently at work on the next Anna Strong novel.

THE ULTIMATE IN FANTASY!

From magical tales of distant worlds to stories of those with abilities beyond the ordinary, Ace and Roc have everything you need to stretch your imagination to its limits.

Marion Zimmer Bradley/Diana Paxon

Guy Gavriel Kaye

Dennis McKiernan

Patricia McKillip

Robin McKinley

Sharon Shinn

Katherine Kurtz

Barb and J. C. Hendees

Elizabeth Bear

T. A. Barron

Brian Jacques

Robert Asprin

penguin.com